The HEARTland—that place between the coasts where real people live. They work and play, laugh and cry, meet and fall in love. If they stumble and fall, they pick themselves up again and continue to fight the good fight. God and family always come first, friends a close second.

You know these people. They are always in the middle of things, the heart and soul of their families and communities. They will give their all for those they love. Their beliefs are unshakable.

In my third HEARTland ROMANCE, **PROMISES KEPT**, you will meet Dr. Kris Holland and aerobatic pilot Matt Walker. Anna Watson tells Karen in **THE RIGHT KEY**: *"Kris and Matt are not together... They have never been able to work out whatever differences they have." "So how long have they been trying?" "Almost a life time."*

After her father's death Kris finds her life in shambles. She suffers a brutal assault, and a malpractice suit is filed against her. She flies to Alaska to stay with family friends only to have Matt turn up. She has never stopped loving him, but she wonders: *What man in his right mind would want her now?* Well, Matt has never claimed total sanity. After all he *is* an aerobatic pilot. He knows it's way past time he faced his feelings for Kris. He will not be walking away...

My fourth HEARTland ROMANCE will be available in the near future at www.lulu.com. You will meet Kendra and hear about Jared in **PROMISES KEPT.** Look for their story, **ON THE EDGE,** coming soon.

I hope you enjoy these characters as much as I have enjoyed creating them. I wish you FAITH, HOPE & LOVE. May God Bless.

Eva O'Connor

HEARTland Series Book 3:

PROMISES KEPT

by

Eva O'Connor

Lulu.com

HEARTland Series Book 3: PROMISES KEPT

by Eva O'Connor

ISBN: 978-0-6151-9185-0

Cover Photograph by Kerry Stewart

God did not promise a smooth flight...
But a safe landing!

...I go and prepare a place for you, I will come back and take
you to be with me that you also may be where I am... John 14:3

To ALL those members of
THE GREATEST GENERATION
whom we have been privileged
to know and love...

To ALL our military heroes
from all wars, past and present...

And to our friends in that exclusive
World of Flight. We have trod the
Heavens and returned to roam the Earth.
Never again content to feel the ground
under our feet, we seek again and always
the wind beneath our wings.

PROLOGUE

(From the Journal of Benjamin F. Walker, December 24, 1945)

> *Christmas Eve! Peace at last! It's been too long since the world celebrated Christmas without war. We made it through--Roy, Bill, Hal and me. Tonight we realized we'd gotten pretty good at watching out for each other--flying as wingmen all these years. We decided not to break up a winning combination and made a pledge to be there--all for one and one for all. . . Roy drew up a contract. . .*
>
> *I don't want to lose touch with these guys. What we have was forged in ice when we flew P-39's in the Aleutians; it survived intact the Hell of Europe as the P-47's brought us through. Blood runs deep, but this bond goes deeper. I hope my children appreciate the legacy we're leaving them. Friendship is the greatest gift of all . . .*

November 12, 1971

Ben Walker pulled the sleek fighter plane into a vertical climb and pushed it over into a spin. His blood raced and his features creased into a smile behind his oxygen mask. *This new design delivered everything the engineers claimed! Superb performance and a joy to fly.* What more could a pilot want?

He leveled out and glanced at his watch. *Time to check in.* He judged this initial test flight an unqualified success, his preflight worrying for naught.

Ben keyed the mike and his eyes widened as a spark arced from it across the instrument panel. The cockpit plunged into darkness, the silence deafening. For a split second time stood still, and then the plane lurched out of control.

"*Mayday! Mayday! Mayday!*" He pulled the lever to arm the ejection system. *Nothing.*

The plane spiraled down, tumbling end over end. Ben slumped in his harness, mercifully unconscious. After falling for a small eternity, the craft plunged through the frozen surface of a lake. Water closed over man and machine and ice began to reform.

PROMISES KEPT

February 23, 1991

The A-10 Thunderbolt pulled up sharply and Matt Walker looked back with satisfaction at the line of exploding tanks snaking across the desert floor. Several of his bombs had hit their mark. *Time to head back.* One could expect only so much luck in a given day, he reflected with a wry grin.

Sudden Hell exploded inside the cockpit. Shrapnel smashed through the canopy and into his left shoulder. Blood splattered across the instrument panel. He fought to maintain control of the aircraft and stay conscious against the pain searing his shoulder. His arm hung useless. *Funny how A-10's could survive almost anything,* he thought with a strange detachment, *as long as they had a pilot capable of keeping them in the air.*

How far was he from Saudi airspace? A SAM had taken out his left engine and exploded behind the cockpit. His instruments spun crazily as the desert floor raced toward him. A smooth stretch of sand lay ahead and he cut power to the right engine. The sturdy aircraft touched down, bucked across the shifting surface, and jerked to a stop. Matt released the canopy and pulled himself out with his right arm. He fell, landed on his good shoulder, and rolled down a sand dune.

Would anyone come? He wondered as blackness threatened to engulf him. It had been twenty years since his father disappeared near the Arctic Circle. All available resources of the United States Government had searched in vain for the top secret aircraft and its pilot. Twenty years . . .

He struggled to think of something else, and unwillingly a face appeared. Blonde curls tumbled around an angelic face with bewitching green eyes and soft inviting lips.

"Kris," he whispered. "Dear God, Kris . . ." His eyes closed. Blood flowed from his shoulder, making a dark stain in the desert sand.

CHAPTER ONE

(From the Journal of Benjamin F. Walker, September 16, 1951)

Today Bill announced he was retiring from the air force. He plans to built a little airfield somewhere in the middle of Alaska--sort of an inn and trading post combination. Marie has other plans. She wants something like a bed and breakfast. One thing I know, once someone has tried her apple pie, they'll be back! Maybe Bill should listen to her...

Matt Walker strained to see into the inky blackness below. The global positioning system on his instrument panel showed him to be directly above Bentley Base, Alaska. In that case, the runway should be visible. Bill always turned the lights on at the first sound of an approaching aircraft.

Trying to ignore the ache in his shoulder, Matt sighed and pulled up for another pass over the base. Weather conditions were deteriorating fast. If he didn't get someone's attention soon, he'd be forced to return to Fairbanks.

Assuming, of course, he could stay ahead of the blizzard. Instrument flying conditions he could handle. *Icing was something else again.*

Kristin Holland awakened, shaking off the effects of her dream. She'd been flying a few hundred feet above a deserted California beach. Waves broke against the shore, wind tore at her hair. She pulled into a climbing turn and made another pass, just above the water, so low she could see the spray thrown up by her prop wash.

She pushed aside the blanket of sleep and sat up. *The sound effects in her dream were too realistic!* She could feel the vibration of the engine. The room echoed from the sound of an aircraft passing overhead—very low overhead! She glanced out the window to see the ever present darkness--typical for this time of year in the middle of Alaska, just south of the Arctic Circle.

Her heart lurched and caught in her throat. A pilot waited up there, somewhere, depending on her to turn on the runway lights so he could land! She jumped up and raced down the hall to the breaker box and pulled the lever. The plane made another low pass and the windows rattled.

Kris looked out to see the lights on and the beacon rotating. The beam from the huge lamp slashed at the impenetrable night. Her breath caught. In the eerie light, she could see blowing snow. *What kind of fool would fly in this weather, anyway?*

She heard the plane again as she ran to the garage. The pilot could see the runway now. But he was coming in way too fast! He had plenty of room to land. What was his hurry?

The plane pulled up to go around again, and she let out her breath in relief. The pilot had been checking the runway before landing. As he made another approach she heard him throttle back to idle. She closed her eyes and mentally followed his motions in the cockpit. She heard the swish as he passed the building, still a few feet in the air, heard the gentle kiss of rubber against tarmac. She hadn't seen it, but she could tell from the sound that it had been a perfect landing.

Kris pulled onto the taxiway as she drove Bill's Bronco down to collect the pilot. She heard the drone of the engine as the plane turned off the runway and began taxiing back. She pulled up before a hangar and got out to open the doors. The snow was falling harder now and the plane coming toward her emerged like a ghost from the mist. It came to a stop beneath a floodlight. The engine died and the propeller spun to a stop. Kris turned for a closer look.

She found herself staring, and her lips parted in mute protest. She recognized the black and red plane sitting in the circle of light. Her father had helped Matt Walker build it. *But what was it doing here?* Her heart pounding, she raised her eyes to the pilot as he stepped down from the plane.

He wore a black flight suit, the red MW on his sleeves matching the logo on the side of the plane. *Convenient initials.* They read the same whether he flew straight and level, or inverted during an aerobatic routine. He removed his helmet and Kris felt her pulse accelerate at sight of his face. *Why not?* Matthew Jordan Walker had never been far from her thoughts, awake or dreaming, for longer than she cared to remember.

He stalked across the tarmac. "Where's Bill?" For some reason that escaped her, he seethed with rage.

"I—he's—a family emergency," she stammered in confusion, shrinking from him as he towered over her. "He and Marie are in California."

"You're in charge?" He glanced toward the hangar.

"Y—yes." *He didn't recognize her, bundled as she was against the cold!* She pulled off her ski mask and raised her eyes to his. "Hello, Matt."

Matt swung back at the sound of his name and stood frozen. Blonde hair whipped around Kris's face and her green eyes sparkled with challenge—a challenge that didn't quite conceal the hurt lurking in their depths.

Matt stared at her, his anger evaporating to leave a dark void. "Kris, darling." His drawl was a masterpiece. "Roy wouldn't tell me where you were and this is the last place I expected to find you."

"I beg your pardon?" The blood drained from her face.

"I've been looking for you for months—" His voice trailed off, his gaze narrowed. "And I've been flying around waiting for someone to turn on the lights. A blizzard is coming—" A gust of cold air tore at his clothes. "Is here."

"Matt, I'm sorry!" She raised her voice as the wind whipped her words away. "I turned them on as soon as I heard you." How could she admit she had been asleep? *And dreaming, no less.*

"How could you *not* hear me?"

She looked at him for endless seconds, then turned away, swallowing all the arguments she might have used in her defense. Pride brought her chin up at a defiant angle. "I've said I'm sorry. It would be pointless to repeat it. After all, you might have called ahead. Do you need help with your plane?"

"I could use a tow bar." He looked around.

Kris went into the hangar to take one from the wall and hand it to him.

"Anything else?"

"No, thanks. I can manage."

Kris watched as he pulled the plane inside. His movements were quick and efficient as he took steps to protect the machine against the harsh cold of the Alaskan interior. Within moments the plane was secured and he picked up his helmet and duffel bag and followed Kris to the Bronco.

Kris could think of nothing to say as she drove back to the inn. Tension crackled inside the cab and her hands clenched the steering wheel. The drive normally took only a few minutes, but the blizzard had arrived in full force and slowed her progress to a crawl. The wipers fought a losing battle against the ice already coating the windshield. She could feel Matt's gaze.

"You don't seem all that pleased to see me." Matt drawled.

She shrugged. "Should I be? I thought you might strangle me."

"I had given myself one more minute before I returned to Fairbanks when the lights came on. No pilot likes to cut things that close."

"So why didn't you call?"

"I gave up trying. I thought maybe the radio was out—or turned off."

Her indrawn breath sounded harsh in the closed interior of the Bronco.

"Is it?"

"I don't know." Her voice was a whisper. "Yanni worked on it just before he left. . ."

"Besides, how was I to know this creature resembling nothing so much as the abominable snowman was the same woman I've been in love with for the better part of eternity—"

The Bronco lost traction on the rapidly forming ice and skidded across the taxiway. By the time Kris recovered and straightened the vehicle, it was much too late for a flippant reply—*assuming she had been able to think of one.* She pulled into the garage and cut the engine.

Matt followed her inside and she stopped to throw the switch that would turn the runway lights off again.

"Bill has a nice operation." Matt glanced around the den, his eyes expressing his appreciation. "I haven't been here in a long time."

"Well, you picked an interesting time to return," Kris said. "This is the worst weather we've had in months, and Bill and Marie left a few weeks ago."

"Where are Yanni and Salina?" He frowned. "You said he left."

"Back in their village. Salina's sister had a baby and they went to help out for a while."

"And left you here alone?"

Kris detected disapproval in his voice and shrugged it off. "They knew I'd be fine." She turned to face him. "What are you doing here, Matt? I didn't know you knew the Bentleys."

The hand he had been running through his hair froze in midair. His eyes were now slits of blue ice. She noticed that his hair brushed the collar of his flight suit. What happened to the military cut she remembered so well? Not that the longer style in any way detracted from his good looks, but it somehow made him appear more vulnerable, less perfectly masculine.

"I told you." His hand fell in an almost passive gesture. "I've been looking for you and I thought Bill and Marie might know something."

Kris stood stunned, her eyes focused on his hand. She had never seen him indecisive before. What was going on? After a moment she blinked and wet her lips, then turned and walked to the fireplace.

"What made you think of them?" she asked. "How did you know I even knew the Bentleys?"

"Of course you know them. Our families have always known each other. Very closely—because of the pledge."

"What pledge?"

He frowned at her. "The pledge our father's made to each other after the war." A tinge of impatience colored his voice.

14

She shook her head. "I don't know what you're talking about. At Dad's funeral Marie explained they had been friends of my parents and offered to help. That's why I came up here—" she broke off. "You said you came up here looking for me, or information as to my whereabouts." She knelt to stir the fire. "Why?"

Matt's hand closed over hers as he took the poker from her. "Because I had to see you. Know you're all right." The words were clipped.

Kris thought she must have imagined his uncertainty earlier. She sat on the hearth and rested her elbows on her knees, her hands clasped to keep them from trembling. "Considering the steps you've taken to get away from me in the past, I don't have the courage to ask what that has to do with anything."

He knelt to tend the fire, on a level with her. His eyes held hers. "Everything, Kris. I was wrong all those years ago. I was wrong last year."

She blinked. "Last year?"

"At Hal's funeral. I shouldn't have left you. I haven't been able to forget how alone you were. I know Scott was there, but—well, something wasn't right. He's all wrong for you, Kris—"

She stood. "Well, this is a first! You and I finally agree on something!"

He caught her hand and rose to stand beside her. His fingers tightened around hers. "Kris, I'm sorry. Please forgive me for being so blind—"

She freed her hand and turned away. "No apologizes necessary. As far as being blind, I'm not sure anything has changed." Her voice was thick with unshed tears. "Let's leave it at that, shall we? Everything has been said."

"No, Kris! I have to explain—"

"Excuse me. I need to get your room ready—"

"Kris, wait—"

She looked back. "By the way, where is Scott?" She stood frozen, dreading the answer, needing to know.

He stared at her. "You don't know? I haven't seen Scott since Hal's funeral. I crashed a few months after that and haven't been competing—"

Kris caught her breath. "An airplane—?"

"No." He grinned. "My sister's car. I wasn't hurt bad—a broken leg—but I haven't raced since. I came up here to get Bill's help with some modifications to my plane. And to try and find you," he added, watching her face.

Kris had stopped listening and was staring at him in disbelief. "You don't consider a broken leg a serious injury?" *What else had he not mentioned?*

"Well, it wasn't life threatening or career ending," he explained.

"Thanks for clearing that up." Kris studied him. "What else did you break?"

His eyes narrowed. "Doctor, this isn't a professional visit." He sniffed. "Do I smell coffee?"

Kris went into the kitchen, came back and handed him a mug. "Don't change the subject. Where there's a broken leg, there are usually other injuries, especially in a car wreck. What? Broken ribs? Collarbone?"

He grimaced. "Both." He reached up to rub the still tender area on the left side of his neck.

She studied him. "How long have you been here?"

His eyes widened. "About ten minutes—"

"I mean in Alaska. The cold is going to cause you a lot of pain. Have you noticed that yet?"

"I've noticed," he said dryly, flexing his left shoulder.

Kris turned away. "I assume you plan to stay for awhile." *How could her voice sound so cool when she felt she was being consumed inside?*

Matt picked up the poker and stirred the fire again. Straightened. "I did, but that was when I thought Bill and Marie would be here, too. Now—"

"Yanni should be back in a couple of days. Don't let me change your mind. You'll never know I'm around." *If only she could say the same about him.*

Matt looked at her. After a moment he nodded. "Whatever you say. Obviously, I can't leave until this storm blows over. Did Bill and Marie say how long they'd be gone?"

Kris shook her head. "Carl was diagnosed with leukemia. His doctors want to do a bone marrow transplant. The last I heard everything was still pretty uncertain." Her voice grew husky as she spoke.

Matt shook his head. "I grew up with Carl. It's hard to imagine—" He broke off. "But I want to know why you're here. Roy wouldn't tell me anything—except to finally confirm that you'd left town."

Kris looked down, trying to conceal the pain she'd hidden since her arrival. Keeping her feelings from Bill and Marie had been one thing. They barely knew her. It would be a lot harder now that Matt was here. "That's a very long story not even my friends know. You never had time for me before. I have no intention of crying on your shoulder now." She turned away. "I'll get your room ready."

Matt watched her go, then turned back to the window. *Dear God, how could I have walked away and left her? Please let me prove myself worthy, and give me another chance to make things right with Kris.*

Kris lit the small gas heater in the guest room. She was shaking so hard she had to strike a second match. She told herself it was just the cold.

She turned to the bed and made it up with fresh sheets and blankets, trying not to think about the man who'd be sleeping in it. Although he'd never really been part of her life, Matt Walker had been a disturbing influence for longer than she cared to admit. She didn't seem to be able to do anything about it. He lurked there in her sub-conscious, waiting for a weak moment.

Dear God, I've never in my life been more vulnerable than I am now, and he shows up in person! I still love him. I always have. Help me to know what to do!

She remembered running into Matt again after he joined the Air Force. *Literally.* He turned from talking to her father as she ran into the office and crashed into him. His hands went out to close around her arms—then she felt them tighten. She took in the flight suit and the Captain's bars, then found herself spinning out of control in the turbulent depths of his blue eyes.

"Matt?" she whispered. She reached out to touch the wings on his chest. "Has it been that long?"

A smile touched his chiseled mouth. "Kristi! You've grown up." His eyes told her he liked what he saw.

What she would have done or said next, Kris didn't know. Hal Holland looked up and saw her. "Oh, Kris, there you are. I need you to do me a favor." He glanced at the man holding his daughter. "I'll see you tomorrow at one, Matt," he confirmed, before turning his attention back to Kris.

She felt the hands drop from her arms and tried to pull herself together, more shaken than she'd ever been by a man's look. *A man's touch.*

"Kris, this is Scott McGraw," Hal was saying. "He wants to look at the racer in Bret's hangar. Can you take him over and show it to him? I haven't been able to reach Bret and I have another lesson in five minutes."

"Sure, Dad." She turned to look at the other man in the room and breathed a sigh of relief. She recognized Scott "Mac" McGraw from his photographs. He was making a name for himself in air racing. His cool gaze felt like a calm sea after what she'd seen in Matt's eyes. She smiled at him.

"Kris Holland, Mr. McGraw." She held out her hand.

As Scott clasped her hand in both of his and returned her smile with a devastating one of his own, she heard the door open.

"I'll see you around, Mac." The deep even tones of Matt's voice made Kris want to turn around and look at him.

Scott looked up. "But, Matt, you wanted to see the racer, too!"

"I saw it earlier. Thanks for the lesson, Hal." The door closed.

"Well," Scott turned back to Kris, "where have you been all my life?"

For the next few weeks, Kris caught only fleeting glimpses of Matt as Scott made every effort to monopolize her time. For her part, she barely acknowledged Scott's existence. On the other hand, Matt intrigued her. No longer the lanky kid she remembered hanging around the airport for a few weeks each summer, he now towered over her and exuded masculinity. She'd never been so aware of anyone, or more confused. The feelings Matt aroused in her dealt with emotions she'd never encountered before. If he'd returned her interest, she would've been in trouble. But on that count, she was safe. After their initial collision, he never indicated that he knew she was alive—in fact, didn't come near her.

Kris returned to the den and found Matt standing by the window with a steaming mug of coffee. He'd unzipped his flight suit to reveal a dark blue turtleneck. Her mouth twisted as she noticed the color of the sweater reflected in his eyes. She tore her gaze away, trying to refocus her thoughts.

"Your room is ready." She swallowed. "It should be warm soon. Are you hungry? I can make lunch."

He looked up. "I am. I've been dreaming about Marie's apple pies. *Obviously that's out.*" His sigh spoke volumes.

"For that I should let you starve," Kris said, her voice lighter now, teasing him. "Let me show you to your room—actually, you may know your way around better than I do. It's just past the bathroom." She held her breath, hoping he'd know the way. It would be much safer to keep her distance.

"I usually get the one across from it." He sounded hopeful, one eyebrow quirked as he looked at her.

"Sorry. I'm not moving out." A smile lurked around her mouth.

His eyes didn't soften. "You still haven't told me why you're here."

Kris looked away. "Is there some reason I should?" She twined her fingers together, the smile gone.

"Because of Hal, maybe." He watched her. "Because of the bond between your father and mine—a bond meant to transcend generations. We're pledged to take care of one another, you know."

"*Since when?*" Bitterness edged her voice. "I believe I once made a similar offer. You turned me down cold." She moved toward the kitchen. "Lunch will be ready in twenty minutes."

Matt picked up his duffel and carried it to his room. He stripped off his flight suit. *What had brought Kris here?* It had been almost a year since Hal's death. Matt knew his loss had devastated Kris. He'd seen Scott at the funeral, not offering Kris much support. She appeared so alone and vulnerable that Matt broke his own cardinal rule of survival and went over to speak to her.

Her fingers clung to his when he reached down to catch them. He couldn't imagine a surgeon having such slender, delicate hands, until he felt their strength. They were perfect for the work she did so well.

"I'm sorry, Kris," Matt said, his voice choked. His own sorrow at losing Hal Holland threatened to overwhelm him. When his father died, Hal stepped in and had always been there for him.

Kris looked at him with Hal's eyes and Matt shivered. Of bottomless jade, they were the only feature she inherited from her father. The same blonde hair and model's figure served Jean White well before she married Hal Holland. The apparent fragility deceived. He knew Kris had all Hal's strength and more.

As he gazed down at her, he again saw and felt the turbulence that rocked him in Hal's office when he reached out to steady her, just days before he left for the Persian Gulf. She felt it too; he knew from the way her fingers tightened around his. At that moment he threw caution to the winds, and under the guise of a comforting gesture, he drew her into his arms.

She clung to him, and he felt her tremble. Then she pulled away and stepped back. "Thank you," she whispered, holding his eyes for another moment. Then she turned to the next person waiting to express their condolences.

"My dear, we're so sorry—"

Matt walked away from her then—for the second time. He didn't look back, and as he left the cemetery rain began to fall, just as it had that first time. Now, months later, he could still feel her trembling body, see the anguish on her face, the sheen of tears in her eyes. But something else now shadowed her features. *Wariness? Betrayal? Could he be responsible for that, too?*

Matt pulled his thoughts back and continued unpacking. His past encounters with Kris had been few and brief. Even so, those meetings always left him shaken and at the very edge of control. His best defense had always been to limit contact with her. But he'd thought about her so much since Hal's funeral that he had to find her. Now she was here, in the last place he'd have ever thought to look. This time he wouldn't be walking away. When he left, he had every intention of taking her with him.

CHAPTER TWO

Matt returned to the kitchen to find a pot of soup steaming gently on a back burner. A plate of sandwiches sat on the counter beside a note from Kris.

Please make yourself at home. Obviously you know your way around. You'll be happy to know I found one of Marie's apple pies in the freezer. You can have it for dinner. Maybe this trip will turn out to be worth while after all.

He poured the soup into a mug and picked up a sandwich, looking out at the storm as he ate. Daylight had broken, such as it was. Even without the blowing snow, the effort would have been pretty meager. Today, it was bleak indeed.

Where was Kris? Matt prowled the house, shooting pain radiating down his leg and through his shoulder. *It would take a lot more than one of Marie's pies for this trip to qualify as a success.* He had no idea the cold would cause this kind of discomfort until Kris explained. *A little late now.* He was stuck here for awhile. Giving in to his aches, he sat down and used a pillow to elevate his leg, then leaned back and closed his eyes.

The pain in his leg was easier to bear than the pain he saw in Kris's eyes and the knowledge that he had put it there. The only thing that would make this trip worth the effort would be to have her look at him again the way she did that day in Hal's office.

Kris pushed open the door and stepped into the kitchen. She put down her lantern and supplies and removed her coat and gloves. Warmth seeped into her hands.

She went into the den, the quietness of the house echoing around her. Embers glowed in the fireplace. Her forehead wrinkled. She thought Matt would at least keep the fire burning. Then she saw him asleep on the sofa.

Kris stirred the coals and threw wood on them, watching as the flames caught. Matt still did not awaken. She straightened and looked down at him. He had changed into jeans and a sweater and lay with one leg elevated. *The one he'd broken?* As she watched he stirred and his brow creased in pain. One hand went to his neck and she remembered the broken collar bone. She reached out to touch him, forgetting how cold her hands were.

"What—?" Matt's eyes flew open and he sat up.

"You're in pain?" Kris swallowed, her eyes on his face. Why did it hurt so much to see someone suffer? *Someone you loved—*

"Never mind that. Why are your hands so cold?" His eyes searched hers. "You've been out. *Where?*"

"I went down to the hangar for awhile." She'd been looking at him in concern, but now he saw her face close.

24

"Why?" *They were in the middle of a blizzard!* Did she find a cold dark hangar preferable to sharing the house with him, Matt wondered.

"I needed to be close to something familiar."

"That's fine, but the wind chill must be—"

"I survived." She turned away. "I'll make dinner."

She had completely shut him out, Matt saw. His jaw tightened. "Don't hurry on my account." He didn't realize how harsh the words sounded until he saw her cringe.

She looked back. "Do you need something for the pain?" She asked because she had to know. Her polite, disinterested voice told him that.

He met her eyes. He sighed. "Do you have anything that will help?"

Kris knew how much the admission cost him. It was a small breakthrough—the first. "I'll see what I can find."

Kris returned with a glass and two white tablets.

"Warm milk?" Matt said. "I haven't been given warm milk since I was three years old." He didn't sound overly pleased that she would give it to him now, either, Kris thought.

"Trust me. It'll relax you and make the medication work faster."

Matt tossed the pills into his mouth and drained the glass, handing it back to her with a grimace.

"I'm sure Bill won't mind if you use his recliner," Kris said. "It'll help if you keep your leg elevated."

"Not so that I can tell." He stood up and limped over to the chair she had pointed out. "This looks complicated."

Kris stared at him. "You fly a million dollar airplane, and make it do things neither God nor man intended. You can figure out a recliner!"

As she left the room, Matt knelt to examine the mechanics of the comfortable looking chair. He couldn't remember sitting in a recliner. He'd always thought they were for old people. Bill wasn't old, was he? Hal Holland hadn't been old. He also hadn't used a recliner. Well, if the doctor thought it would help, he might as well give it a try, he decided, a smile tugging at his lips.

Matt opened his eyes and put a hand to his head. His eyelids felt heavy, weighted. The glow from the fire cast a soft light over the room. A blanket lay across his legs. Unconsciously, he groaned.

Kris appeared beside him, putting a hand on his arm and touching his forehead. Even in his stupor, he could see the concern on her face.

"What happened?" His tongue felt sluggish. He tried to speak again, and Kris put a finger to his lips.

"Don't try to talk," she whispered. "I'll get you something to drink."

He tried to sit up and she pushed him back. "Don't move yet. Wait until I get back."

Matt lay with his eyes closed. He didn't have to be told twice to lie still. He hadn't felt like this since he was eighteen and got drunk for the first and only time.

Kris returned. She brought the recliner to a sitting position and held the glass for Matt. He drank the water without protest. Then he looked at her, his eyes narrowed, questioning.

"I'm sorry." Kris met his gaze without flinching. "We seem to have overdone the pain medication—"

"We?" He stared at her in disbelief.

"A little input from the patient might have helped," Kris said, her voice dry. "You apparently don't have a very high tolerance—in other words, a little goes a long way."

He sat up, resting his forehead in his palms for a moment. "I don't think I've taken anything since I got back from the Persian Gulf. I'd been living on pain killers for almost a year." He leaned his head against the back of the chair, his hands resting on the arms.

"Were you addicted?" Her voice soothed, like a healing balm. It also hypnotized. Words seemed to come of their own volition.

"I don't know. But I haven't taken anything since I left you. I figured I deserved the pain." His words tumbled over one another, slightly slurred in the rush. "Besides, if I couldn't have you, it didn't really matter."

Kris sat back, dropping onto a footstool, her lips parted. "What makes you think you *couldn't* have me? You're the one who left." She held her breath for his reply.

"Because I couldn't bear to share you. Scott told me about your arrangement." His voice trailed off, his eyes closed.

"Arrangement?"

The sharpness of her voice brought Matt's head up again. He tried to focus on her.

"What arrangement?" Kris repeated. "What did Scott tell you?"

Matt shrugged. "The next morning, after I ran into you in Hal's office, Scott said he took you to dinner and dancing—and then to bed."

"And you believed him?" Kris breathed.

Matt shrugged, winced. "It was standard practice for Scott."

"I see." She stood up, fighting back tears. "So while I worked hundred hour weeks serving my residency, living on snatches of sleep, and spending every waking moment worrying about you—praying for you—you thought I was living the good life with Scott!" She pressed her lips together and turned away. "I'm sorry about the medication. I just wanted to help—"

Something in her voice penetrated the fog in his mind. "Kris, wait—"

She looked back. "I'd rather you didn't stand—*yet*."

"When I want your advice, Doctor, I'll pay for it." He gained his feet, swayed.

"Because if you fall, I'm not sure I can catch you," Kris went on, her voice even now, reasonable.

He caught the back of the chair and ran a hand through his hair. "What happens next?" His voice softened. He couldn't get too upset when all he wanted was to pull her into his arms.

"Food will help if you can eat. If not, you'll have to sleep it off." She watched him, not trusting this sudden cooperation.

"What about fresh air?" He looked hopeful.

"*At thirty below?*"

"I seem to remember making a similar remark when you came back from the hangar. As I suspected, it isn't such a good idea. What's for dinner?"

"Are you sure?"

"It's worth a try. Besides, you *promised* me apple pie." He quirked an eyebrow in her direction.

"Can you make it to the kitchen or would you like me to bring a tray?"

"I'll make it to the kitchen," he said through clenched teeth. "My image has suffered enough damage for one day."

"What image is that?" Kris asked, unable to resist teasing him. "If it's the macho one you're worried about, doubtless it will survive intact."

He grimaced. "Remember I owe you for this. Your time will come." But she could hear the laughter in his voice. She allowed herself to relax, ever so slightly.

Matt awakened with a burning thirst. He'd turned the heater down before going to bed and now he shivered. He found a robe behind the door and pulled it on.

Matt entered the kitchen and stopped short. Kris sat at the table, a laptop computer and books spread before her. Rather, *she'd been sitting*. Now she sprawled amidst the clutter, her cheek resting on an arm crooked beneath her head. He walked over to touch her shoulder. She didn't stir.

"Kris—" He started to shake her when he glanced at the computer screen. He reached over to turn it for a better look. His brows knit as he scanned the contents.

Malpractice? Kris? That explained a lot, including Roy's evasiveness. All Matt had been able to get him to say was that Kris had taken a leave from the hospital. When he checked with the hospital, they had been even more close-mouthed than Roy.

"What on earth!" Forgetting the need for stealth, he spat out the exclamation.

Kris sat up, blinked, and yawned. Then she saw Matt reading the report she'd been studying and came instantly awake. She reached out and pressed a button and the screen went blank.

"Is this what you call getting even?" she asked, her voice cold. "If it is, I think all scores are settled."

Matt turned away and opened a cupboard door. "I came in to get something to drink and found you asleep. I tried to wake you and saw what you were reading. What's all that about a malpractice suit?"

"I'm afraid that's none of your business." She tried to keep her voice even, controlled.

Matt shrugged. "Would you like anything?"

Kris pushed her hair back. "Water, please."

"Don't you think you should be in bed?"

"Sleeping isn't something I do very well anymore." She took the glass. "Except like this—work until I fall asleep. I can't seem to schedule it."

His eyes narrowed. "Were you sleeping this morning—yesterday morning—when I arrived?" A frown creased his brow. Was that why it had taken so long for her to awaken and turn the runway lights on? *Because she had fallen asleep from exhaustion?*

She swallowed. "I went to bed about this time. For once I did sleep. I was having a wonderful dream—about flying along the beach south of Crescent City. That's why I didn't hear you at first. The sound seemed part of the dream. I'm sorry. And I don't know what's wrong with the radio. Yanni had a few problems with it, but thought he had it fixed before he left."

"Forget it. I checked it out and it seems to be working. Maybe the weather was interfering with the signal." He made a dismissive gesture. "That must've been some dream." He watched her as he leaned against the counter, drinking his water. Her hair tumbled about her face, her eyelids drooped, and her lips invited his kiss. He felt a familiar surge of desire.

Kris shrugged. "That's all I seem to have left." She stood and snapped the computer closed. She stacked the books in a pile and picked them up.

"Don't let me run you off," Matt quipped. "I'm going back to bed. My conscience is clear—I've been sleeping like a baby. Either that—or your medication."

Her breath caught and her eyes lifted to his. At sight of the sheer misery he saw there, he drew in his breath and expelled it sharply.

"I'm sorry. I didn't mean to hurt you, Kris! I was only teasing—"

"Forgive me for not being able to appreciate your sense of humor just now," Kris said, turning to leave.

"You could try talking about it," Matt suggested. "That might help you sleep. And I'm a good listener."

She stopped and turned back. "Thanks for the offer, but I never learned to talk about my problems." She held his gaze until he looked away. She knew he remembered saying those same words to her years ago in the hangar at Holland Aviation. Then he walked away, across the tarmac in the rain. She had not spoken to him again until Hal's funeral.

Matt stood there for a long time after Kris left. He turned his empty water glass between his fingers. Then he looked around the room. He would give a lot to know where Kris kept those pills that knocked him out so effectively. He needed them if he planned to get any more sleep tonight.

Kris awakened from a restless sleep and looked outside. It was dark out but yesterday's storm appeared to be over. She had to clear the runway of snow as soon as possible. There was a good chance Yanni would be coming back today. She went through the kitchen to pull open the door to the garage.

"Good morning," Matt called from the den. He stood up and walked toward her.

Kris turned. "Did you have breakfast?"

"I managed." His eyes narrowed. "Where are you going?"

"I have to clear the runway." She turned to open the door again.

"I'll help—"

"No, thanks."

"How long will it take?"

"About forty-five minutes," she replied. "If I can get the plow started."

"I'll give you an hour and then I'm coming to find you." He looked at her again. "Let me help."

"I can't, even if I wanted to. Bill has insurance on everything and you aren't covered." She didn't know if that was true or not, but it sounded logical.

"Who cares about the insurance—"

Kris met his eyes, held them. "Please, Matt. I need to do this—*alone.*"

Matt studied her. The expressive green eyes were haunted by personal demons he could only begin to guess at. He pushed his hands in his pockets and turned away to keep from reaching out and pulling her into his arms. "Be careful, Kris."

She almost weakened. It had been so long since anyone seemed to care. Her lips parted, then she changed her mind. She opened the door and stepped into the garage.

Matt watched from the window as Kris drove the snow plow back and forth across the runway, carefully pushing the snow between the runway lights, uncovering them as necessary and making sure they remained clear. She had apparently been able to start the plow with no trouble and seemed to be making good time. He glanced at his watch. She'd been gone forty minutes.

Kris pushed open the door and removed her gloves. As warmth and feeling returned to her hands, a cut on her wrist began to bleed and pain washed over her. She went to the sink.

"There you are." Matt walked into the room. "I was about to launch a search and rescue mission. What happened?" His tone turned to concern as he hurried toward her.

Kris held her hand under the running water. The cut now bled profusely. Matt reached for her arm.

"Don't!" Kris said, her eyes filled with pain. "Haven't you heard of blood borne pathogens?"

"I have," he replied, ignoring her warning. The cut slashed across the back of her wrist and he pulled the edges together and held them to slow the flow of blood. "However, I would put you at a very low risk. You're a doctor—"

"Who could have caught almost anything from a patient."

"Again a low risk. At any rate, I'm willing to take a chance. I don't enjoy seeing anyone in pain, either."

"I can do that," Kris said, reaching over to hold the wound closed.

Matt rinsed and dried his hands. "Where do you have bandages?"

"Above the sink. There should be a first aid kit."

She watched as he began wrapping her wrist. When he finished she looked up to meet his eyes. "Thanks. It feels better."

"How did you cut yourself?" Matt felt himself drowning in the shimmering depths of her eyes. If he didn't watch himself, he would pull her into his arms in the next heartbeat.

"I grazed my wrist against the blade when I put the plow away. It didn't start bleeding until I came in here and began to warm up."

"Have you ever been told you need a keeper?" Matt teased, trying to lighten the mood, to make her smile. Apparently that was not the thing to say. He watched as tears flooded her eyes.

"Well, the right person hasn't applied for the job." Her voice sounded choked. She turned to leave the room.

"Kris!" He caught her arm and turned her to face him. She pushed against him blindly, contacting the tender area around his collar bone. He flinched and released her.

Kris stared in horror, stricken that she'd caused him pain. "I'm sorry," she whispered, reaching out to touch him.

"You have some real problems, Kid." Matt's voice was not mocking, or accusing—merely stating a fact.

Kris met his eyes, nodded.

"Is there anyone you can talk to? I know you don't think you know me well enough—but from where I stand, it looks like I'm all you've got."

Kris turned away. "No, there isn't anyone I can talk to. And you're right. I don't know you well enough."

"Don't you think it might be time to change that?" Matt held his breath as he waited for her reply.

Kris looked at him. "Once upon a time, I thought so. You didn't."

"I've admitted I was wrong, Kris. I would give anything if I could play that scene again."

"Really?" Her eyes widened in mock interest. "And what do you think you might do differently?"

34

"I know exactly what I'd do," he grated. "We were alone in the hangar—alone at the airport. Rain fell incessantly. A pile of camping gear lay in the corner." He turned away. "I wanted to push you down on one of those sleeping bags and kiss you until you begged me to make love to you."

A brief moment of silence. "Why didn't you?" Kris whispered.

He whirled back to face her. *"Why didn't I?"*

She shrugged. "I wouldn't have put up even a token resistance."

CHAPTER THREE

(From the Journal of Benjamin F. Walker, July 12, 1968)

We buried Joey today. I wish I could do something to help Hal and Jean. Hal is a zombie and Jean keeps holding on to Kristi. Beth managed to get Jean to lay down for awhile and I held Kristi. She didn't cry once. She seems to be as much in shock as anyone, although I know she's too young to understand. She's the most beautiful child. Those green eyes are going to cause a lot of heartache one day . . .

I know Hal blames himself for Joey's death, but he couldn't have known that the construction workers left the transformer unsecured. Joey had Hal's sense of curiosity. I know I'm being selfish, but it's a miracle that Matt wasn't with him. Those two were virtually inseparable, doing everything together. . .

Matt put aside his father's journal and sat for a moment, letting sadness wash over him for all the losses in his life.

He'd taken one of the pills from the bottle Kris gave him. She told him she trusted him to regulate his own dosage better than she could. He knew what reaction to expect and he hated taking any medication, she reasoned. The pain in his leg had dulled, but his mind still raced.

Over and over, he kept replaying her words to him just before she turned and walked out of the room. With each repeat of the scene, his smoldering desire for her fanned into a conflagration.

Kristin Holland had been a problem for him from the moment he turned and bumped into her in Hal's office. He couldn't remember the last time he'd seen her. She'd been away at college and then medical school and their time off never seemed to mesh. She had somehow grown up without his being there to notice. Boy, had she grown up! His lips twitched at the knowledge that his father had pegged Kris a heartbreaker at the age of two!

Matt stood and walked to the window. Daylight had broken and Kris had turned the runway lights off to conserve energy. How could she be so conscientious about everything else, and neglect her own health? Matt shook his head. He had to figure out a way to get her to talk to him. Maybe then he would be able to help her.

His memories persisted and Matt frowned. The encounter in Hal's office left him so shaken that he decided to avoid further contact with Kris. Added to that, the next morning Scott staked his claim to her. To try and win her didn't seem worth the effort. He knew he would be leaving for the Persian Gulf within a week. His strategy worked until the last day.

He stood in the hanger looking at Hal's Piper Cub, remembering all the joy of his first flight in it. He'd said good-by to Hal and his mother. His orders had come to rejoin his unit for deployment to Saudi Arabia and Desert Shield. He reached out to stroke the varnished wooden propeller and sensed someone else in the hangar. He knew before he turned who would be there.

Kris stopped when she saw him, then moved forward. She reached up to touch the propeller as he had.

"Did Dad teach you to fly in her, too?"

Matt nodded. "Too? When did you learn to fly?"

"Ten years ago. This is still my favorite plane. Dad's, too—I think."

"I can understand that. I have to admit it rates pretty high with me." He ran his hand over the propeller again.

She studied him. "I saw the picture Dad has of you with your A-10. You must be pretty happy in the air force."

He frowned. "Why do you say that?"

She shrugged. "You're smiling. I haven't seen you do that since you've been back. Not that you ever smiled that much—"

"You've hardly seen me at all."

"I wonder why," Kris said, watching him.

"Maybe because you've been with Scott most of the time." He hadn't meant to say that. It slipped out.

She threw him a glance he couldn't interpret. "Not really." Kris walked around the plane, unconsciously doing a preflight inspection. She reached up to touch a frayed piece of fabric. "I realize I don't know you very well anymore, but I hoped we could be friends—now that you're back."

"I don't think that's possible," Matt replied.

Her head jerked up and she stared at him. Color flooded her face. "I'm sorry—"

"Is that what you want?" His voice had changed, husky now, and a little strained. *"For us to be friends?"*

Her breath caught. She moved toward him, her steps slow and uncertain. She shook her head.

Driven by something too strong to resist, he reached out to touch her face, to draw the back of his knuckles down her cheek. Her skin felt like silk. He brushed his thumb across her mouth and felt it tremble. Her lips parted.

He never knew who made the first move. He heard a groan and didn't know which of them uttered it. His arms, seemingly of their own volition, reached out to imprison her. Crushing her against him, he bent his head and kissed her as if she were the sustaining force in life.

Moments later—or perhaps longer—he put her away from him. He reached out to fasten a button on her shirt with hands that were none too steady.

"What—?" She looked at him through eyes cloudy with desire. She began to tremble.

"I can't do this, Kris." He drew her close again, burying his face in her hair. "I'm leaving tomorrow for the Persian Gulf."

Matt turned as he heard Kris enter the den and felt his breathing constrict as he looked at her. She'd changed out of her ski suit and her hair hung down her back in cascading waves of gold. Jeans hugged the impossible slimness of her hips while a sweater gently outlined every curve.

Kris looked up and caught his expression. "What's wrong?" When he didn't answer, she frowned. "What are you thinking?"

He moved toward her. "About the night I left for the Persian Gulf."

Pain slashed across her face. Her eyes closed and he knew the memories were still as vivid for her as they were for him. "Don't!"

He caught her arm, the one with the cut above the wrist. "Are you going to let me help now?" He saw that she'd already replaced the bandage he put on earlier. The new one was neater and more compact. *Could he not do anything well enough for her?*

She shook her head. "You're a guest—at least until Bill and Marie return. They can put you to work if they want."

"And you aren't a guest?" Why was she here and how long did she plan to stay? *And what about the malpractice suit?*

"Not since they left and I offered to take care of the place. They knew I had experience around airports."

"But how can you afford so much time away from your job?" He followed her into the kitchen.

She froze for an instant, and when she spoke, she chose her words with care. "Some things are more important than others," she said, her voice a little too casual.

"I won't argue with that, but perhaps you'd care to elaborate." He knew from Hal how important being a doctor was to Kris. She'd given up everything for it. And many of her weeks as a resident had been longer than the hundred hours she'd mentioned last night.

"Friends, for instance," Kris said, glancing at him. "Especially when you have as few left as I have. When I came up here, Bill and Marie were doing me a favor. I had a chance to return it."

"Why did you come up here?" Maybe the best way to find out what he needed to know was to ask.

"At Dad's funeral I saw Bill and Marie again. I'd met them several times, but I didn't know them well. They told me to come to them if I ever needed anyone or anything. They said they'd be here. I never imagined actually taking them up on their offer, until two months later, when I looked around and that was the only option I had." She shrugged. "You appear to know Bill and Marie—and Carl—a lot better than I do." She began cleaning the sink.

"Yes, because of the contract. I've known them all my life. I was born here."

Kris looked at him. "You said something about that yesterday—about a bond between our fathers—and a pledge to take care of one another. Tell me about it."

"They made a pact after the war—Dad, Hal, Bill, and Roy Ferguson. They flew lend-lease planes to Fairbanks along the Alaska Highway to hand over to the Russians—and they were with the Eleventh Air Force during the Aleutian campaign."

"I knew Dad and Roy did that, but I didn't know about Bill and—I'm sorry, I didn't know your father—"

"Ben Walker." Even now, Matt found it hard to speak his name.

Kris glanced at him, turned back to her work. "I've heard that name. Dad talked about Ben a lot. I assumed they had been friends." She frowned. "There's a parchment scroll—some kind of contract—in Dad's office, and Bill has one in the den—" She looked at Matt, her eyes wide. "Is that—"

He nodded and dropped down on a barstool. "They shared a lot more than friendship. Bill and Dad settled here after the war. Your mother was never strong enough to live in Alaska so Hal went south. When Dad died, Mom didn't want to stay here alone, but before we left, I knew Bill and Marie as a second set of parents and Carl as a brother.

"We went to California and I got to know Hal. In the pact, they all pledged to care for each other's families and children if anything should happen to any of them. Roy drew up the contract you saw as a reminder. Hal honored his part of that agreement by always being there for me. Now that he's gone, everything has fallen to Bill and Roy. That's why you're here, and why I felt I could come back when my life took a low turn."

Kris stopped working, looked at him, her eyes iridescent through a sheen of tears. "What a beautiful story!" she whispered. "Dad never talked about it. How did you know?"

"Mom told me when we still lived here. Marie confirmed it. Hal never talked about it, but he did talk about his friendship with my dad." Matt shrugged. "I know it had to be hard for Hal to have me around, after losing Joey, but—"

"Joey?" It was an idle question. Kris continued cleaning the sink.

Matt froze, staring at her. *"Kris, look at me!"*

Startled at the intensity in his voice, she looked up.

"Joey—your brother," Matt said, his eyes holding hers.

"I didn't have a brother."

Matt felt the blood drain from his face. "Dear, God!" he whispered. "How could they have done this to you?"

"Matt, what are you talking about?" Kris wet her lips, suddenly uncertain. Her hands shook and she clenched the sponge in a death grip.

He ran a hand through his hair. "I thought you knew." His voice strained with anguish. "How can I be the one to tell you? You had a brother, a year younger than me, five years older than you. He died when he was seven. I can see why you wouldn't remember or understand—you were only two. I just never thought they wouldn't have told you about him."

"How is it that you know so much more about my family than I do?" Kris couldn't look at him, afraid of the emotions that swept her. "It sounds as if Dad replaced Joey with you, and obviously you considered him a father figure."

"Perhaps. It worked for us."

Kris shrugged. "Yes, quite well." She tried to mask the bitterness in her voice.

"Kris, there's no reason to be hurt. Hal loved you very much." Matt struggled for words to comfort her.

"I never doubted his love. But he never really had time for a daughter in his life. Now I know why I could never measure up." She looked at Matt, swallowing her pain. "If all this is true, why weren't we together more as kids?"

Matt shoved his hands in his pockets. "That was mostly my fault. I became pretty anti-social after I lost my Dad. And I still hadn't gotten over Joey. Hal helped Mom send me to military school where they hoped I'd settle down. I did, more or less to their expectations."

Kris kept polishing the sink, anything to avoid looking at Matt. "Beth remarried a few years ago, didn't she?"

"Yes—someone she met through the flight school—another pilot." Matt watched Kris, so intent on her work.

"So you get along with him?" Kris desperately sought for anything to divert the conversation, to give her time to deal with what she'd just heard.

"Well enough. We have common interests, he's good to Mom and she loves him. I don't think I have a right to ask for more in a step-father."

"And Tracy? You wrecked her car—"

"Yes. She doesn't fly. She married an investment banker and lives in Arizona. They have three daughters, two of them twins. He isn't too thrilled with her right now because she let me drive her new Jaguar, but other than that, he's okay. She's happy. Dad would be pleased for them—for Tracy and Mom."

"What about for you?" Kris finally looked at him.

Pain flashed in his eyes. He turned away. "I'm afraid he'd have disowned me by now." He walked out of the room.

With the kitchen spotless again, Kris began preparing lunch. The few hours of sunlight had faded. The sense of being in a time warp where nothing was real weighed on her. Even Matt's presence added to it. The story he told her must be true. Strange she hadn't heard it before. Had everyone just assumed she knew—about Joey and about the pledge between their families?

She remembered Beth Walker's kindness during her mother's illness and after her death. Kris had been reluctant to accept her friendship. What a difference it could have made if she'd known that Beth was there for her, just as Hal had been for Matt. Unwilling tears flooded her eyes and she tried to blink them away.

Matt glanced into the kitchen as he passed by and came to a stop. Kris still stood by the sink, her head bowed. He could see her shoulders shaking. As he watched, she reached up to brush at her face.

Kris looked up as she felt a hand on her arm. Matt looked down at her with the turbulent blue gaze that had altered the course of her life once before. Her eyes closed over the tears flowing unchecked down her cheeks.

"Please go away!"

The husky plea went unheeded. *"Not this time."* Matt lifted her in his arms and carried her into the den. He sat down on the sofa, still holding her.

"Now cry. As much as you need to. We may be getting somewhere."

Kris tried to check her sobs. She struggled briefly and Matt's arms tightened. He pressed her head against his shoulder. "Don't fight me, Kristi!" His lips brushed her hair. "I wouldn't hurt you again for anything, and neither will anyone else as long as I'm here!"

Kris relaxed at the endearment. Her father had called her Kristi as a child. *Her mother, too.* Feeling safe and protected in Matt's arms, she turned her face into his shoulder. He stroked her hair as her tears soaked his sweater.

Matt was alone in the den when he heard the radio crackle. He hurried over to answer the call.

"Bentley Base, this is Yanni."

"Bentley Base here. Come in, Yanni. How's it going, buddy?"

"Bentley Base, who am I talking to?"

"This is Matt. I flew in yesterday."

"Hey, Matt! That's good news. I've been a little worried about leaving Kris alone. I'm calling to tell her that I won't be back for a few more days. Do you think she can handle it?"

"I know *we* can," Matt replied. "How are Salina and Brandi and the baby?"

"All are fine. Josef has a son. He is happy. Is Kris all right?"

"Fine." Matt hesitated. "Do you need to speak to her?"

"Not really. Take care of her, okay?"

"I will. Let us know when you decide to come back."

"Will do. Yanni, over and out." The radio went silent.

Matt flipped off the transmitter and turned away with a frown. *What else could he have told Yanni?* Kris was far from all right. She had cried herself to sleep in his arms and he carried her to bed. She slept so soundly now that she appeared dead to the world. He'd been checking on her every half hour or so.

Matt turned back to the radio, an idea taking shape in his mind. He looked up a number and began to transmit.

Matt tore his eyes away from Ben's journal and sprang to his feet as a cry came from Kris's room. Long strides carried him across the hall. He had left the door ajar and now he pushed it open with such force that he had to catch it to keep it from banging into the wall.

He had not undressed her when he put her to bed, but had removed her boots, belt and sweater. Now she slept with the blanket thrown aside, her shirt pulled free of her jeans and several of the buttons unfastened. As he watched she twisted restlessly, flinging an arm across her face.

"Scott, please!" The words came to him clearly. "Don't do this. Don't—"

Matt dropped to his knees beside the bed, catching her wrist. Some instinct told him that she didn't need to wake and find him towering over her.

"Kris, sweetheart, wake up!" His words were low and husky. With his other hand he stroked her cheek with a feather light touch.

In the dim light from the hallway, Matt saw her open her eyes and slowly turn her head to focus on him.

"Matt." The whispered word was joyous, spoken almost reverently. The tension drained from her body to leave her collapsed against the pillows. "I prayed you would come."

Matt sat down on the edge of the bed and gathered her into his arms. "Shshsh, darling! You were having a dream."

She melted against him. "A nightmare." Fully awake now, she trembled. "That's why I don't sleep much. When I sleep soundly, I have nightmares."

"*Nightmares about Scott.*" Try as he would, Matt could not keep the harshness out of his voice.

He could feel the tension building in her body again and when she struggled he placed her back on the bed. He studied her face in the dim light.

"I think you'd better tell me about the nightmares."

Kris sat up and wrapped her arms around her knees. "There's no reason to." She had withdrawn. "I did pray that you would come, but you only show up in my dreams. That doesn't count. This doesn't involve you."

"Does it involve the reason you left your job, California, everything you've worked for—"

"Everything I worked for didn't mean much anymore without someone to share it. And after the malpractice suit I didn't have much left to fight with." She rested her forehead on her knees. "Yes." It came out a muffled sigh. "The nightmares are caused by the reason I left—*the final straw.*"

"Do Bill and Marie know about the nightmares? Do they know the reason you came here?"

"They didn't ask. They just accepted that I needed to be here."

"Has being here helped?" Matt pursued relentlessly.

His tone finally got through to Kris and she straightened, glancing at him in the semi-darkness. "You know, when you changed careers, you should have become a lawyer." Her voice was dry.

Matt did not smile. "Funny. Roy said the same thing when I tried to coerce him into telling me where you were."

Kris held his gaze. "He couldn't tell you. He could only talk if—" Too late she realized what she had almost said and clapped a hand over her mouth, her eyes wide and tragic.

"*If what, Kris?*" Matt's hands shot out to grip her shoulders. "What is so terrible that you can't tell me; that Roy can't tell me? We're supposed to be in this together. Roy isn't supposed to choose between you and me. Bill and Marie aren't supposed to choose—"

"Then don't force them to."

He stared at her, and his grip relaxed. He released her. "You did."

She shook her head. "Bill and Marie don't know. I never suspected that you would ask Roy. Roy is sharp enough in his own right to know better than to tell you."

"And why would he decide not to tell me?"

"Because he cares about you. He cares about everybody, but you and I are the children he never had, the children of his best friends, and we were near by. He knows us better. I had no one else to go to—and—" She swallowed, unable to go on.

"Kris." Matt's voice came out a low growl of frustration. "How much more do you think I can take? Talk to me!"

"I can't! Not now."

"Because I let you down? Because I walked away and left you at Hal's funeral? I've been looking for you for months, Kris."

He stood up and walked to the window. "It took a few months to realize that Scott wasn't for you. Whatever you had with him, he wasn't there when you needed him. When I held you at Hal's funeral, I knew everything I felt for you was still there, as strong as ever, and you knew it, too. I ran scared again." He turned back. "But I've found you now, and if it takes the rest of my life, I promise I will make you forget anything you ever felt for Scott."

A strangled sob escaped before Kris buried her face in a pillow. Her shoulders heaved with emotion.

Matt crossed to her, caught her face between his hands. "Kris?"

She swallowed, brushing her fingers across her lashes. "Oh, Matt, will it always be the same with us? *Just in time to be too late.*"

"Don't say that!" He sat on the edge of the bed. Light from the hall shadowed his face. His robe gaped open at the throat, and Kris could see his bare chest. She wanted to touch him, to feel the hard wall of muscles, to bury her fingers in the hairs curling over it. Aching with need, she ran her tongue over dry swollen lips.

Matt's gaze focused on her mouth, then dropped lower. Her shirt held together precariously with only a couple of buttons. He reached out and closed those that had slipped loose. He could feel her breath against his neck and he steeled himself against the temptation she posed. He didn't want her like this.

Kris sighed. "Why do you have to have so much control?" Her wistful voice was tinged with frustration.

"Because I need it—especially around you. I remember very well what happens when I lose control."

She studied him from beneath her lashes. Finally she shrugged. "It hardly matters anyway. It's far too late—"

His head jerked up. Even in the dim light, he couldn't miss the incredible sadness of her expression. Against his will he reached out to touch her, resting his hand against her face.

"Kris, what happened?" His voice was the merest whisper, so careful was he of frightening her. "What hurt you? Why did you leave California?"

She shrugged again. "Actually, it all started when you didn't happen to me. What did happen is a nightmare I can't share. With *anyone*, and especially not with you." Her eyes pleaded with him for understanding.

"What could be worse than losing Hal and facing a malpractice suit?"

She turned her face away, staring out the window. "Scott."

Matt stared at her averted profile. "Scott? What do you mean, *Scott?*"

"Just that. Scott." She lay back and pulled the blanket up under her chin and closed her eyes. A moment later he heard her even breathing.

Matt reached out to touch her cheek. She stirred, but did not awaken. He sat there in the darkness for a long time, looking at her. Then through the open door he heard the radio crackle again.

"Bentley Base, this is Counselor."

Matt stood up and left the room, carefully closing the door, and hurried to answer the radio.

Matt paced back and forth in the den like a caged animal. Roy had refused to budge when Matt grilled him for information on Kris. But somehow what he wouldn't say had given Matt more insight than he could possibly know. Roy and Kris were protecting someone. Someone, presumably, that Matt knew as well. It didn't take a rocket scientist to guess that someone was Scott.

Matt paused to look at Bill's parchment copy of the contract hanging on the wall. Aside from being in love with Kris, he had inherited an obligation to help her—one he intended to take seriously this time. Something told him he had violated the spirit of the pact when he walked away from her, but then his own survival and well being had been tenuous at best. He hadn't been able to deal with his own problems at the time, let alone a relationship.

Yes, he told himself bitterly, his father would have disowned him for giving in to his own weaknesses and not fighting harder for what he wanted where Kris was concerned.

Matt reached out and lightly touched the aged parchment. "You're right, Dad," he whispered, his voice husky. "Kris is a heartbreaker! But we both know she's worth it."

CHAPTER FOUR

A hand touched his and Matt looked up to see Kris beside him. He closed Ben's journal and laid it aside, then turned to her. He reached out to clasp her arms.

"Kris? How do you feel?" He could hear the huskiness in his voice, knew his eyes revealed way too much. He could feel her softness through the thin shirt and fought the desire to pull her into his arms again. Reluctantly, he let his hands drop.

She sat facing him. "How long did I sleep?" She pushed her hair back and drew a hand across her mouth.

"Almost twenty-four hours, give or take those few minutes last night when you woke up." His glance swept over her, missing nothing. Her eyes were clear and bright with no trace of last night's tears. She seemed rested and more relaxed than he'd seen since his arrival. With her hair tumbling around her face, she also looked about twelve years old and very vulnerable. Matt felt a sudden fierce protectiveness surge through him.

"Last night? Did you come into my room, or did I dream you?" Troubled green eyes searched his face.

Matt grinned. "Oh, I was there. You had a nightmare. But you did say I only show up in your dreams. Whether or not I showed up again after you fell asleep—"

She punched his arm, her mouth curving into a smile. "All right. I guess I asked for that."

"You look much better than yesterday," Matt said. His eyes roamed her face. *That was an understatement.* She looked wonderful.

"Have you heard from Yanni?" Kris changed the subject, pushing her hair back with another restless gesture.

"He called last night. He won't be back for a few more days. I assured him that we could handle it."

She looked up to meet his eyes. "*We?*"

He grinned. "We. Yanni put me to work."

She wrinkled her nose. "You don't play fair."

"Maybe you should remember that." He held her gaze long enough to convey that he was no longer talking about Yanni or Bentley Base.

Kris lowered her eyes. "How is the baby?" Her voice sounded strained and she twisted her fingers together.

"Fine. Josef has a son." Matt watched her.

Kris smiled, a little wistfully. "I wish I could see him. I hope he doesn't look like Josef!"

Matt laughed. "Short round men don't appeal to you?"

"Only if they're under three or over seventy."

"Speaking of someone in the *latter* category," Matt said, his voice casual, "I talked to Roy last night."

"Roy?" Her eyes flew to his face.

"Roy Ferguson," Matt confirmed.

She stared at him, wet her lips. *"My lawyer?"*

"And mine."

Kris stood up and whirled away from him, her hair swinging around her shoulders.

"Kris—"

"And what did you talk about?"

"You. Hal. The rest of the family."

"And?" Her eyes flashed with suspicion.

He sighed. "And the malpractice suit against you. He only confirmed what I already suspected. In fact you mentioned it yourself last night, whether or not you remember."

She stood perfectly still. "Anything else?"

"I'm afraid not."

She let out her breath in relief. She reacted by turning on Matt. "How could he tell a stranger—why would he betray a confidence—?"

"I'm not a stranger, Kris. Roy knows that. He's part of the pact, too, remember? We talked about that last night. After you went back to sleep, I had to find out what we're dealing with. I'm worried about you."

She wet her lips. "Well, aren't you going to ask?" Her voice, flat and brittle, fought to conceal the pain her eyes betrayed.

"*Ask what?*" Matt shook his head. What did she expect him to do? Obviously something that would hurt her.

"If I'm guilty." Her lips compressed and she held her head high, pride battling to overcome the tears welling in her eyes.

Matt stood up, eyes narrowed slits of anger. "I don't need to ask." His voice was clipped and formal. "Roy did assure me, however, that all charges were dropped by the Medical Review Board. You still have your license." He took a restless turn around the room as he spoke, then turned to pin her with a questioning gaze.

Kris shook her head. "That's not good enough. I don't know if I'm guilty or not! *Can you understand?* The world thinks I killed a child. Her parents believe I did. I relive that night every time I close my eyes. Whether I'm cleared or not, I don't know if I can go back into another operating room!"

Before he had time to think about the consequences, Matt crossed to Kris and pulled her up into his arms.

"It's all gone," she whispered, clinging to him, hating herself for her weakness. "Everything in my life is gone! That's why I'm here. I have nowhere else to go!"

Matt's arms tightened and he stroked her hair and back, trying to comfort her. Any words he might use to reassure her would be empty and meaningless. After a moment he led her back to the sofa and sat down beside her. He brushed the hair from her face.

"Can I get you a drink? Coffee?"

She shook her head. "May I ask you something?" Her voice was hesitant, afraid almost. She wet her lips.

"Sure. I'll try to answer."

"Tell me about Joey." Her eyes were troubled. "I need to know."

Again she saw pain slash across his face and heard his harsh intake of breath. Her hands went out to catch his.

"I'm sorry! I didn't realize how hard it would be for you. I just— there's no one else I can ask." A tear rolled down her cheek.

"Kris!" He swallowed the emotion in his voice as his hands clasped hers. His eyes closed for a moment, remembering. A smile touched his lips.

"Joey was so proud of you," Matt said. "He thought having a little sister was the greatest thing in the world. We were visiting that summer and you were walking. He took you everywhere with us and introduced you to everybody as 'my baby Kristi'.

"Of course having you with us got a lot of attention, because you were so cute. So was Joey. You looked so much alike, blonde curls, green eyes. Before long I was as taken with you as he was. You even had my Dad twisted around your little finger, and he wasn't one to get mushy a lot.

"Hal had just bought the airfield and was having some new runways put in. A crew was laying electrical conduit for the lights and had gone home for the weekend.

"I had picked up a summer cold and was running a fever that afternoon. You had gotten a little cranky, too, and Jean put you down for a nap. Joey was not one to sit still for long so he wandered off on his own."

Matt paused to look at Kris. Her fingers clutched his and she was holding her breath, her eyes wide and riveted on his face. He closed his eyes.

"I was watching television. Some western series. The picture flickered once, then went blank. At the same time, all the lights went off. I remember hearing you cry and Mom and Jean went into the nursery. I followed because everything was dark, and I was a little scared.

"Jean picked you up and I overheard her say something to my mother about another squirrel in the transformer. I went cold and began running through the house looking for Joey because I remembered he had been fascinated by all the electrical work going on.

"About that time Dad and Hal came in from outside. I grabbed Hal's hand and told him he had to find Joey. I was crying. I guess I already knew."

Matt paused and Kris reached up to brush a lock of hair back from his face. "You never got over it, did you?" Her voice was tender with compassion. "Yesterday, you said—"

He opened his eyes. "I couldn't even look at you after that. And we had gotten very close. You would run to me as often as to Joey. With him gone, you tried to turn to me." He shook his head. "That was the first time I let you down. As you grew older, you began to look even more like Joey. I couldn't handle it. I began to find excuses not to go with them when Mom and Dad went to visit. My feelings for you were so mixed up with what I felt for Joey. That's why we weren't together more as kids. *Because I was afraid.* Even then, I couldn't handle my feelings for you."

Matt picked up a photo album from the coffee table. "I was looking at this last night. Marie has pictures that go back to the beginning of time. Pictures of Joey. Pictures of the three of us. Pictures of Dad and Hal."

Kris reached for the book. "Show me." She let it fall open. "Tell me about them."

Matt nodded. "There's some passages in Dad's journal you need to read, too. About the pledge. And about Joey. Someone should have told you all this long ago."

"Maybe it's something you were meant to do. Maybe we can help each other heal."

Matt looked at her and nodded again. "I'd like that." He bent over the album, pulling half of it onto his lap. "Let's start at the beginning."

Matt tensed and looked up, listening intently. Kris closed the album, her eyes searching his face.

"What is it?" They had been looking at photographs for what seemed hours and she stretched.

"A plane." Matt still strained to hear and at last Kris heard the faint sound of an engine.

"Yanni?" She asked in a whisper.

"I don't think so. What's he flying?"

"The Cherokee." Kris could hear the plane clearly now. "I think it's Bill's plane!"

"I think you're right!"

Kris went down the hall to turn on the runway lights, a signal that someone had heard the plane and would be along to collect the occupants. She stepped into her ski suit.

"Wait for me."

Kris turned to look at Matt and felt her breath catch. Funny how something as simple as a battered leather jacket could transform him from the gentle comforter of a moment ago to someone who sent her pulse rate into overdrive. She swallowed and reached for the keys to the Bronco.

Matt's hand closed over hers. "Allow me."

As they drove out of the garage, they could just distinguish the plane swooping down for a landing.

"It is Bill," Kris said. "I thought he would call and give us an agenda."

"I wonder if Marie is with him." Matt didn't look at Kris, but concentrated on driving.

"If she is, I'm afraid it'll be because they decided she wasn't a suitable donor for Carl."

"Is there anyone else?" Matt asked, his voice reluctant.

"I don't know. They've already ruled out Bill because of his age."

They were silent as they drove to the hangar. Matt jumped out to open the doors. "Do I need to move my plane?"

Kris shook her head. "There's plenty of room for him."

They turned to watch the aircraft taxiing toward them. The day was clear and crisp, the sun low on the horizon. Kris thought how different this was from the morning that Matt had arrived—how long ago? Four days. She sighed, her brow creased with worry. The fact that Bill and Marie were back so soon could not be a good sign.

The plane came to a stop and Bill cut the engine. Matt walked around to pull the door open, Kris just behind him.

Bill looked up, his face lighting with pleasure. "Matt! We heard from Roy that you were here. I've never been so glad to see anyone!"

"What's going on?" Matt asked, clasping Bill's hand.

"I have Marie in here. She's pretty weak. They only let me bring her home because I assured them that we had our own personal doctor to take care of her—" He looked past Matt to Kris. "Kris, love." Matt heard the tenderness in Bill's voice, saw the affection in his eyes.

Kris pushed past Matt. "How is she?" Kris frowned. "You know you're a fool, Bill, for doing this."

"I know." He stepped down from the plane. "But she wouldn't have it any other way. Once we knew Carl was going to be all right, she couldn't rest until she came back. She's been worried about you."

Kris threw Matt a guilty look, then turned back to Bill. "Let me look at her. I'm glad about Carl."

"Yes." Bill's sigh held a world of relief. Kris squeezed his arm before climbing into the plane.

A few minutes later Bill handed the slight figure of his wife into Matt's waiting arms. Marie touched his face.

"Matthew, dear," she whispered. "I'm so glad you came back to us!"

Matt dropped a kiss on her forehead. "I'm glad I'm here, too." His voice husky with emotion, his arms cradled their precious cargo as he carried Marie to the Bronco. Kris installed her in the back seat, her head on Bill's lap.

"Drive them back," Matt said, catching Kris's hands briefly. "I'll put the plane away. Come back for me after you take care of Marie."

Kris nodded, dragging her gaze away from him, and climbed into the Bronco. She drove as fast as she dared, being careful to avoid any bumps.

It took half an hour for Kris to get Marie settled into her room. Although weak and exhausted from the trip, Marie looked surprisingly well, considering the ordeal she'd been through. Kris knew she was far too close to the upper age limit to have been the ideal choice for a bone marrow donor.

Bill hovered beside the bed. "Stay with her for awhile." Kris touched his arm. "She should go to sleep soon. I have to go back for Matt."

Bill dropped down on the bed beside his wife. Kris saw him reach for Marie's hand and bring it to his lips. She turned away, tears stinging her eyes. After more than fifty years they were still so much in love!

Kris was somber as she drove back to the hangar, still thinking about Bill and Marie and the kind of love that lasted through the decades. Once she had dreamed of finding a love like that—before Matt had sent her emotions into a nosedive from which she had yet to recover.

She didn't see Matt and brought the Bronco to a stop. She left it running and went into the hangar.

"Over here," Matt called. "I just found an old friend."

Kris followed the direction of his voice and found him standing beside a bright yellow plane with high wings and a black lightning bolt down the side. A brown and red logo of a small bear adorned the tail.

Matt's eyes glowed. "Hal taught me to fly in this over twenty years ago! I soloed in her. He said if I learned to fly a Piper Cub, I could fly anything."

Kris swallowed. "I remember. You told me before—the night you left for Saudia Arabia."

Matt glanced up. "I never did ask how you got up here." His voice was suddenly too quiet.

"I think you just figured it out." Kris walked over to touch the propeller. Her eyes were full as she gazed at the plane. She trailed her hand gently over the bright fabric. "I flew up here in the Cub four months ago."

Matt stared at her. "What did you say?"

"You heard right. I learned to fly in this plane, too. I told you that. When I put Holland Aviation on the market, this was the only plane I kept. I couldn't part with it. I packed up a few things and shipped them up here, added a wing tank and carried extra fuel in the front seat. It took over two weeks to make the flight, what with the weather and only being able to fly VFR. But I wouldn't have missed it for the world."

"What route did you take?" Matt still looked at her as if he couldn't believe what she'd told him.

"The Alaska Highway, of course. Remember lend-lease and all that?" Her voice gently mocked as she met his eyes.

"You're a fool!" Matt sounded angry.

Kris looked at him. "I won't argue that point, coming from such an obvious expert, but could you be a bit more specific—"

"If you'd gone down, you might never have been found." His harsh voice accused. "How could you take a chance like that?"

She crossed her arms over her chest. "I thought of all that. I flew out to Colorado to talk it over with Gregg Watson. You may remember him?"

Matt threw her a glance. "Do you really think there's much chance I could forget him?"

Kris held his gaze for a long moment. "Well, Gregg and I are still friends, and Dad had a lot of respect for him as a pilot. I thought he would be adamant about me not making the flight, but I had it all planned out. When I presented it to him, and he saw that I was determined, he gave me the best advice he could.

She turned away. "Among other things he suggested that I sign up for a survival course with *Extreme Expeditions*. One of his buddies from Special Forces started the program a few years ago—"

"Jared Hall," Matt said.

"You know Jared?" she asked. "I didn't think he was with the group that rescued you."

"He wasn't. He tried to hire me. They mostly use helicopters, but sometimes they need a fixed wing craft. I still hear from him occasionally. He keeps saying that if I ever want to stop *playing at flying* he could use a real pilot."

Kris studied him. "Well, anyway, after I got back from that, I felt a lot more confident about making the flight. I called Gregg every night and he plotted my course. He's supposed to send me the map." She looked at Matt again to see that he still seethed with anger. "I know you don't understand., but I *had* to do this."

Why was he so angry? She reached out to touch the plane again, as if seeking reassurance. She shrugged. "I made it. Why are we fighting over water under the bridge?"

As she looked at him, Matt saw a sheen of tears in her eyes. His heart pounded at the thought of how easily he could have lost her. He looked back at the plane, shoving his hands into his pockets to keep from reaching for her. "How much?" he asked. *Anything to change the subject.*

Kris stared at him, then her look turned incredulous. "For the Cub? You can't believe I'd sell the only thing I have left that means anything to me!"

"This is the *something familiar* you mentioned the other day," Matt said, as realization dawned.

Kris nodded, swallowed, as she struggled with deep emotion.

A brief silence. "How much?" Matt repeated.

Her glance turned to scorn. "You don't have that kind of money."

"Don't be ridiculous! I want this plane!" He walked around it again, his fingers caressing the wooden prop.

"Would you trade the racer for it?" Kris baited.

He looked at her. "You can't fly the racer!"

"No, I can't. But I have my answer." She pushed her hands into her pockets. "Perhaps I can get another answer."

Matt straightened and turned to her. The sun was just setting and she could see the blue glint of his eyes. He waited for her to go on.

"The night you left for Saudi Arabia—" she began.

She felt Matt tense as he stood beside her.

"Why did you kiss me?"

He didn't move a muscle but she could feel the tension in him.

"I couldn't help myself," he said, his voice bitter. "I shouldn't have. I didn't want you to know how I felt."

"Why not?" The strained whisper tore through him. She stared at him, trying to understand.

"I didn't think I had a right to feel the way I did."

"Why not? If you cared for me, why shouldn't I know?"

"I thought—well, there was Scott."

A tremor shot through her, but she managed to control her voice. "What about Scott?"

Matt sighed. "I told you already. He said you had an understanding. He made it sound like an informal engagement, at the very least."

"And you weren't interested enough to find out differently?"

"And just how was I to do that?" Matt shrugged. "Every time I saw him during the week before I left, all he talked about was taking you dancing, taking you to dinner, even—"

"Even?" Kris prompted, wetting her lips. The color had drained from her face.

"Taking you to his apartment," Matt said. He stared out across the runway. "He implied, not very subtly, that you spent your nights with him."

"And everything that encompasses," Kris whispered. She could barely breathe. "I hoped I had misunderstood the other night when you were still groggy from the pain killer." She turned and walked to the Bronco. "I can see why you weren't interested after that."

Behind her she heard Matt closing the hangar doors. Her breath frosted in the cold air as she blew it out in little puffs. Matt joined her and they got into the vehicle. He didn't look at her as he shifted gears.

Kris leaned her cheek against the window and closed her eyes as she felt her heart break all over again. *A love that spanned the decades.* Her mouth twisted. Such an opportunity only came along once in a lifetime and, thanks to Scott, she had never had a chance with Matt.

Kris managed to make it through dinner as Bill filled them in on Carl's operation. The bone marrow transplant had gone off without a hitch. Carl's wife and her parents were with him, and would stay until he went home. Hopefully, he would be well enough to spend Christmas in Alaska.

Kris gave Bill the news about Josef's baby and the fact that Yanni and Salina would be gone for a few more days. Matt told Bill about his flight up from California in the racer. Kris also heard for the first time the details of Matt's car wreck. She poured coffee for them and turned away to begin clearing the dishes. Matt stood up to help her.

Kris smiled and shook her head. "Please, let me do it. I enjoy hearing you and Bill talk."

Matt frowned, but sank back in his chair. After a moment Bill picked up the conversation again.

Kris finished the dishes and turned to leave the room. Bill looked up.

"Sit down, young lady," he said, his voice brusque. "We need to have a talk that's long overdue."

Kris looked at him, something in his voice alerting her. She lowered her eyes. *"You know."* A statement. Flat. Emotionless.

"I know—*now*. The question is, why didn't you tell us?"

She met and held his gaze. "It isn't exactly casual dinner conversation."

"And we aren't exactly casual acquaintances." Bill stood. "Kris, you aren't guilty."

"Thanks for the vote of confidence." Her lips trembled and she pressed them together. "But a child is still dead and I have to live with that—"

Bill made an impatient gesture. "What happened, Kris? Why do the parents think they have a basis for suing you?"

"I don't want to discuss it." Her voice was still flat, controlled. Too controlled. It could break at any moment.

"How can I help, if I don't know what happened?" Bill glared at her in frustration.

"You can't help, Bill, but thanks for caring enough to ask." Kris tried to hold his gaze again and failed.

Bill sat down and raked a hand through his graying hair. "Roy Ferguson came to us. He said you won't do or say anything in your own defense; that you want to settle out of court. He thinks you're so disillusioned by what happened that you may never practice medicine again. Why, Kris? Why won't you put up a fight?"

66

She stood for a moment, head bowed. Matt watched her and when she looked up, he saw tears glistening in her eyes.

"Do you have any idea what it's like to devote your life to helping people and then have everything you've done thrown back in your face?" She made a helpless gesture, her hand clenching into a fist. "It negates every thing I am. I don't know how to go back. I don't know what to fight with the next time it happens."

Bill cleared his throat, started to speak again, to try and reason with her.

Matt pushed back his chair. "I think that's enough for now. I raked her over the coals pretty thoroughly already." He put out a hand to lead her from the room.

Bill looked after them, a smile lurking in his eyes, his expression reminiscent. Gradually, it changed to one of brooding concern.

Matt paused outside Kris's room and let his hand fall. "Are you all right?" He knew very well that she wasn't. He could feel the fine tremors when his hand rested on her arm. Again, he pushed his hands into his pockets. It was either that, or pull her into his arms.

She looked at him. "You know, for someone I thought reasonably intelligent, you ask stupid questions." In spite of everything, Matt could hear a trace of humor in her voice. He thought of Hal and a smile touched his lips.

"Okay, so you're not all right," he grated. "Is there any thing I can do?" He watched her face for a response.

"Nothing comes to mind." Her voice was flippant.

Matt frowned and reached to catch her chin and tip her face up. "You don't have to act tough for me, Kris."

Her eyes met his, and Kris knew immediately that was a mistake. His eyes looked black in the dim hallway, black and captivating. She felt the pulse in her throat begin to race and wondered if he could see it.

Matt felt himself mesmerized by the look in her eyes. He wondered if the sirens in mythology, known for luring sailors to their deaths, had green eyes. Unwillingly, his thumb moved to stroke along her jaw line. He heard her draw in her breath and her lashes fell. She wet her lips and Matt suppressed a groan of desire.

"I'm not—acting tough," Kris managed, her voice a mere whisper. "It's just—you can't help."

His hand dropped. "Would you let me if I could?"

Her eyes opened. "What do you have in mind?" The humor was back in her voice, stronger this time.

"I don't know. Maybe I could beat up somebody—or even break something." His eyes were teasing now and Kris relaxed.

"I think you've broken enough things lately—bones at least." She studied him, a smile on her lips. "Something tells me you could be a lot of fun under different circumstances. It's too bad we didn't know each other a little better growing up. A friend would've been nice."

"What's to prevent you from getting to know me now?" Matt asked.

Kris's smile vanished. "Until a couple of days ago, I would have said it was you." Her lips trembled. "But I guess I have Scott to thank for that, as well." She opened the door and stepped into her room.

Matt stood there for a moment. His mouth twisted as he remembered the stormy encounter when he walked away and left Kris standing in the rain after his return from Saudia Arabia. He hadn't been thinking about Scott then, or his relationship with Kris. *He'd been too busy feeling sorry for himself.*

He hadn't been ready to settle down, Matt tried to rationalize to himself why he hadn't given himself a chance with Kris. Just back from Desert Storm, and still recovering from his career ending injuries, he threw himself into his racing and aerobatic training. After working with Hal Holland, he won everything he competed in. He couldn't regret that decision.

He realized that Kris now found herself at a similar crossroads in her life. He hadn't been willing to let her in back then. He'd had to work through his problems alone. Was it possible that he wouldn't be able to help her? That she would have to make it through this alone, just as he had. Something cold and icy clutched at his heart.

Not if he had anything to say about it!

CHAPTER FIVE

Kris looked out at the black arctic night. Her father had loved this land as had Ben Walker and Bill. She thought about Matt's story of the friendship between these men. That explained a lot. Bill treated her as the daughter he'd never had and Marie gave her love without reservation.

At first it had been hard for Kris to return Marie's affection, scarred as she was by her relationship with her mother. They had been too close—Kris taking care of her mother when she was still only a child herself. She couldn't remember not wanting to be a doctor. She couldn't bear the thought of anyone suffering.

Kris sighed as her thoughts turned to the malpractice suit filed against her a few weeks after her father's death. She found herself all alone and disillusioned, thinking that had to be the lowest point in her life. *But worse was yet to come.* Reluctantly, she made the decision to flee to Alaska, to people she hardly knew.

Kris stood with bowed head. She'd have to tell Bill and Marie the whole story. They deserved to know. Matt, too, she supposed. She would have to risk it. Her mouth twisted at the irony of it all. Scott had led Matt to believe he was in love with her. And Matt, with his inborn sense of honor, had kept his distance. *If only things could have worked out differently!*

Her thoughts switched channels. She'd seen depths to Matt in the last few days that surprised her. Knowing he was Beth's son, she understood their origin. Never having had a chance to know him as a person, she'd fantasized about him as a devil-may-care pilot. He was that, but so much more. And the better she got to know him, the more she ached for those years they should have had together—for the relationship that was no longer possible.

Kris glanced at her watch and decided to check on Marie again before getting undressed. She made sure that Marie still slept soundly, then went to the kitchen. The house was so quiet she assumed everyone must be in bed.

She carried her hot cocoa into the den, intending to drink it before the fire while she looked at the photo album. Too late, she noticed the light beside the chair where Matt sat reading. He looked up and slowly focused on her, as if pulling his thoughts back from a long way.

"I'm sorry," Kris said. "I didn't mean to disturb you." The last thing she needed now was to be alone with Matt. She turned to leave.

"You're not," he said. Then, "I thought you went to bed." *Hadn't he walked her to her room himself?*

"I wanted to check on Marie, and I developed a sudden craving for hot cocoa." She held up her mug.

He grinned. "Did you make enough for me?"

"I didn't know you were still up." She perched on a foot stool. "What are you reading?" She glanced at the thick leather volume open on his lap.

He looked uncomfortable for a moment, shrugged. "Dad's journal."

"Oh?" Kris wondered if she was treading on sacred ground. Matt might not want to discuss something so personal.

"Mom gave it to me before I came up here," Matt explained. "I guess she didn't think it would mean anything to me earlier—and she suspected I was coming up here to do some soul searching. Some of it—" He paused. "Some of it is pretty heavy stuff."

Kris saw the play of emotions across his face. She felt her throat tighten, struck again by the depths to this man whom she barely knew, yet seemed to have known always.

Matt glanced up and caught her expression. He saw the sympathy and understanding in her eyes, and something more. *Wistfulness? Yearning?*

"You might like to read it," he offered. "There's a lot in here about Hal. It helps me—well, I never got to know my dad that well, and it explains a lot of things about Hal that I didn't understand before."

Kris looked at him, aching with the love she felt for him—love that could never be fulfilled. She made a restless movement and stood up. "Matt, what happened to your father—to Ben? How did he die?"

She had partially turned away and at his harsh intake of breath, she looked back. His eyes were closed, pain contorting his face into a grimace.

Kris knelt before him, almost spilling her cocoa. "I'm sorry, Matt! I shouldn't have intruded—"

"No, it isn't that." He reached out to stop her and felt her tense at his touch. His hand fell. "I'm sorry." His voice hardened.

"Please—I just—" Kris broke off as she saw his expression close. What could she say? The damage was done. *Scott had seen to that.*

She turned away. "Good night, Matt."

"Kris."

She stood still.

"When I left you earlier, you implied that Scott had influenced my opinion of you—perhaps even kept me away from you—"

She laughed unexpectedly—a bitter, broken sound. "Didn't he?"

His head came up. "Why do you say that?"

"Considering what Scott told you—" she broke off, shrugged. "I'm surprised you could bring yourself to touch me to begin with. I can understand that after thinking about it for a year, you wouldn't want to have anything to do with me."

"Where did you come up with that?" His voice was incredulous as he stared at her.

"It all fits. And it was my fault that anything happened in the first place. I realize that now. That must have done a lot to reinforce the image Scott had already planted in your mind—" She broke off. Her lips trembled and she pressed them together.

Matt walked over to her. "What's this all about, Kris? At the time I couldn't bring myself to burden you with what I had become. You said it didn't matter, but it mattered to me. I didn't want to hurt you. I don't want to hurt you now. Do you want me to leave?"

Her eyes locked with his, her lips parted. "No. That's the last thing I want. You need to be here. You need Bill and Marie—as much as I do."

"Forget what I need," he grated. "What do you need?"

Kris felt tears burn behind her lashes. "What I need isn't possible." She stared at Matt for a moment longer, then turned and fled.

Again Kris stood by the window in her room. No, she didn't want Matt to leave, she told herself. But how could she go on being in his presence when her feelings were so volatile? The overwhelming awareness she'd always had for him flamed into a conflagration of desire when he was near. How could she keep it from consuming her? Although he had never returned it, the love she had given him completely and without reservation had strengthened over the years until it now threatened to destroy her.

Marie got out of bed the next afternoon. She sat in the den with Bill and Matt. Kris could hear their voices as she worked. They sounded happy and comfortable with one another. Kris fought down a wave of loneliness. She knew they wanted her to feel she belonged, but she was reluctant to join them. There were still too many things they didn't know. *Things she had to find a way to tell them.*

Bill and Marie walked into the kitchen that evening to find Kris and Matt arguing.

"How was it any more foolish than your flying up here?" Kris asked Matt, her voice heated.

"There isn't any comparison," Matt replied. "I can fly four times as fast as you, I have IFR capabilities—"

"And if you'd gone down, they might never have found you," Kris cut him short, throwing his words from the day before back at him.

Matt's eyes flew to her, and for a brief moment she saw agony in them, quickly concealed. She remembered last night and the pain on his face when she had asked him how his father died.

74

Bill laughed. "This sure brings back old times."

Kris and Matt both turned as he helped Marie into a chair. She looked at them with a smile. "Doesn't it? Ben and Hal used to argue constantly, but for all that, I don't think any two men ever loved each other more."

"And one thing we learned," Bill put in, "was never to jump in on their arguments. They'd unite against you so fast your head would spin."

Kris swallowed convulsively and turned back to the sink. "It's good to see you up, Marie. Are you feeling stronger?"

"Very much so," Marie replied. "What with you and Matt spoiling me like this." She looked at Matt. "Where'd you learn to cook, Matt?"

He grinned, carrying a steaming casserole to the table. "I'm afraid it's one of the little necessities that comes with being a bachelor."

"A situation you could remedy at any time, I'm sure," Marie said. "Don't expect that line to get you any sympathy!"

"I didn't," Matt relied, unruffled. "But I hear enough of that from Mom and Tracy. Why is it that all the women in my life can't wait to see me married?"

"It isn't that we can't wait," Marie explained. "It's just that we're amazed it hasn't already happened. How old are you now, anyway? Thirty-five or thirty-six, I believe. Carl is thirty-eight. And he has a ten year old son."

"Well, maybe he was luckier than I've been. If the right girl came along—I let her slip away." Matt tried to keep his voice casual. It took all his will power to keep from looking at Kris.

"And you've given up looking?" Marie watched his face.

"I didn't say that. But to put the record straight, I've never actually 'looked.' I believe that if I'm meant to meet someone, I will."

"Without any effort on your part?" Marie persisted.

Matt glanced at her. "Meaning what?" He knew from experience that Marie was not above trying to trick him into revealing more than he wanted to.

"If this person comes along, how will she know that you're interested?"

"I'll work out the tactical details when the time comes," Matt assured her, his eyes laughing.

Kris had been listening to this exchange a bit uncomfortably. Now she turned to put a salad on the table. She looked up and caught Bill's eye.

"Now Kris here," Bill said, reverting back to the start of the conversation, "learned to survive without cooking. All I ever see her eat is fruit and cheese and salads."

"Which sounds about right for a busy surgeon," Matt put in. "What do you expect her to do? Go home and cook a seven course meal?"

Bill and Marie exchanged glances and smiled.

"What?" Matt demanded, pinning them with his gaze.

Bill shook his head, grinned. "Nothing's changed. Ben would jump to Hal's defense in a heartbeat—and vice versa."

Matt's eyes narrowed. "Well, stop picking on her." He pulled out his chair and sat down across from Bill.

"I wish I could," Bill sighed. He waited until Kris had taken the other chair. "I promised Roy I'd try to persuade her to go back and fight the malpractice suit. The hospital is still holding her job for her. It seems that surgeons of her caliber are hard to come by."

Kris drew a sharp breath. "Do we have to talk about this now?"

"Yes, dear, we do," Marie said. "We owe it to Hal to try and help you. And we can't help if we don't know what you're facing."

"I'll tell you everything after dinner," Kris promised. "I'll *try* and tell you everything," she amended after a moment. She carefully avoided Matt's eyes, although she could feel him looking at her. Her appetite was gone now, such as it was. She picked up her water glass and sipped.

Matt saw her hand tremble as she replaced the glass. A surge of helpless frustration washed over him. Why couldn't he help her? But more than that, how many of her problems had he caused himself, however inadvertently?

Kris waited in the den for the others to join her. She held a mug of cocoa, her hands wrapped around it for warmth; also to keep them from trembling.

Marie settled into a comfortable chair and Bill lit his pipe. Matt was still in the kitchen making coffee. Kris waited until he brought in a tray, then turned back to the little group. Bill and Marie were watching her expectantly.

Kris walked over to stand before the fireplace. She carefully placed her mug on the mantle and looked at Bill.

"I'd like to apologize for not telling you all this earlier," she began. "I didn't know how. And I was still trying to come to terms with most of it."

"Tell me about the malpractice suit." Bill's voice was gruff— something Kris knew he did when struggling with deep emotion. That knowledge brought a lump to her throat, making it even more difficult for her to talk.

She shrugged. "I've asked Roy to settle out of court." She marveled that she could sound so calm, so matter-of-fact. She felt as if a mild breeze would shatter her.

"Kris, you can't do that!" Bill exploded.

"Think about this, my dear," Marie urged. "You're talking about your future—everything you've worked for."

Kris looked at her. "Do you really think I've been able to think of any thing else? All I know is that I can't fight it. I can't go to court—I've seen what happens—" She put a hand to her head and closed her eyes.

After a long silence, Bill cleared his throat. "I think you'd better tell us what's behind the case against you."

Kris drew in her breath, her eyes going to Matt, seeking something she could not define. But it was there in his eyes. She relaxed fractionally and sat down on the hearth. Matt leaned against the mantle.

"It happened a couple of weeks after Dad's funeral. I had emergency duty that weekend. A major crash involving a station wagon full of migrant workers and a city bus occurred that evening. A total of fifteen people were injured, eight from the station wagon. Three later died, including a little girl who required emergency surgery. Her name was Melinda Morales. She had massive internal injuries.

"I was told we had parental consent by the nurse working admission. Both parents had been in the car, neither injured badly. They didn't speak English, but the nurse was bilingual. It never occurred to me to check that we had their permission. It hadn't come up before and I didn't have any time to waste if I intended to save this child."

Kris stood up to pace for a few steps. "I couldn't save her. She'd lost so much blood that she was already in shock. We did everything we could—" She drew a long, painful breath before she continued.

"I got off duty at midnight. I went home and took a sleeping pill and woke the next morning to a call from the administrator of the hospital telling me he needed to talk to me. When I arrived he told me a malpractice suit had been filed. Apparently I'd performed the surgery without parental consent and against the family's wishes.

"The maternal grandmother was there. Her religious beliefs were such that she didn't believe in seeking medical help. God would cure all. According to her, if I hadn't touched Melinda, she would have survived. In the space of eight hours, I found myself not only charged with unethical practice, but also accused of murder. Melinda's parents stood by, stunned, bewildered almost. I found myself wondering how much they understood of what was going on.

"No one at the hospital believed the charges, but neither did they have any advice to offer. I was given a mandatory leave of absence while the Medical Board reviewed the case. There was nothing to do but pack up my things and go home." Her voice faltered and she paused for a moment.

Finally Kris turned back to Marie and Bill. "While I waited for a decision from the Medical Review Board, I put Holland Aviation on the market. At Dad's funeral you told me to come to you if I needed anything. I didn't know what I needed or what you could do when I cabled I was on the way.

"The only thing I remember about the two weeks it took to fly up the west coast and pick up the Alaska Highway is the sense of escape. You greeted me with open arms—more than I deserved or expected. Again, I'm sorry I wasn't open with you." She started to say more. Hesitated. She still wasn't being open—not about everything.

Bill shifted as if his chair was uncomfortable. "But according to Roy, the Medical Review Board threw out the charges. You still have your license. You aren't guilty."

"Tell that to Melinda's parents." How could she sound so casual when she was dying inside? Kris wondered.

Marie twisted her hands together. "Where was Scott during all this?

He was with you at Hal's funeral. You haven't mentioned him—"

"Perhaps we—" Bill tried to intervene.

"You're right that he was at the funeral," Kris said, her voice clipped. "But he was not with me."

"Then what was he doing there?" Marie frowned.

"The presumption was that he was paying his respects. I happen to know that he was gloating."

"Kris!" Marie's shocked voice rang with disapproval.

"Why do you say that, my dear?" Bill's quiet voice broke the silence that followed Marie's outburst.

"First of all, why does everyone presume that Scott and I had, or have, a relationship? I was never interested in him. Dad didn't care for him, and he hated Dad."

"Forgive me," Marie said dryly. "From everything I've heard, he pursued you relentlessly."

Kris shrugged. "Perhaps he did. I never did anything to encourage him and I was too busy to notice—at least until it was too late."

"Why didn't Hal care for him?" Bill asked. "Do you know?"

"I do. To his credit, Dad never said anything against Scott. I had my own misgivings about him. For one thing, I was afraid to fly with him. Aerobatics was Dad's life, but I've never been comfortable with them. The one time I went up with Dad for a demonstration, he stopped the routine as soon as he realized I was having problems. I never trusted Scott to be so considerate.

"I decided to check Dad's student files. He kept a profile on everyone he trained—or turned down, as far as that goes. He listed Scott as unsafe and undisciplined and refused to give him instruction."

"Do you agree with that analysis?" Bill pressed.

"I read his profile on Matt and another student that I know, Gregg Watson. They seemed to be pretty close to the mark. I felt he must be right about Scott as well. And, yes, his summation supported the conclusion I had already reached."

"You don't think Hal might have been just a bit prejudiced as far as Matt's abilities were concerned?" Bill asked, watching Kris closely.

Kris shook her head. "He was harder on Matt and demanded more of him than his other students." She threw an unwilling glance at Matt.

"Why do you suppose he did that?"

"Because he knew how good he could be." Kris could not look away from Matt, but held his gaze. "He said over and over that Matt flew like his father. He had the same instinctive judgment, the same coolness." She turned back to Bill. "As for Gregg Watson, I trusted Dad's opinion enough that I went to him for advice before flying the Cub up here. Dad felt he was the safest pilot he ever trained."

"So Scott held a grudge against Hal." Bill mused. "Do you think his purported interest in you may have been an attempt to get back at Hal?"

Kris turned back to Bill, opened her mouth to speak, closed it. Finally she nodded. "He admitted as much."

"When?"

Kris made a restless movement, trapped. She would have to tell them everything now. She swallowed convulsively. "He showed up at the airport one evening. *Very drunk.*"

She felt Matt raise his head to stare at her. It was impossible for her to look at him. She cringed inside. How could she possibly go on?

Something in her voice alerted Bill. "When was this?"

"About a week after the malpractice suit was filed. I was cleaning out Dad's office, trying to get the school ready to put on the market."

"Were you there alone?" Bill's voice was quiet.

"I had been doing paperwork for hours. I decided to walk out to the hangar. Look at the planes. I was feeling—I guess a little sorry for myself."

"Were you alone?" Bill repeated.

Kris raised her head to meet Bill's eyes. For some reason he was the only one she could look at.

"Why do I get the feeling you've talked to Roy?" she asked him, trying to keep her voice light and failing miserably.

Bill nodded, his eyes full of concern and sympathy.

Kris sighed. "If you talked to Roy, then you know why no one else knows. Are you sure I should go on? I don't want to talk about this. I don't know if I can—"

"What is it, dear?" Marie urged. "You know we're all family here."

"Please—" Kris said, her voice strangled.

"Roy and I discussed your concerns, which he shares. I told him I would accept responsibility. Finish your story. You went out to the hangar," Bill prompted, his voice gentle. "You were alone, and Scott showed up drunk."

Kris nodded, turning away. "He was very upset. Ranting and raving. I gathered that Dad's death cheated him of whatever revenge he'd been plotting."

"Which was?"

"He figured the ideal revenge would have been for me to fall in love with him and marry him. If he could make my life miserable, he thought that would be just retribution against Dad. The only problem was, I hadn't cooperated. Not only had I not fallen in love with him, I hardly acknowledged his existence. That was a blow to his ego—which was always considerable."

"And then what? Cheated of his revenge against Hal, what did he do?"

Kris drew in her breath. "He decided to take it out on me. As he explained, he would rather things remain civilized, but I left him no choice."

"What did he do?" Bill persisted when Kris fell silent.

She raised her head, her eyes pleading. "Bill, you already know! Don't make me go into detail—"

"Tell us, love. You have to say it. We can help." Bill held her gaze for a long moment.

She searched his face. She had to trust his judgment. He wouldn't ask her to do anything that would hurt her, would he? Her glance fell and she moistened lips that had gone dry.

"I—" she swallowed with difficulty. "I knew he was drunk and I knew there wasn't anyone else around to hear me if I called for help. I tried to keep him talking—maybe distract him enough to make a run for it. I—almost succeeded." She pushed back her hair and put a hand to the back of her neck.

"Someone had left a tow bar attached to a plane. I tripped over it as I turned to run. The next thing I knew he was on top of me, hitting me. He was so drunk he wasn't very coordinated. I scratched his face and kicked him. I was finally able to knee him in the groin. He rolled off me and clutched himself, moaning. But by then my clothes were in tatters. I had a cracked jaw and ribs, and bruises all over my body. My mouth was bleeding. I ran out of the hangar and he didn't follow. It was almost a month before I recovered, and that was when I cabled you that I was coming up here."

Marie stared at her, aghast. "Scott assaulted you? Tried to—"

"I prefer not to dwell on what he had in mind," Kris said, her voice controlled. "By the time I got away from him, I was very close to losing consciousness. In fact, when I got back to the office and locked the door, I did pass out for awhile. If I hadn't managed to hang on—" She broke off as a shudder rocked her. "He was quite mad. I don't think he would have stopped beating me."

Kris pressed her lips together to keep them from trembling in the silence that followed. She hadn't known what to expect from Bill and Marie, or from Matt, for that matter. In actuality, they were strangers to her. *If only someone would say something!*

A hand touched her and Kris looked up into Matt's eyes. He pulled her into his arms, gathering her close.

It took a moment for her to react and then she tensed and tried to pull away. "No, please!" she whispered in anguish.

"I'm not Scott, Kris." There was a thread of steel in Matt's voice. The arms cradling her were gentle and protective, and she hadn't a chance of escaping their hold. After a moment she relaxed into his strength, a single sob escaping her as she felt the weight of the world fall from her shoulders.

CHAPTER SIX

Matt felt the tremors that shook Kris and he bent his head over hers. He stroked her back, comforting, trying to lend her his strength. He struggled to control his own trembling and the white hot rage threatening to engulf him.

Marie looked at them, her expression wistful. She'd long had a suspicion that Kris was the one Matt let get away. She saw a different side of him with Kris here, a side she'd never seen when he visited alone. Also, it was obvious to her that Kris cared deeply for Matt. Was he aware of her feelings?

Bill was thinking much the same thing. He wasn't sure how well Kris and Matt knew each other, but he'd suspected for some time that her involvement with Scott McGraw was superficial at best.

Watching Matt's face as Kris talked, it was obvious to Bill that Matt thought she was in love with Scott. *Had that kept him from pursuing her himself?*

Perhaps Matt wasn't as much his father's son as Bill had always thought. On the other hand, maybe he was too much like Ben Walker.

After a moment Bill stirred. "What is happening to the flight school? You said you put it on the market."

Kris straightened and Matt released her. She looked at Bill and pushed her hair back, adjusting her train of thought. "His chief flight instructor, Bret Brown, is running it for the time being, but yes, it's for sale."

"Do you have to sell it?" Bill asked.

"What options do I have? I'm only a private pilot. I can't instruct or teach aerobatics."

"But you know what kind of people to hire," Bill argued.

"Oh, I see," Kris said. "*We've written off my career?*"

Bill's impatient gesture spoke volumes. "*I* haven't, but it sounds as if *you* have." He held her gaze. "I'll buy the school. We have to keep it in the family."

"The family?" Kris echoed.

"Yes," Marie said. "*The family.*"

Unwillingly, Kris looked at Matt to find him watching her. She laced her fingers together. "Actually, I've been thinking that the only way I can work again is in private practice. I thought I'd use the money from the school to open my own office, perhaps with a couple of other doctors."

Bill nodded. "As long as you haven't given up. We'll support you."

"Thank you," Kris said. She looked at Marie, saw the tiredness on her face. "I think you should go to bed," she told her. "That is, if you still trust my diagnosis. It's too bad you didn't know about the malpractice suit before Bill committed you to my care."

Marie's eyes flashed with hurt. "As a matter-of-fact, we did know. Roy came to visit Carl and we mentioned you were here. He's so desperate for you to take some action on your own behalf that he told us everything he knew, begging us to use any influence we had. That's why we had to get back, and I do have faith in your diagnosis. Incidentally, do you happen to have any of those pain pills left?"

"Oh, Marie, I'm sorry!" Kris knelt before her. "You shouldn't have stayed up so long—" She broke off, blinking at the tears stinging her eyes.

"Nonsense." Marie looked past her to Matt. "Do you think you could give an old lady a lift?" she asked him.

Matt bent over her. "*An old lady*, no. But for *you*, anything." He lifted her into his arms.

Kris walked ahead of them to open the door and fluff up the pillows. Matt placed Marie on the edge of the bed and left the room. The door closed with a click.

Kris helped Marie off with her robe. She filled a glass with water and handed her a couple of pills. Marie popped them into her mouth, drank, and looked up.

"Tomorrow we talk," Marie said, her voice firm. "I know you're in love with Matt. What's going on in that quarter?"

Marie saw the pain that swept across Kris's face before she looked up to meet her eyes.

"Let's talk by all means," Kris replied. "Maybe together we can figure it out. I've tried for years, and I still don't know what's going on or why."

Marie lay back and Kris pulled the covers over her. Marie again saw a sheen of tears in the green eyes lifted to hers and her throat tightened with emotion.

Kris turned away. "Remember, I'm a very light sleeper if you need anything. Send Bill for me." She opened the door, closed it gently, then turned and bumped into Matt.

Kris stared at Matt as her mind played back the conversation with Marie. *Could he have heard it?* The door had been closed. *Did it matter?* He had to know how she felt about him. She had never been able to hide it.

Matt's hands went to her shoulders. "Are you all right? Is Marie all right?"

Kris wet her lips. "Fine. Marie's fine."

"Come into the kitchen," Matt said, catching her hand and pulling her after him.

She followed him without hesitation. He pulled out a chair for her. "I made some fresh cocoa. I don't believe you've finished a mug yet." He sat down across from her and picked up his own drink.

Kris looked at him, the treacherous tears threatening again. He was so kind and considerate, so strong and gentle. She recalled the conversation with Marie. Why couldn't Matt have been interested in her instead of leaving the field open for Scott? Now it was too late.

"I didn't mean to make you cry," Matt said. He reached across to flick a tear from her cheek.

Kris drew in her breath. She reached for the mug of cocoa and sipped it. "Thanks." Her voice was thick with her effort to control it. "I'm not used to having anyone think of me like this—do things for me." She slowly traced her finger around the rim of the mug.

Matt reached across to touch her face. "I haven't thought of much else since I bumped into you in Hal's office."

She stared into her cup. "Well, now you have something else to think about. I don't think you're interested in the wreckage Scott left." She looked up, forcing herself to meet his eyes.

He didn't look away. Instead he reached out a finger to touch a tiny scar, barely visible at the corner of her mouth.

"Did Scott do that?" The touch was almost a caress; the look in Matt's eyes her undoing.

Kris gave a strangled gasp and pushed her mug away. She stood up, but Matt was faster.

"Kris—" He caught her and pulled her into his arms. "I deserve to have you think that way about me. After all, I was foolish enough to believe Scott and not what I felt when I was with you." He held her away from him. "Please! Let me at least be your friend. You need someone."

Kris looked at him, wet her lips. "Is that what you want? *For us to be friends?*" She perfectly mimicked the words he said to her the night he had kissed her with such devastating thoroughness. "You were right. It was too late for friendship from the moment I crashed into you." She held his gaze for a moment, then turned and walked from the room. Matt stared after her.

"She's right, you know." Bill spoke from the doorway. He crossed to drop down in the chair Kris had vacated, his eyes searching Matt's face.

Matt held Bill's gaze for a moment, then looked away. "Yeah, I know," he sighed. *Mere friendship with Kris would never have been enough.*

"Do you know that she's falling in love with you—if she isn't already?"

Matt stood. "That really isn't your concern—" he began, his eyes flashing blue lightning.

"You're under my roof at the moment. That makes it my business."

Matt stared at him, grinned, and shook his head. "Fair enough. I've been in love with her from the moment we collided in Hal's office, about a week before I left for the Persian Gulf."

"So why haven't you done something about it?" Bill asked.

"I thought she was interested in Scott. He even told me they had an understanding. And when I returned from Desert Storm, I had nothing to offer her. *I didn't have anything to offer myself.*"

"She was interested in Scott—not that Scott was interested in her? I can accept the first a lot easier than the second." Bill's gaze pinned Matt ruthlessly as he waited for him to answer.

Matt sighed and dropped back into his chair. He drew a hand across his face and looked up. "I'm not sure what I thought. I was so mixed up after the war—being discharged from the air force—my injuries. No woman could want the shambles left of what I had been. I didn't give myself a chance to know her, to see if she might return my feelings. I ran scared, threw myself into my training, and with Hal's help, I've won everything there is to win in aerobatics and air racing."

Bill looked at him. "And what do you have to show for all that now?"

"A shelf full of trophies and a very cold bed," Matt replied without hesitation.

"I can see that at least you've been thinking about it." Bill stood. "You may be Ben's son after all."

Marie sat by the window the next morning while Kris changed her bedding. She watched the younger woman with a tender expression. Kris was so different from her mother. It had amazed Marie that Hal Holland could fall for a clinging vine like Jean White. She'd always felt that Ben Walker's choice of Beth Jordan made more sense. She shook her head, a slow smile touching her lips. Love didn't always make a lot of sense, she reflected.

Kris looked up to catch Marie's secretive little smile. "And what's that all about?" she teased. "You must be feeling better."

"I was thinking about all those years ago when we were still children, younger than you and Matt. The war was over and Bill and I were married. Ben and Hal were still single and they spent a lot of time here. They didn't meet their wives until after the Korean conflict. Then Beth and Jean became part of our lives, too. Your mother was never happy here so Hal took her back home. And of course after Ben was killed, there were too many memories here for Beth. She went to California and Hal helped her get on with her life."

"Matt told me some of the story the other day," Kris said. "I'd never heard it." She walked over to stand by the window beside Marie's chair. Glancing outside she saw that it was still dark. *So what else was new?*

She looked back at Marie. "I think it might have helped if I'd known about the contract. Beth tried to be kind to me after Mother died, but I completely shut her out."

Marie nodded. "I know. Beth talked to me about you. Hal did so much for Matt. She wanted to be able in some measure to return the favor. She felt so inadequate that she couldn't get through to you."

Kris shook her head. "I didn't know how to relate to her. My life was always so tied up with taking care of my mother. I think I resented other women who were still alive, because she wasn't. It took several years to outgrow those feelings."

"And you never had anyone tell you about other feelings you would experience—such as meeting that special man you were meant to spend the rest of your life with."

Kris met her eyes. "Is there such a man? I'm not sure I believe that anymore?"

"No? Well, I believe you've met him. I think you know you have. You've known from the beginning."

"Let's get you back into bed," Kris suggested, helping Marie stand and leading her across the room. Her pulse raced. She was afraid she knew what Marie was leading up to.

Marie settled back against the pillows and patted the bed beside her. "Are we ready for that talk?" she asked. She was watching Kris and saw panic in the eyes that met hers before Kris turned away.

"I've never been very good at talking," Kris said, clasping her hands beneath her chin.

"But I've always been good at listening," Marie said. "That should make it easier for both of us."

Kris looked back at her and Marie patted the bed again. Kris crossed to sit beside her, not knowing how to refuse Marie's gesture, wanting to talk, and yet afraid.

"I don't bite," Marie said with a smile, trying to get Kris to relax. She'd grown fond of Hal's daughter. At first it had concerned her that she looked so much like her mother. But Marie quickly learned that all similarities ended with the physical.

It saddened Marie to know how deeply Kris had been hurt by life, but the strength she exhibited was a source of comfort. She was indeed Hal Holland's daughter and that told Marie what she was made of. But Marie also understood the gentleness and vulnerability that were part of her make up.

Kris twisted her hands together. "You think Matt is the man I was meant to spend my life with." She looked at Marie.

"What do you think?" Marie probed.

"I thought there was something when we met again just before he went overseas. But that was all I had. He never gave me a chance to know him, to find if I liked him—or more."

"Tell me about that meeting." Marie's voice was gentle.

"He was in the office. I'd gotten a message that Dad wanted to see me. I was running late and I came charging through the door and literally ran into Matt's arms. I was completely mesmerized as I stared into his eyes. I felt as if I were in a tornado—or a plane spinning out of control."

"And?"

"Dad looked up and saw me, introduced me to Scott, and asked me to take him to see a plane he was interested in. Matt turned away and that was the end of that. He never came near me or spoke to me again. Until that last night, just before he left."

"And what happened then?"

"I wandered into the hangar and Matt was there. I tried making small talk. The tension was so thick you could feel it. Then he kissed me, ravaged me, actually. It was everything I'd ever imagined a kiss from him could be." A smile touched her lips.

"And?"

"He pushed me away. He said he couldn't do—the things we'd been doing—he was leaving the next day for the Persian Gulf."

"Did you see him again when he returned?"

"I tried." Kris stood up to pace. "He was cold, remote, a stranger. I spent a year thinking about him, dreaming about that kiss, praying for him to return. All I got for my efforts was *I'm sorry, Kris. It shouldn't have happened*."

"Tell me about meeting Scott." Marie said.

Kris blinked. "I *hardly* saw Scott. Bumping into Matt sent my emotions into a tailspin. I was so upset when he insisted on avoiding me."

"In his defense, he knew he would be leaving soon," Marie said. "He didn't want to start anything on such short notice."

"It started without any effort on either of our parts," Kris said, her voice dry. "If he had just been willing to talk about it! I would have understood."

Marie could understand Kris's conflict, her uncertainty. Matt Walker was a man who made a powerful impression on everyone he met. For someone as young and inexperienced as Kris had been, it had apparently been an overwhelming one.

"I was so confused," Kris went on. "I'd never met anyone who affected me the way he did—made me feel the things I felt."

"Tell me about those feelings," Marie urged, her voice a breath of sound. *Kris needed to talk about this.*

Kris stood up, moved to the window. "I guess it was like the proverbial moth to the flame. I was frightened of what I felt, but at the same time I wanted more—to be closer to him. I was only inches from him, his hands on my arms. I wanted him to put his arms around me, bend his head those few inches. I was ready to die there, in his arms, knowing that was where I belonged." Kris stopped speaking, and realized she was trembling. She wrapped her arms across her chest.

"I never had any doubt how I felt about Matt." She looked at Marie. "I didn't admit those feelings to anyone—not even Dad. Matt—should have known. I didn't do a very good job of hiding my attraction to him."

"Do you think he feels anything for you?" Marie asked.

Kris shrugged. "At one time I thought he did. But now I know how Scott poisoned everything by telling Matt we had a relationship." She put a hand to her mouth. "And I can see how everything I did after that would only confirm that I was the kind of woman Scott made me out to be."

"And are you that kind of woman?" Marie asked. "If you aren't, Matt will realize it soon enough."

Kris shook her head and came back to sit beside Marie. "Before I met Matt again, medical school had been my whole life—that, and Dad, and the flight school. I had just started my residency. I hadn't had time for a relationship with anyone. After Matt, there couldn't be anyone else. I—"

"You're still a virgin?" Marie's voice was gentle.

Kris swallowed, nodded. *"Virginity."* She laughed. "Funny how tenuous something like that is. Matt could have had it at any time—with total compliance on my part. And because of that willingness, I'm sure it has never occurred to him that I'm—still *untouched*, as the saying goes."

"In his defense, Matt was in a rather difficult position," Marie said.

Kris glanced at her. "In what way?"

"He has a very strong sense of honor, as did Ben and Hal—the two men who shaped his life. I'm sure he found the thought of a relationship with you quite difficult while Hal was alive because of the closeness they shared. What if Hal didn't approve of him for you?"

"An interesting concept," Kris agreed, "but I can't quite buy it. Matt is strong willed and focused enough that if he wanted something, he would find a way to have it. Look at the way he rebuilt his life after he was discharged from the Air Force."

"Matt has been very reserved ever since Ben was lost." Marie was thoughtful. "I think he is afraid of losing someone else he loves like that again.

95

He was at a very vulnerable age when Ben's plane went down. And the fact that they never found his body or the wreckage meant that Matt didn't have the kind of closure he needed upon losing his father. I'm not sure he knows how to love, Kris. If you really want him, you may have to teach him." Marie paused. "You know as well as I do that it will be worth your effort."

Kris shook her head. "It's too late, Marie! I don't even know how to live with myself after all that's happened. How can I possibly have anything to offer Matt?"

Marie's eyes filled with sympathy. "My dear, you owe it to yourself to let him make that decision."

Kris sat alone in the darkness, thinking about her conversation with Marie. At last she knew about Ben Walker's tragic disappearance. She understood now why Matt was so paranoid at the thought of her flying alone! She shuddered. No wonder he had been a discipline problem and was sent away to military school by Hal and Beth when he was twelve.

She thought about the factors that had shaped both their lives, turning them into the loners they were. His father had disappeared suddenly without a trace, leaving him torn, shattered, vulnerable.

The years he had spent in military school, she had spent watching her mother die slowly from a deteriorating muscle disease. In the end, the once beautiful woman was a shell, totally dependent on others for every need.

Was it possible, as Marie said, that Matt did not know how to love? He had so much to offer—so much gentleness and warmth. *And that first kiss had shown such promise!* A sad smile touched Kris's lips. She ached with desire for all that she had never had a chance to have; knowing, in spite of Marie's words, that she no longer had anything to offer that Matt desired.

CHAPTER SEVEN

Bill straightened, put aside his wrench and looked across the hangar. Matt stood deep in thought, studying the engine of his plane. He and Bill had discussed several modifications and Matt now considered a suggestion from Bill. They'd been in the hanger for a couple of hours, long enough to become thoroughly chilled.

"Let's go get some coffee and warm up," Bill said. "And I think it's time you told me the real reason you left the field open for Scott with Kris. And why you still aren't going after her."

Matt threw him a glance filled with resentment. "You know, I don't usually welcome such intrusions into my personal life—"

"Then it's high time you did," Bill returned. "Ben isn't here to give you advice and neither is Hal, although I would think he found it rather hard to talk to you about his daughter."

"He didn't know—" Matt began.

"Of course he knew. Anyone who sees you together can't help but see that you're crazy about each other—"

"Maybe that was the problem," Matt replied. "I doubt that he ever saw us together. We've hardly been together—until now."

"And that was to clear the way for Scott, perhaps?"

"Now just a minute—" Matt protested.

"Go ahead," Bill urged, meeting Matt's eyes. "I want you to tell me you didn't let Scott have Kris—figuratively speaking, that is. I could tell last night when Kris was talking that you thought their relationship had a lot more depth than she claims."

After a moment of strained silence Matt placed his wrench beside Bill's and ran a hand through his hair. "I suppose I did," he admitted.

"And now?" Bill insisted.

"And now what?" Matt stared at him, seething with anger.

"I'd say Scott is out of the picture."

"You think so?" Matt's voice held a thread of steel. "Will he ever be gone for either of us? Last night when I held her, she tried to pull away. Will she ever be able to stand having a man touch her again?"

Bill looked at him, rolled his eyes heavenward. *"Ben, I'm afraid I may fail you on this one,"* he said under his breath. Then his gaze returned to Matt.

"If I remember correctly, she stopped struggling and you held her for several moments. Do you think just anyone could have done that?"

Matt wasn't listening. He swung on Bill, his blue eyes dark with violence. "The next time I see Scott, I will beat him to within an inch of his life!" Matt shoulders slumped. "The way he did Kris—" He could not go on.

Bill reached Matt in a heartbeat, slipping an arm around his shoulders, feeling the tension in him. "No, you won't," he said with absolute conviction. "Why do you think Roy was so adamant about not revealing Kris's whereabouts or what had happened to her? Even if you weren't in love with her, you would feel an obligation to fight her battles—because of the contract. Incidentally, Roy realized immediately that you're in love with her. As I said, you don't hide it very well. Neither does Kris. *Except, apparently, from each other.*" Bill's voice was dry.

Matt straightened and studied Bill's expression. "What makes you so sure that I won't make Scott pay—?"

"Because I told Kris last night that I would accept responsibility for your knowing what happened. I also know that you won't pick on someone weaker than you."

"*Weaker?*" Matt sounded incredulous.

"Perhaps not physically, although if he makes a habit of drinking like that, he soon will be. I was referring to emotional and character weaknesses." Bill studied Matt as he spoke.

An attempt at a grin lightened Matt's features. "You did this to me when I was a kid. When I was ready to beat up Carl for pulling Tracy's hair."

"Yeah?" Bill said with a grin of his own. "I'm still good at it." He put his arm around Matt's shoulders again. "How about that coffee?"

"Later," Matt said. "I think I'll stay here. I need some space."

Bill nodded in understanding and crossed the tarmac to the Bronco.

Matt slumped down on a stool and stared into the murky nothingness around him. It wouldn't be long until dawn—such as it was. An overhead light had provided illumination while they worked. He reached over and flipped it off.

The cold creeping into his bones seemed appropriate somehow. So did the aches that seemed even worse this morning. His whole body was racked with pain. This somehow seemed symbolic of his life without Kris.

Matt stood and thrust a hand impatiently through his hair. The thick curls felt strange, having grown out from the military cut he usually wore. He wondered briefly if Marie would feel well enough to cut it soon, or if he should fly into Fairbanks.

The stress of being around Kris was beginning to take its toll, he admitted to himself. He was ready to accept how much he wanted and needed her—*how much he loved her.* But this time she was the one who wasn't willing to listen. After hearing her story last night, he couldn't say that he blamed her.

The fact that Kris seemed so desperately alone tore at Matt. He cursed Scott for his attack on her. At a time when she needed someone most, Scott had turned against her. And because he himself was a coward, he hadn't been there to protect her. Matt frowned as he realized that a lot of what he was feeling was guilt.

Matt heard the Bronco returning and looked up to see Kris step out of it. She wore a dark green flight suit with emerald stripes. He knew even at this distance what those colors would do for her eyes and groaned inwardly.

His eyes followed her as she crossed to the hangar. The morning was fairly mild and she wore her hair loose with no cap or ski mask covering it. Standing in the shadows he didn't try to hide the desires stirring in him.

Kris saw him and walked over to put the keys in his hand. "Hal said you could take the Bronco back. I'm going to fly over to the village to see Brandi and the baby."

"In the Cub?" Matt asked, raising his head to pin her with his gaze.

"What else?" Kris asked. It was almost light now and he could see her eyes shining with excitement. "I'll have almost five hours of daylight and with the wing tank, I have plenty of fuel. No sweat."

"Could you make it with a passenger?"

"I've flown to the village with both Yanni and Bill. I can refuel there if I need to." She was too preoccupied to see the trap Matt was setting.

He straightened. "Then you just got a passenger."

Kris stared at him, her lips parting. "I don't particularly want a passenger. Besides, someone has to take the Bronco back."

Matt was already walking toward the vehicle. "I'll have Bill bring me back. Don't leave without me!"

Kris stared after him and then set about getting the Cub ready for flight. She hadn't flown in weeks, what with Bill and Marie being gone. This was her chance to be alone with her thoughts, to unwind. Now she could feel her nerves coiling into knots. If Matt went with her, relaxing would be the last thing she'd do.

She wondered again how long she'd be able to hold up to his constant presence. Just thinking about him was detrimental enough. She feared having him around in person would prove to be more than she could endure. She couldn't stand the thought of his pity, knowing he would never have anything more to offer.

Kris put warmed oil back into the engine and pulled the plane out of the hangar before the Bronco returned. Matt got out and Bill shouted something to him before driving off.

Kris tied the plane down and chocked it, then began pulling the prop through to distribute oil evenly to all cylinders. *Routine. Methodical.* Just what she needed.

Matt's hand closed over hers. "Let me do that."

Kris didn't move her hand from beneath his right away, but leaned her face against her arm. This was anything but routine and methodical. *This was the last thing she needed.*

"Kris?" Matt bent close to her ear, his breath stirring her hair. She straightened and moved away.

"You don't want me along?" His eyes met hers, blue and piercing, demanding the truth.

She shrugged. "It isn't that I don't *want* you along. *I wanted to be alone.*"

"I think you've spent too much of your life alone," Matt said flatly and saw her face close.

"You don't know the half of it." Her voice had turned bitter. "But that being the case, I don't see any arguments for changing now."

"Meaning what?" He glanced at her.

She turned away. "You figure it out."

Matt pulled the propeller through a few more times and then stood behind the engine, one hand holding onto the door frame while he spun the prop. The engine sputtered a couple of times and caught. He nursed the throttle until it ran smoothly. After checking the oil pressure, he left the engine to warm up and looked around at Kris.

She stood a few feet away, forming her hair into a braid. Matt watched, fascinated, as her fingers moved in and out of the golden strands.

Kris finished her hair and turned to him. "Would you like to fly?" She tried to meet his eyes, failed, and dropped her gaze.

Matt knew how hard it was for her to make the offer. He shook his head. "Maybe coming back. I'm a little rusty."

"I guess I should fly from the front. If you sit up there, I won't be able to see any of the instruments."

"Hal always said you didn't need instruments to fly a Cub," Matt reminded with a grin. He wanted to see her smile.

She nodded, shrugged. "All the same, I like knowing they're there."

"If you're ready to get in, I'll untie her."

Kris climbed into the front seat and did a quick check of the instruments while she waited for Matt to get in behind her. She put on her headset and flipped on the radio and intercom. Then she advanced the throttle and moved forward onto the taxiway.

It had been a long time since he'd been back here, Matt reflected as he gave himself over to watching Kris handle the plane. Most of the time, it was Hal's broad back that he'd stared at. Fortunately, he'd been tall enough to see the instruments over Hal's shoulder. Kris was right. If he sat in front, he would completely block her view of the instrument panel.

Kris did an engine run up and mag check and set the altimeter. She closed the door and moved onto the runway.

"Ready," she said over the intercom. In the next instant she shoved the throttle forward and they were skimming down the runway. Then, effortlessly, it seemed, they were airborne.

Matt drew a deep, soul-releasing breath. This was real flying. However fast and high powered the planes he flew in the service and in racing, nothing could beat this for the pure joy of flying.

Kris wished she could see Matt's face. She heard the indrawn breath and interpreted it correctly. Whatever he'd done in flying so far, Matt was still a pilot from the old school, just like her father. *Just like her.* She sighed. It was too bad they couldn't share more.

The Athabascan fishing village nestled in a valley along a narrow river. A crude runway lay to the north of the village and Matt studied the layout of the community as Kris made her approach. The landing strip was of little concern, he knew. There was virtually no wind today and Piper Cubs were very much at home on grass or dirt fields.

Kris had called Yanni before she left to see if anyone in the village needed anything special in the way of medical attention. Her bag was fully stocked, although as a whole these were a healthy, hardy people and Yanni knew of no particular problems.

As she throttled back and turned base, Kris saw a Jeep moving away from the house that belonged to Salina's sister. Yanni was on his way to pick them up. She turned final and lined up with the runway. Seconds later, they touched down in a perfect three point landing. She taxied to the end and turned the plane around, then cut the mags and unbuckled her seat belt.

Yanni yanked open the door. "Kris!" He practically lifted her out of the plane and enveloped her in a bear hug. Then he looked up at the man who stepped out behind her.

"Matt!" Kris found herself abandoned as Yanni threw his arms around Matt. Matt returned the embrace. "Man, it's been years!" Yanni said without stopping for breath. "I heard all about Desert Storm and the shrapnel in your shoulder. I can't tell you how glad I am to see you. For a while it didn't sound as if you were going to make it . . ."

Kris stopped listening, staring at Matt. Her stomach turned over and she forced herself to take a deep breath. She knew Matt had been injured in Desert Storm. He'd been in the hospital for months, and upon his release had been discharged from the Air Force. That would've been just before she saw him that last time. *When he'd told her it was all over. That there was nothing between them.* She'd never put it all together before. She turned away blindly to get her bag out of the plane.

Kris sat in the back of the Jeep as Yanni drove them to Josef's house. Matt sat in front and the two men talked nonstop. It was obvious to Kris that there was a deep love and friendship here. Everyone seemed to like Matt and he cared for them in return. A fresh wave of regret for what she could not have washed over her.

Matt visited with Yanni and Josef while Kris checked out Brandi and her baby. Salina came out and gave Matt a hug. He gazed down at her affectionately. She was a contrast to her husband in every way—dark and slim and quiet. Yanni was loud and outgoing with the physique of a grizzly bear. As unlikely as it might seem, Matt knew that Yanni was totally and willingly enslaved by his wife.

"So are you keeping Yanni out of trouble?" Matt teased.

She smiled. "Of course. But you know without me, he would get in big trouble."

Matt nodded. "I have no doubt of that. I'm glad to see that you're still willing to put up with him."

"Ah, here is Kris with little Phillipe," Salina said as she glanced up. "You must admire Josef's son."

Matt looked around and saw Kris with the baby cuddled in her arms. His breath caught. The expression on her face was of such tender wistfulness that he felt his heart contract. She should have children of her own. *His children.* Matt caught himself as he realized the direction his thoughts had taken.

Somehow he went through the motions and said the right things to Josef. Kris finished her visit and Yanni drove them back to the plane. As he climbed in, Matt realized that Kris hadn't spoken directly to him since Yanni arrived to pick them up.

Kris didn't offer to let him fly the plane back and Matt sensed that she needed the diversion. He settled back and enjoyed the beauty of the terrain below as the plane skimmed along at a few hundred feet. The aches he felt this morning seemed to be worse now. Was it from the cold? Or perhaps being folded into the back of the small plane?

The sun was setting when they landed. Bill apparently heard them coming and turned the runway lights on for good measure. Matt pushed the plane into the hangar and drained the oil while Kris unloaded her supplies. The temperature was dropping rapidly with the approach of darkness. Finally there was nothing left to do and Bill still hadn't arrived with the Bronco.

"You've been awfully quiet," Matt commented at last, uncomfortable with the silence between them.

"Guilty," Kris replied.

"Is something wrong?" His gaze searched hers.

"Does something have to be wrong?" He heard tears in her voice.

He moved closer and tilted her chin to look into her face. "It doesn't have to be, but I know it is. You seemed so happy until we got to the village." He tried to remember what had happened to cause the change in her.

Kris turned away. "Just something I overheard."

"Do you want to tell me about it?"

She shook her head and glanced at her watch. "Let's walk back. Something must have happened. Bill should have been here ten minutes ago."

Matt didn't reply and Kris looked at him. "Well?"

He grimaced. "My leg's been aching all day and being scrunched up in the plane didn't help."

Something flashed in Kris's eyes. "Why didn't you tell me? You weren't flying. I could have given you something for the pain. Or we could've come back sooner."

"You needed to be there," he said. "You were in your element today, Kris. I know why you're a doctor. What I don't understand is how you can give it up—"

"Who says I've given it up?" Her voice was impatient. "I just haven't decided how to fight, yet, that's all. I—" She broke off. "I'm walking back. If you want to wait here, I'll come back for you as soon as I can."

"I'm sure Bill will be here in a couple of minutes."

Kris shook her head. "I can't wait. I have a feeling about this."

Matt reached down and zipped up the leather jacket she had on over her flight suit. "Then we walk." He turned away to fasten his own jacket.

They didn't meet Bill as they walked the quarter mile back to the inn, and Kris's concern grew. What could have happened? He must have heard her arrive, because he'd turned on the runway lights. She pushed open the door to the garage and saw that the door to the Bronco was open.

"Kris, thank God you're here!" Bill's voice, muffled with pain, came to her. "Is Matt with you?"

"Yes, we're both here." Kris followed the sound of his voice as her eyes adjusted to the light. He lay at the base of the steps that led into the garage, one leg twisted beneath him.

"Bill, what on earth?" Kris drew in her breath and knelt beside him. "What happened? Where are you hurt?"

"Slipped down those blasted steps. Did it once before. Was a lot younger then." He was speaking in short clipped sentences full of pain. "Something twisted this time. My back, my hip, my leg—I'm not sure. I thought it best—not to move."

"Good thinking." Kris attempted to examine him. *Nothing obviously broken.* "I'm going to try to get you to a more comfortable position and put some blankets over you. Do you know if there's a stretcher or backboard around?"

"There's a stretcher in the storeroom," Bill managed, his voice weak.

"I'll get it," Matt said before Kris could reply. "I saw it the other day." He hurried into the house.

"Is Matt doing all right?" Bill asked, looking at Kris to gauge her reaction.

She sighed. "His leg is hurting. You know, the one he broke when he totaled his sister's new Jaguar. I warned him that the cold would cause him a lot of pain, and today he chose to over do it a bit."

"So now you have three invalids," Bill said, watching her. "Poor Kris."

She shrugged. "Well, that's what I do—or used to do."

"And will do again," Bill said, looking into her eyes.

"Yes," Kris replied. "And will do again."

He nodded with satisfaction. "You wouldn't be Hal's daughter if you gave up."

CHAPTER EIGHT

An hour later, an exhausted Kris finally had Bill settled into bed. She gave him a mild sedative, then went into the kitchen. Matt handed her a mug of hot cocoa. She wrapped her hands around it, sniffing in appreciation.

"You're spoiling me." Her sigh was heartfelt.

Matt caught her arm as she turned away. "Kris, we have to talk—"

"Oh? About what?" She swung around to face him.

His hand dropped. "Scott, maybe. What he did to you. *To us.*" His eyes were dark and troubled as they met hers.

"I think I'd rather talk about Desert Storm." She couldn't keep the pain out of her voice, but her gaze didn't waver. "What it did to you. *To us.*"

He winced. "Maybe they're part of the same thing." His voice was too quiet, sounding somehow defeated.

Kris felt her control slipping. She put the cocoa down and turned away to begin unzipping her flight suit. She'd been too busy to take it off until now, and it had grown uncomfortably warm.

Matt watched as she removed the garment. Underneath it she wore snug fitting jeans and a pink silk turtleneck that clung to every curve. His gaze lifted to hers.

Kris stopped breathing, mesmerized by the look in Matt's eyes. She could read his hunger and need and knew it was mirrored in her own face. Her lips softened and parted. She had no more power to resist him than she had that night in the hangar—before he left for the Persian Gulf.

Matt found himself no longer fighting his own desires, but hers as well. With a supreme effort he turned away. He ran a hand unsteadily through his hair, his breathing ragged and uneven. His gaze focused on the darkness outside the window.

Pain seared through Kris. *Scott!* Matt would never touch her again because of Scott. She'd been right. He had no interest in the wreckage Scott left behind. She gathered up the tattered remnants of her self control, picked up her flight suit and left the room.

"We do have to talk." Kris's spoke from the darkness behind Matt.

He looked up from Ben's journal and turned his head to see Kris standing a few feet away. She moved to the fireplace and stood with her hands clasped behind her. She wore a flannel shirt over the turtleneck and her hair hung loose. Matt held his breath.

"Can you fly Bill's plane?" she asked without preamble.

The question was so far removed from anything he expected her to say that Matt could only stare at her.

110

Kris picked up the poker to stir the fire. "Because if you can't, I need to call Yanni. We have to get Bill to a doctor."

"You're a doctor—"

She shook her head. "*A hospital*, then. I need x-rays. He's obviously in pain, but I can't find anything broken, and only a few bruises. He may only have torn muscles and ligaments, but I can't take any chances."

Matt stood and pushed his hands into the pockets of his jeans. "I need to make a few landings to be legal, and I'd prefer to do them during daylight. Yanni did say they're coming back tomorrow, but it'll probably be late."

"I've never checked out in Bill's plane and I'm not instrument rated," Kris said. "There's something else to consider. If you fly him, it'll just be the two of you. I have to stay here with Marie."

Matt nodded, watching her, silent and brooding.

"I'm open to suggestions," Kris said. "I can keep him sedated while we wait for Yanni and Salina. Then I can go with him and Yanni while you and Salina take care of Marie."

Matt made a gesture of resignation. "You have to make the decision. I'll do whatever you need me to do—*legality be damned*."

"I'd like to see how he's doing in the morning," Kris said. "Of course, at his age—" She reached up to push her hair back. *"Dear God, I don't know!"* Matt could see tears of frustration sparkling in her eyes.

"Let's give it 'til then," he said. "You're too tired to make a rational decision now, anyway."

Kris looked at him. "Thanks for the vote of confidence." Her voice was dry, almost brittle.

He frowned. "What does that mean?"

"That under the right conditions, you think I'd be capable of making a rational decision. You don't have much reason to assume that from what you've seen—and learned—since you arrived."

"I know you're under a lot of stress—and frankly, you're holding up a lot better than you have any right to. Considering you won't let anyone help." His eyes held hers until she looked away.

"I've never had anyone I could turn to. I don't know how." She made a restless movement. "I couldn't go to my mother because she was never well and I didn't want to worry her. And as much as I loved him, Dad never knew what to do with a daughter. I couldn't share my problems with him."

Matt hesitated. "As I've said before, I'm here."

She shook her head. "It's kind of you to offer. But I can't see how going to the problem will solve it."

"Kris—" His hands clenched into fists as he fought for control. He walked over to the fireplace to stand with his back to her. "All those weeks in the hospital, the only thing I could think about was you."

"Then why—" she whispered, then broke off when he turned to her.

"There wasn't much left of me, Kris. Nothing of the man who had kissed you before he left. I was bitter. *Broken. Battered.* You didn't want that."

Her mouth twisted. *"Wanna bet?"*

"Will you answer a question for me?" He raised his eyes to hers, blue, piercing. *Impossible to hide from.*

Kris swallowed. "I'll try."

"Do you believe that I want you? That I can still want you now that I know about the malpractice suit and Scott?"

Her lashes fell. She twined her fingers together, brought her hands up to clasp under her chin. When she looked up, Matt still watched her. Slowly, she shook her head, her mouth trembling.

He released his breath in an explosive sigh. "I thought as much." He jammed his hands into his pockets again. *"Now do you understand how I felt?"*

"Kris?" She turned as her door opened after a light tap. She reached to switch on a lamp. Matt strode across the room to hand her Ben's journal.

"Read this," he said, leaning over to point to a passage. "It starts here, and goes on for about a page." His eyes were a dark intense blue and he seemed to radiate restless energy. He knelt beside her chair.

Kris looked at him, could not define the expression in his eyes, and finally turned her attention to the pages before her.

Bill the peacemaker strikes again! Hal and I were having a Class A argument—I don't even remember what it was about. But Hal was getting madder and madder and I knew it would only be a matter of time before he took a swing at me.

Just then Bill tripped and fell down an incline into a ravine. It took us twenty minutes to get him out. He couldn't walk, not even stand. By then we were exhausted.

It was Hal's idea to make a litter. We found some branches we could cut and used our coats, tying them together. Boy, was it cold without them!

Bill was blue and almost comatose. If he talked at all it was to murmur incoherently and call out for Marie. We were scared.

After we got him on the litter we had to carry him for miles. We finally made it back to the base. At which point, Bill stood up under his own power, saluted, and thanked us for the ride.

We stared after him in open-mouthed disbelief that we had been so completely had. Then Hal began to laugh. About the same time I realized what had happened and started laughing, too. Hal offered to buy me a drink and we sat in the canteen pondering the lesson Bill had taught us. We would only survive if we stuck together . . .

Matt watched Kris as she read. He heard her draw in her breath, and watched the growing amusement on her face. She laughed as she handed the journal back to him.

"Oh, Matt! Do you think that's what Bill's trying to do this time? But why? What could he hope to gain?"

"If so, his intent is apparently to teach us a lesson. Hopefully, we'll be smart enough to figure out what it is."

Kris frowned. "I have a sneaking suspicion I may know. He apologized for adding to my patient load." Her eyes suddenly pinned Matt. "By the way, did you take anything for those aches?"

"No, Doctor, I did not."

"But why?"

"I may have to fly tomorrow," he explained patiently.

"Matt, trust me, those pills won't affect your flying. I'm a doctor, and I'm a pilot. I know. Are you still in pain?"

"Like you wouldn't believe."

She wet her lips. "Please take something!" Her eyes pleaded with him.

His silence told her he would not be swayed. She sighed and glanced at the clock, then looked at Matt, taking in his jeans and sweater. "You haven't gone to bed yet?"

"I had a lot to think about. Apparently I'm not keeping you up. You're still dressed and apparently wide awake."

Kris shook her head. "No. I was doing a bit of soul searching myself. I sort of promised Bill I'd make at least a token effort to clear my name."

"Did your visit to the village have anything to do with that decision?" Matt's quiet voice told her he understood.

She glanced at him. "You see entirely too much, Captain!" A smile danced in her eyes as they met his.

He stood up. "You'd do well to remember that." He strode from the room, not trusting himself to look back.

Kris sat deep in thought for several moments after Matt left. Finally, she prepared for bed and reached over to set her alarm for four-thirty. Rolling onto her side, she tried to fall asleep.

She heard Matt go into his room and the house grew quiet. As she imagined Matt getting ready for bed, she groaned and buried her face in the pillow. She remembered his expression as he watched her take off her flight suit. His look made her feel desirable—cherished even. He asked if she could believe that he still wanted her, now that he knew everything. A faint ray of hope glimmered briefly and a wistful smile curved her lips as she fell asleep.

Kris moved silently through the house and turned the knob to Bill and Marie's bedroom. If Bill did indeed intend to put something over on them, as the passage from Ben's journal suggested, then this was the time of day when he'd be most likely to let down his guard.

A night light in the adjoining bathroom cast enough light for Kris to see Bill in bed with Marie, his arms around her. That was *not* where she'd left him. Not wishing to disturb Marie more than necessary, Kris had asked Matt to set up a cot in a corner of the room. Kris had left Bill in it, in an agony of pain.

She felt a movement and turned to see Matt beside her. Without thinking, she put a finger to his lips to silence him and moved aside so he could look in. In the dim light, she saw him smile.

Matt stepped back, drawing Kris with him, and closed the door. When they were a safe distance away, Kris stopped.

"What are you doing up?" She found it hard to breathe, with Matt so close to her. She could almost feel the heat from his body.

"I heard a sound and hoped to catch Bill—well, doing something incriminating." Matt jammed his hands in the pockets of his robe to keep from reaching for Kris. He had found her desirable earlier. Now, with her standing before him in nothing but a pair of silky pajamas, his ability to resist her had all but deserted him.

"You couldn't have heard me," Kris said. "I didn't make a sound."

"Maybe not enough to wake someone," Matt agreed. "But since I wasn't asleep—"

"You didn't take anything—" Kris tried to keep the impatience out of her voice. Nagging wouldn't help, not with someone like Matt.

"We've been over that already." The words were a low growl of warning.

Kris turned away with a sigh. "Lack of sleep will affect your flying more than anything I could give you."

"What are we going to do about Bill?"

"I think we should let him call the shots. When I suggest x-rays, if he agrees, and you're up to it, we'll fly him to Fairbanks. This could still be for real. If he protests, or suggests we wait a few days, or wait for Yanni, then we'll wait. He isn't a fool. If he's really hurt, and in pain, he'll want help."

Matt nodded. He put his hand to his throat and turned away. "I need something to drink." Kris followed him into the kitchen. She could see him in the dim light from the hallway as he found a glass and opened the refrigerator.

"Do you want anything?" Matt turned to look at her.

"No—thanks," Kris managed. "Nothing to drink."

"Food?" He raised an eyebrow. "That'd be a first."

What would he do if she told him that what she wanted was more basic than food or drink? Kris wondered. She wet her lips, unable to take her eyes off him.

Matt closed the refrigerator and raised the glass to drink. His hand went to his throat as he swallowed and Kris saw him wince.

"What's wrong?" She went to him and reached up to touch his face. He caught her hand and jerked it away as if he'd been burned.

"I'm sorry!" Kris stared at him. "You looked as if you were in pain. I wanted to help."

"Kris!" He caught her face between his hands, his gaze roving hungrily over it. She felt his tension. Then he relaxed. "I'm tired of being in control," he murmured. "It's killing me! *I want you, Kris!*" He bent his head and his mouth closed over hers.

Kris thought she must be dreaming, but when she slipped her hands inside his robe, Matt groaned and gathered her closer. Her hands went from his chest to clasp around his neck. His lips against hers were hard and demanding. Hers softened and parted.

Kris felt her blood ignite in a surge of passion. She wanted Matt to touch her. She melted against him. *She'd been waiting all her life for this!*

Then slowly, through her stupor, Kris realized that all was not well. Something had registered when she touched his face, but he hadn't allowed her to follow through. *His body was much too warm!* She felt his neck and face and brought her hands to his chest. Then she drew back to look at him.

"Matt." Her fingers grazed his face, her voice gentle. The passion of a moment before had fled as if it had never been. She was a doctor again. "I'm sorry, but you have a raging fever. No wonder you couldn't sleep. How does your throat feel?"

He looked at her, trying to focus—to remember. He brought a hand up to touch his throat again. "I don't know—raw and scratchy, I guess."

"It sounds like you're coming down with the flu." Kris took his arm and led him toward his room. "How long have you felt like this?"

"Since this morning. I never thought—"

"How long does it usually last when you get the flu?"

He stopped and looked down at her. "I hate to disillusion you, Doctor, but I've never had *'the flu'*. I don't have a clue how it affects me."

She stared at him. "Well, I'll try to make it simple. Those aches that were so bad this afternoon, that raw and scratchy throat, this burning fever— those are going to be facts of life for anywhere from three or four days to a week or so. All you can do for it is drink lots of liquids, take aspirin, and stay in bed. You most certainly will not fly. And if you don't take care of yourself, flu can easily develop into pneumonia. The fact that you've never had it before doesn't tell me anything—except that you'll be a very difficult patient."

"What about you? Isn't the flu contagious?" Kris could hear the concern in Matt's voice.

"Extremely."

"I just kissed you—"

"Don't worry about it." She tried to sound casual. "I always get a flu shot." *But had she this year?* For the last several months, that would have been the last thing on her mind.

CHAPTER NINE

Kris sat beside Matt's bed where she had spent the past thirty-six hours, sleeping fitfully when he slept, waking to bathe him when he burned with fever.

She walked to the window, stretching to get the kinks out of her back and shoulders. Thankfully, Yanni and Salina had returned, and Yanni promised to relieve her as soon as he took care of a couple of chores.

Kris had assigned Salina to take care of Marie and Bill and cautioned her not to come near Matt. She couldn't take a chance on Marie catching the flu at this critical stage when her immune system was rebuilding itself.

Kris glanced around the room. The only illumination came from a small shaded lamp in the corner. She saw Ben's journal lying on a chest. Matt had offered to let her read it if she was interested. She would take it with her when Yanni came to stay with Matt.

Kris changed into pajamas and curled up in a chair. Long past the point of exhaustion, she still felt too tense to fall asleep. She saw Ben's journal lying on the bedside table and reached for it. Opening it to the first page, she blinked at the childish scrawl. She didn't remember the handwriting from the passage she had read the other night.

They still haven't found Dad or the plane. I've decided to keep a journal like he did. Then when they find him I'll be able to tell him everything that happened—

Kris gasped in horror as she realized this couldn't be Ben's journal. She checked the date of the entry. *Thanksgiving Day, 1971*

She closed the journal to look at the cover. Now she could see that it was bound in dark blue leather. Ben's had been dark green with gold veining. *In the dim light of Matt's room, she had mistakenly picked up the wrong journal!*

Feeling like an intruder, Kris let the pages feather through her fingers. Suddenly she froze, mesmerized. Her hands clenched as she stared at the page where the book had fallen open. She couldn't have put it down if her life depended on it. *She had seen her name.*

Matt opened his eyes and blinked. His eyelids felt as if they had grit behind them. He tried to focus and saw Kris asleep in a rocking chair beside the bed, a quilt pulled over her. He glanced at the window. It was light out, early afternoon. *Already?*

He threw back the covers, swung his feet to the floor, and folded over as dizziness washed over him. He felt hands on his shoulders and looked up into Kris's face. His eyes closed again as she lowered him back to the pillow.

The next time he awakened Kris was gone. It was dark out, but he could see the empty chair with the quilt draped across it. He closed his eyes and remembered her as she slept in the chair.

He heard the door open and looked up. Kris brought in a tray and put it on a table beside the bed. She sat down and reached over to feel his forehead.

"Good," she said. "You haven't had a temperature for several hours now. Your color is better, too. I thought you might be hungry."

Matt tried to speak, moistened his lips. Kris held a glass of water for him and he put his hand over hers to steady it as he drank. He lay back.

"What happened to me?" he asked, his voice hoarse and cracked. "The last thing I remember is kissing you—at least I think I kissed you—and now I feel as if I've been run over by a freight train."

Kris smiled, laughter sparkling in her eyes. "I never knew my kisses packed such a wallop!"

He gave her a dark look.

"Okay," Kris relented. "While we were kissing—it took a while, but I noticed you were much too warm. I realized you had a very high temperature."

He shook his head. "I wouldn't know. That's the way I always feel around you." He met her eyes for a moment.

"Have you really never had the flu?" Kris asked, bringing the conversation back to a level she could deal with. "You didn't recognize any of the symptoms?"

"Not for what they were. I thought the aches were just the cold affecting all those newly healed broken bones the way you told me it would—that and being folded up in the back of the Cub all those hours."

"Well, you had a pretty rough time." She stood up. "You've been here for four days—mostly delirious. Yanni and I took turns giving you cold baths to bring your temperature down. Until late last night I was sure you were going to develop a text book case of pneumonia."

Matt had stopped listening. "Did you say you gave me baths?" he asked, his eyes burning into hers.

"And why not? Admittedly, doctors usually don't do such mundane tasks, but I didn't have a nurse to assign it to."

"I think you know *that* is not my concern," he grated.

"Matt, I am a doctor."

"Why didn't you at least put some clothes on me?"

Obviously he didn't enjoy being administered to by her. "Something like pajamas, perhaps?" she asked innocently.

"Well, yes." The look he threw her told her that he didn't appreciate her amusement at his expense, either.

"We tried. I found some of Bill's old pajamas. If you own any, you keep them well hidden. But between the chills and fever, they kept getting soaked and we had to take them off for the baths, anyway. Besides, you didn't seem very comfortable in them."

"You're enjoying this, aren't you?" he growled. But at last a smile touched a corner of his mouth.

Kris laughed. "Maybe a little."

"Kris, about that kiss—" Matt looked uncomfortable.

"I'm not sure I want to talk about that kiss." She turned away to begin folding the quilt.

He sighed. "We should."

She shook her head. "Not if you're going to tell me you didn't mean it—that you're sorry it happened. After all, you couldn't bring yourself to touch me until you were delirious—"

"I just wanted to say that I hope you don't catch this. You've been through enough lately."

She stared at him, wet her lips. "I appreciate your concern." She held the quilt in front of her, smoothing it over and over.

"It's a lot more than concern, Kris. I want to kiss you every time I look at you. Before, I was the one who held back. This time, I'm ready and you aren't. It isn't easy. I'm afraid I'll frighten you away if I go too fast—or remind you of Scott."

She turned away. "You couldn't possibly remind me of Scott. I can forget him if you can." She hesitated for a moment, as if to say more. Then, "I'll send Yanni to help you dress."

"Kris—"

She looked back. "I'm glad you're feeling better. And don't worry about me catching the flu. Franz came out several weeks ago and gave us all shots." The door closed behind her.

Matt sank back against his pillow. A moment later the door opened and Yanni walked in. He gave Matt a dark look.

"Now what?" Matt asked, glaring at this man who had been more of a brother than anyone he'd known.

"If you can't figure it out, far be it from me to try and explain—"

"What did Kris say?" Matt demanded.

"Oh? So you do know her name is Kris." Yanni's soft guttural voice mocked him. He pulled jeans and a shirt from a drawer. "Would you like a shower?"

"I would." Matt threw back the covers. "But first I'd like to know why my love life seems to be everyone's business, including yours?"

Yanni's brows rose innocently. "Your love life, is it? And you're speaking of Kris in that context?"

Matt shook his head and took a step toward the bathroom. He swayed and Yanni caught his arm.

"Hold on, Scout. You aren't ready to slay dragons yet. It's probably just as well that you aren't interested in a damsel in distress—however beautiful she may be."

"Hold still!" Yanni said a couple of hours later. "I'll have a little trouble explaining to Kris why I cut your throat after all we went through to keep you alive the last few days."

Matt grinned. Yanni had cut his hair and now tried to shave him. The haircut hadn't been a problem. An expert, Yanni kept in practice by cutting the hair of all the male villagers. But sporting a full beard in keeping with his rugged physique, shaving was somewhat less familiar to Yanni.

"As I was saying," Yanni picked up his train of thought, "Kris didn't leave your side for the first thirty-six hours. I guess she slept a little in the chair beside your bed. But it wasn't until yesterday afternoon when your fever broke and you fell into a normal sleep that she finally got some rest herself. This has been pretty rough on her, what with three patients and all. She's worn out."

"By the way, how's Bill?" Matt remembered to ask.

"Just a little bruised. When I got back, Kris asked if he felt he needed to go to Fairbanks for x-rays. He wanted to wait a few days. He could move around by then. Kris assigned Salina to take care of him and Marie. She didn't want either of them getting anywhere near you—just in case."

"Just in case—what? Kris said they all got flu shots." Matt frowned.

"We did. But that doesn't mean we can't catch a different strain, or even get a mild case of the same one. In Marie's case—" Yanni shook his head. "It's a chance we can't take."

Matt groaned as realization dawned. "Because she donated the bone marrow for Carl's transplant. I didn't think of that."

Yanni wiped the soap off Matt's face and looked at him critically. "Then she shanghaied me to help with you. She's strong, but you were pretty delirious most of the time. It took both of us to handle you."

Matt groaned. "Did I say things?"

After a moment of hesitation, Yanni nodded.

"What? What did I talk about?" Matt insisted.

"Matt, you really don't want me to tell you—"

"I have to know," Matt said. "Who else can I ask?"

Yanni sighed. "Well, you talked about Ben and Hal. You went on and on about a train—I never did figure that out."

"Train was a dog Hal gave me," Matt said. "What else?"

"You relived the Persian Gulf and getting your plane shot up. And you cursed Scott a lot." Yanni smiled, but it didn't reach his eyes.

"Did I—" Matt swallowed. "Did I talk—about Kris?"

Yanni began putting away his shaving kit. "I need to go check the runway—"

"Yanni?" Matt's quiet voice stopped him. There was a note of desperation in it.

Yanni turned back. "I don't know. I wasn't in the room all the time. On a bet, I'd say you did."

"What do you think I said?"

"I have no idea. I only know she'd been crying a couple of times when I came back into the room."

Matt drew a harsh breath that ended in a fit of coughing. When he recovered, Yanni was gone.

Kris sat at her desk going through a packet of papers from Roy when she heard a tap on the door.

"Come in!" she called, and froze as Matt stepped through the door. "Hello, stranger." Her voice was husky. "I like the haircut," she added.

"Hello, yourself." He closed the door and leaned against it. He ran a hand over his hair, cut again in his usual military style. "Thanks. So do I."

Kris stared at him and the impact of his gaze made her tremble. His face was pale and thin, now that it was clean shaven. The plaid shirt and jeans didn't fit as snugly as they had a few days before. But he looked much better now than the last time she'd seen him.

She allowed herself to relax a bit. He was going to be all right! Without warning, tears flooded her eyes. She turned away and put the papers on the desk. Then she buried her face in her hands.

"Kris!" Matt crossed the room, kneeling to catch her shoulders and turned her to face him. "What's wrong?"

"I was—frightened." The words came out jerkily as she struggled to catch her breath between sobs. "You were so ill—and I couldn't help you—"

"That's not what Yanni told me," Matt soothed. He wanted to pull her close and comfort her, but he couldn't vouch for his self-control, even in his weakened state.

Kris drew a deep breath and dug in her pocket for a tissue. Matt took it from her and blotted the tears from her face. She stared at him, lips parted.

Matt felt himself drowning in her tear drenched eyes. Her damp hair curled around her face. He trailed a knuckle down her cheek.

"Yanni said I made you cry—things I said—" His voice was strained.

Her breath caught. "No!" she protested. "It wasn't *things* you said. I didn't cry *because* of you."

"*Then what?*" He brought her hands together inside his.

"I—was crying *for* you—because—" Kris broke off, pressing her lips together as they trembled.

"*Because?*" he prompted.

She tugged at her hands, but he didn't release them.

"Because," she held his gaze, "you needed someone, and I wanted to be there for you—if only you had let me!"

He bowed his head and his fingers tightened on hers. "I wish I had. More than anything—*I wish I had!*"

"Matt." She put out a hand to touch his face.

A crash sounded from inside the house, making them both jump.

"I'd better check that out," Kris said, standing. "And you need to sit down." She hurried from the room.

Matt sank into her chair and leaned back and closed his eyes, marveling at how weak he felt.

Kris stepped into her room and closed the door. She leaned against it, a bemused smile playing around her mouth.

"What happened?" Matt asked from across the room.

Kris jumped, surprised that he hadn't returned to his room. "Oh, that. Salina's pregnant." She glanced up to see Matt staring at her in total incomprehension.

"She dropped a stack of dishes and burst into tears," Kris explained. "Yanni was beside himself. He'd never seen her come apart like that. According to Marie, breaking dishes is common among expectant mothers in this family." She sounded skeptical.

Matt nodded. "I know that's how Mom and Tracy always found out." He looked at Kris. "Are you sure about Salina?"

Kris shrugged. "I talked to her for a while. I haven't done any tests, but it seems pretty obvious."

"Do they want children?" Funny how easy it was to picture Yanni as a father, Matt thought.

"Oh, yes. Especially after all this time with Phillipe." Kris's face took on a dreamy expression. Then she straightened away from the door, shaking her head to dispel her thoughts. "I need to check on Marie and Bill. Do you need anything right now?" she asked, looking at Matt.

He shook his head. "Nothing. I'm just—tired."

Kris nodded. "That's normal. You will be for a few more days. Just try to relax, and get plenty of rest." She sighed, a smile playing around her mouth. "Actually, the easy part is probably behind us. The hard part will be to keep you from over doing it now that you're better."

Matt grinned. "No, thanks. I can do without a relapse. I'm going to be the best patient you've ever had."

Her eyes widened. "That I'll have to see to believe."

Kris returned from her rounds. Bill was doing so much better that she felt sure he'd been faking most of his injuries. He was more than capable of doing so, according to the passage in Ben's journal. What lesson had Bill intended to teach them, Kris wondered? Apparently Matt's illness forced him to change his plans. She shrugged and decided to check on Matt one last time.

"Matt?" Kris pushed open the door to his room and found it dark.

"I was just going to bed." The voice came from behind her, a little raspy and very sexy.

Kris turned to see him wearing pajama bottoms and nothing else. In the dim light from the hallway he looked piratical—lean, dark and dangerous. She could almost see him in a white blouse, open down the front, a scarlet sash around his waist. Light glittered dully off the chain around his neck.

"Marie dug up some of Carl's pajamas," Matt said, his lips twitching. "They fit a little better than Bill's."

Kris swallowed. "Whatever you say. I came to see if you'd like anything to help you rest."

"I do feel achy," Matt admitted.

"Get in bed and I'll bring you something. Yanni is with Salina. I'm all you've got so I hope you have a good night."

"Is Salina all right?"

"Yes. It's just—Yanni needs to be with her." Kris turned away. "I told him I could manage."

Matt threw back the covers and sank down against the pillows. He couldn't remember ever feeling this tired, this drained of strength. He closed his eyes.

"Matt." Kris sat on the bed, holding a glass of some fizzing liquid. He sat up and eyed her suspiciously as he reached for it.

"It's just an over-the-counter pain reliever. It works on aches and fever," Kris explained, her glance amused.

Matt closed his eyes and grimaced as he swallowed the contents. His eyes were accusing as he opened them to look at Kris. "That's the worst stuff I've ever tasted," he said. "Are you sure you aren't trying to kill me, Doctor?"

"And why would I want to do that? After all the work Yanni and I put into getting you well again—" Kris kept her voice light, teasing.

"He said almost the same thing." Matt still held the glass. He handed it back to her, his hand brushing hers as she took it from him.

"Would you like anything else to drink—juice or lemonade?" Kris asked. She touched his forehead to find his temperature still normal.

"I just had some water, thanks." Matt closed his eyes, reveling in her touch. Her hands felt so good against his skin. Now they were cool and professional. But even in his near delirium, he could remember them around his neck when he'd kissed her.

Kris drew her hand away from Matt's face. He was asleep. She straightened and tucked the blankets around him. Her fingers brushed against his cheek, lingering for a moment longer, her need to touch him almost overwhelming. She swallowed a sob that threatened to surface. Would she ever have that right, she wondered miserably? *Or would their timing always be off?*

CHAPTER TEN

Kris sighed and closed her door. She needed to get some sleep. Four of the other five people in the house were now dependent on her to some extent. Bill should be all right in a couple of days, and once Salina developed a proper routine of diet and rest, she'd be fine, too. Matt needed a few more days to regain his strength, but apparently he had recovered from the worst of the flu. Hopefully, no one else would catch it—Marie, in particular. If the flu shot they had gotten covered this particular strain, odds were they would all stay well.

She removed her robe and slipped beneath the covers. The cold empty bed brought a lump to her throat as she thought of Matt alone in his bed. *Alone and sick.* If only she had the right to comfort him, to care for him, to cradle his head against her and stroke his hair.

The depth of her feelings for Matt overwhelmed her. They had from the beginning. Back then she hadn't been fully aware of what was happening.

Now, she knew she had loved him totally and completely from the very first. There could never be anyone else for her. *Was it too much to hope that somehow he meant it when he said he still wanted her?* In spite of what Scott had told him and what he now knew about the malpractice suit and Scott's attack?

If she believed the passages from his journal, which she had read shamelessly, Matt had been as affected by her as she by him. Initially, his loyalty to Scott had made him hold back. Then his war experience and injuries had left him bitter and disillusioned. Unable to accept himself as he was, he didn't feel anyone else would want him, either. Rather than burden her with his problems, he had chosen to reject her, somehow thinking to save her the trouble of later realizing she didn't want half a man after all.

Kris swallowed the bitter thought that she had been found so shallow and lacking that Matt never gave her a chance to prove what she was made of. Didn't he realize she had spent most of her childhood taking care of her invalid mother? He had to know—

Kris sat up, eyes wide and heart pounding. *Of course Matt knew about her mother!* She swung her feet to the floor and began pacing in agitation. Was that the answer? Knowing she had sacrificed her teen years for her mother, had he thought it unfair to ask her to do the same for him?

She put her hands to her temples as her head began to throb. Matt had written something to that effect in his journal, although at the time she read it, Kris didn't realize what it meant.

She dropped to her knees beside the bed and buried her face in her arms as hot tears soaked the quilt.

Dear God, please help Matt heal, and if it be Your will, please let there be a place for me in his life!

Kris carried a tray into Matt's room and put it on the table. He still slept, turned onto his side away from her. One arm lay on top of the blanket. She reached out to trail her fingers down the length of it, remembering the strength and feel of it around her, gathering her close.

Matt stirred and rolled onto his back. His eyes opened, a dazzling blue.

"Good morning," Kris smiled. He did look good this morning. His color had returned to normal and he seemed rested.

"Hello." He raised himself to a sitting position. "Breakfast in bed?"

"This'll be the last," Kris said. "If I'd known you were doing this well, I wouldn't have bothered."

"You ought to see it from this side," Matt replied. "I don't know if I agree with your choice of adjectives."

"Did you sleep well?" Kris dropped down on the edge of the bed to touch his forehead. "Your temperature is normal."

He threw her a glance. "If you say so." He took the glass of juice she offered. "You *ought* to know how I slept. Is it common practice to repeatedly overdose your patients?"

"Oh, Matt, what did I do now?" Kris wailed.

"I don't know. The last thing I remember is drinking that foul stuff. That—and your touching me. It only seems like a few minutes and here you are with breakfast. I never sleep so soundly." He slanted a suspicious look at her.

"Are you rested? Or do you feel drugged and sluggish?" Kris's voice was brisk, professional.

"No. I feel rested. Not as achy." He raised his arms and stretched. He still wasn't wearing the top to his pajamas and Kris watched the muscles in his arms and chest ripple and flow in coordinated perfection.

133

"Good." Kris swallowed, her mind frantically searching for some coherent thought. "You have to remember how much you've been through. Sleep is your body's way of healing itself. You've been lucky to go thirty-five years without getting the flu. Most of us have to put up with it every year or so—or we did before shots became available." She broke off as she realized she was babbling.

"Thirty-six," Matt said.

"I beg your pardon?"

"*Thirty-six.*" He reached for a piece of toast. "I had a birthday somewhere back a few days ago. *Quite a celebration.* I wonder if Yanni gave me a bath that day."

Kris stared at him. "Oh, Matt!" She reached out to touch his hand, then her face brightened. "That must be what those packages are that Yanni brought from Fairbanks. You were already sick when he got here so I told him to leave them in the den."

"Packages?" Matt's voice was casual. *Too casual,* Kris thought.

"At least one came from Phoenix," Kris said. "The other address didn't mean anything to me."

Matt smiled. "Either Tracy or my nieces—and probably Mom. Thanks for telling me." His eyes held hers.

"Glad to help. When exactly was the big day?" Kris feared she was babbling again, his look so disconcerted her.

"The sixth. What's today?"

"The tenth. You're right—you didn't have much of a birthday. The second day was the worst for you. I think we both gave you baths." She stood up, busying herself with the tray. "Do you need Yanni to help you dress?"

"I can manage." He looked at her. "When is your birthday, Kris?"

She looked startled. "Oh—not for ages," she evaded. "I have to check Marie." She hurried from the room.

Matt stared after her. It seemed to upset her that he asked about her birthday. Maybe she thought she no longer had anyone to send her cards or gifts. Perhaps she didn't realize the size of the family their fathers had created for them. She might not know they were there for her, too. Matt frowned. Didn't she understand the legacy that was theirs to carry on?

Marie sat at the table watching as Kris mixed a cake. She looked so lovely with her hair pulled back in a long braid, one of Marie's aprons wrapped around her. So like her mother, Marie thought. *And yet so different.*

"What do you mean, he doesn't like chocolate?" Kris was asking. "Everybody likes chocolate." She looked at Marie triumphantly. "I know he likes hot cocoa. He drinks it—"

"He may like it," Marie amended an earlier statement. "But chocolate cake is not Matt's favorite. Lemon is."

"Lemon?" Kris's face screwed up into such an expression of disgust that Marie laughed.

"Have you ever had lemon cake?" she asked.

"Why would I when I could have chocolate?" Kris reasoned. "What's next? I have the eggs and sugar—"

Bill limped into the room to sit beside Marie. "What's going on?"

"Cooking lesson," Marie replied.

"And about time, too," Bill drawled. He looked at Kris affectionately, his face brightening at sight of her.

135

Kris stuck out her tongue. "Be nice, or you won't get any," she threatened. Her laugh pealed, light and carefree.

"What are we making?" Bill asked, pretending interest.

"Lemon cake." Kris wrinkled her nose again and Marie smiled.

"Lemon cake," Bill repeated. He glanced at Marie. "Matt's birthday?"

"A few days ago—while he was sick," Marie said. "I forgot it myself, but I don't think it matters. He felt too bad for us to do anything then, anyway." She reached over to give Bill a light kiss on the cheek. "We need you to keep him distracted while we finish the cake."

Bill returned the kiss. "Your wish is my command." He stood up and limped away.

Marie returned her attention to Kris. "You remind me so much of your mother," she said. "Although I don't remember seeing her make a cake."

Kris shook her head. "My grandmother Holland made cakes. Big thick chocolate ones!" Her face sobered. "I seem to remember so much more about her than I do about my mother."

Marie chose her words carefully. "Unfortunately, by the time you were old enough to remember, Jean was ill. She was a lovely person, sweet and gentle. You have a lot of her personality traits."

"Really?" Kris stirred the batter vigorously. "I don't remember any that I would want."

"My dear—"

"I've tried very hard not to be like her. I hate that I even look like her. All I remember is the selfishness and the temper tantrums—"

"That was the illness, Kris. Not the real Jean." Marie studied her. "One trait you inherited in abundance and it obviously didn't come from Hal."

136

"And what might that be?" Kris asked to be polite, not having any real interest in knowing.

"The tendency to care too much. That's what makes you such a wonderful doctor. It also makes it hard for you to face the malpractice charges—"

"I don't know that I'm all that wonderful," Kris protested.

"Of course you are. Look how you stayed with Matt—"

Kris looked at her. "We both know that is an entirely different issue. I would have stayed with him whether I was a doctor or not."

"My point exactly. I saw Jean do the same with Hal when they were first married. I've never seen two people so in love. I worried at first, they were such opposites. But Hal fell for Jean like a ton of bricks. I had given up on him meeting the right girl—"

Kris stared at her. "Are you saying my parents loved each other?"

Marie looked at her in confusion. "Of course they did. Why do you ask such a question?"

Kris shrugged, a lump forming in her throat. "Oh, I don't know. I guess that was something else I wasn't privileged to witness."

Marie felt her eyes fill with tears. "My dear, losing Joey affected your parents terribly. They never recovered. Jean lost the will to fight the crippling disease that showed up shortly after you were born. And Hal—Joey was his reason for living, and he blamed himself for his death. He couldn't give Jean what she needed when she became ill. It was always hard for him to show his feelings—"

"Yeah?" Kris said. "Tell me about it!" A tear rolled down her cheek. She brushed it away, leaving a flour smudge.

Marie reached out to put her hand over Kris's. "Kris, they loved you. No one could have been happier than they were when you were born."

Kris shrugged, sniffed. "Sure. But once they lost Joey, I was obviously a poor substitute. Don't worry, Marie. It's all right. I learned at a very young age how to live without love. It wasn't until after my mother was gone that I realized my father did love me—in his way. We became close, as close as possible for two people who had trouble showing their feelings. Of course, I always worshipped him, from the moment I knew who he was. I don't know if he knew that. *I didn't know how to tell him.*"

Matt watched from the window in the den as Yanni and Kris exercised the dogs. He had spent the morning with Bill who had come in to discuss the modifications Matt wanted to make on his engine. From there Bill began to reminisce about Ben and his dream of building and flying the racer with Matt. He had heard the stories before, but Matt never grew tired of hearing Bill talk about Ben and Hal. After a couple of hours Marie came in and requested Bill's help. Matt had returned to his reading for awhile before wandering over to look out the window.

Matt knew Yanni's huskies were his pride and joy. He worked with them every day that he could manage. They flew to the village with Yanni and Salina. At least one of them accompanied Yanni on most flights. In his native tradition, Yanni treated then as part of his family.

Now Yanni showed Kris how to make them work alone. They didn't need to play. They loved and enjoyed working. He hooked each separately to a small sled and let them take turns pulling Kris. That way, they learned to work independently. It took both of them to pull Yanni's weight, and in that they learned teamwork.

Kris appeared to be enjoying the workout, too. She'd taken a couple of tumbles in the snow and gotten up again. Now she shook the snow out of her cap after a third fall. Yanni said something to her and she nodded eagerly. They traded dogs and hers began pulling the sled up a small rise.

Matt continued to watch, envying Yanni his easy relationship with Kris. Loneliness, like a mantle, settled over him. As he turned away, a flash of movement caught his attention. Looking back he saw that Kris had fallen again. Only this time something had gone wrong. The husky bounded effortlessly across the snow, Kris bouncing along as he dragged her in his wake.

Without thinking, Matt grabbed his jacket and jerked open the door. By the time he reached Kris, Yanni had managed to catch the dog and pull him to a stop. Matt dropped to his knees beside the limp form.

"Kris!" She lay on her back and Matt gently brushed snow from her face. Yanni untangled the reins wrapped around her hands.

"Can we move her?" Matt's voice came out a hoarse croak and Yanni's gaze swung to him in concern.

"I'll move her. You better get back inside. You're still *recuperating,* remember?"

Matt ignored him, feeling for a pulse and checking her arms and legs for broken bones.

Yanni squatted beside him, taking over and running expert hands over Kris. "She's stunned, but if she wakes up and finds you out here, we've got bigger problems than her injuries to worry about." He threw Matt a glance he couldn't interpret. *"Uh-oh. Too late!"* Kris groaned and Yanni helped her to a sitting position.

"Is Buck all right?" She looked around for the dog. Her glance fell on Matt and her eyes widened in shock. *"What are you doing out here?"* .

Matt shrugged. "I saw you fall. What was I supposed to do? Let Buck pull you all the way to Fairbanks?"

"I doubt they'd have gotten that far," Yanni intervened. "Come on Kris, sweetheart. Can you stand?"

He helped her to her feet. She took a couple of experimental steps.

"A little wobbly, but that will pass." She looked up at Yanni. "Do you need help with Buck?"

"I can manage." He reached out to touch her face. "Take care of yourself. Are you sure you're all right?"

"Perfectly."

Yanni looked at Matt. "Get her inside. And you, too. I'm not ready to play nursemaid again." He turned back to Kris. "Kris—" He still sounded worried.

"Yanni, I'm okay!" Kris assured him. "Buck needs you more than I do! Take care of him and tell him I'm sorry. It was my fault for losing my balance. Thanks for your help." She turned and walked back to the inn. After a heartbeat Matt followed her, leaving Yanni looking after them, a mixture of amusement and concern on his face.

Matt closed the door and leaned against it, watching Kris. She looked at him as she removed her gloves.

He reached for her hand. "You know, you could've let go of the reins." The light in his eyes told her he was teasing.

"Good advice. Next time, I won't wrap them around my fingers. Yanni tried to warn me."

Matt looked up from her skinned and bruised knuckles and pinned her with his gaze. "What else?"

"What else?" Kris swallowed.

"Where else are you hurt? You put me through this, remember?"

She shrugged, winced. "Well, I know that most of my ribs are bruised. I don't think any are broken, but I wouldn't be surprised to find some scrapes and scratches. My shin is—"

Matt reached out a finger to touch her face. "You have a bruise on your cheek," he said, the smile now gone from his eyes.

Kris drew in her breath. "I think the best thing for me to do is take a hot bath and see what still hurts. You could ask Marie if she has a bottle of witch hazel and bring it to me." Kris realized she was babbling and sighed.

"Witch hazel?" Matt looked skeptical.

"Yes. It works wonders on scrapes and bruises."

"I'll see what I can do."

Kris finished her bath and returned to her room. She stood by the bed, one foot resting on a chair as she examined a painful scratch on her thigh.

The door opened and Matt stepped into the room. He froze at sight of Kris. She'd twisted her hair into a knot and stood with her back to him. Her robe gaped open, allowing him a tantalizing glimpse of shapely leg.

"Don't you knock?" She straightened and pulled the robe into place.

"I didn't realize you'd finished your bath. It took Salina a while to find the witch hazel. You told me to bring it to you." He held up the bottle.

"Thanks." Her voice sounded husky, her throat constricted.

Matt stared at Kris for what seemed an eternity. "Well, you should be able to handle it from here, right?" He turned away. "Let me know if you need anything else."

"Thanks," Kris whispered, staring after him, willing him to stay, knowing it was impossible for him to do so.

Matt looked up as Kris stepped into the den. He drew in his breath as he saw she'd put on another silk sweater, this one a soft green.

He stood and went over to look down at her. "How do you feel?" His hand came up to touch her face.

She shrugged. "Sore. Battered." She tried to keep her voice light, but his closeness made that impossible.

"Kris, what on earth—" Matt's voice was more harsh than he intended. "What was Yanni thinking—? How could this have happened?"

"It wasn't his fault," Kris defended. "I accept the blame. I lost my balance on the sled and Buck thought we were playing. I—" She broke off.

"I'm sorry." Matt's thumb traced her lips. "Do you have any idea how it makes me feel to see you hurt?"

"I know how I felt when you were sick," Kris whispered. Her hand went up to close around his wrist.

"I can't even hold you," Matt said. "I'd hurt you." His voice was strained, his eyes smoldering.

"I'd be willing to risk that," Kris whispered, wetting her lips. She stood motionless, trying to ignore the effect of Matt's touch, burning through the pain of her injuries. She wanted more. *Needed more.* She heard rapid breathing, harsh and uneven, and realized it was her own. She bowed her head, humiliation washing over her as once again Matt refused her invitation.

"I'm sorry." She swallowed. "You'd think I would learn not to throw myself at you. Forget—"

142

"Kris." With a groan Matt reached for her and drew her into his arms.

She might have been made of porcelain, so gently did he hold her, Kris thought. His hands stroked lightly, magically down her back. *Soothing. Healing.* She let out her breath in a sigh as she felt the tension drain from her body.

"Are you going to be able to sleep tonight?" Matt asked. Kris might be relaxed, but her closeness was having quite the opposite effect on him.

"Maybe a little," Kris said, moving fractionally away from him.

"You aren't going to be able to move tomorrow," he predicted. His mouth twisted in a grimace.

Kris swallowed. "Probably not. I may have to get Yanni to fill the hot tub." Her head came up. "Why didn't I think of that before? That's what Bill needs, too, for all those sore muscles of his."

Matt cleared his throat. "Hot tub?"

"It's over in the guest quarters. Since no one's here this time of year, it's pretty much forgotten." She looked at Matt. "It'd be good for all your aches, too." She pushed her hair back. "I should've thought of it days ago."

Matt turned away. "Can I get you anything?"

"I'll just take a couple of aspirin," Kris said. Then, "Thanks, Matt." Her voice was a whisper of sound.

Matt watched her leave. He drew a deep breath and closed his eyes.

Dear God, please let me somehow deserve Kris. I know I've never been there for her, but that's all changed. The only thing I want in life now is to take care of her, to love her...

CHAPTER ELEVEN

Matt awakened with a start and glanced at the clock. *Almost seven.* After Kris left he felt tired and went to his room for a few minutes. Apparently he had slept for several hours. He pulled a sweater over his shirt and ran a comb through his hair, silently thanking Yanni for trimming it.

Matt found the den empty and wandered out to the kitchen. He was getting hungry. With Kris hurt, he wondered who would cook tonight. The lights were out in the kitchen and he fumbled around for a switch.

"Happy birthday, Matt!" The room echoed with the sentiments. Matt glanced around the room, a smile lighting his face. Bill and Marie sat at either end of the table. Yanni and Salina were on one side, Kris on the other.

Kris smiled and looked happy. Matt realized no one else knew she was in pain. She hadn't told Yanni she was hurt, had brushed her injuries aside. He'd bet she wouldn't worry Bill and Marie.

Matt moved into the room. "I thought I'd missed out on this a few days ago. Who do I thank?" His glance swept the group.

"It was a group effort—" Kris began.

"Your doctor thought it would be good therapy," Yanni quipped. He raised a glass of wine. Apparently not everyone had waited for him, Matt thought, noting Yanni's nearly empty glass. They must have been ready, and turned the lights off when they heard him stirring.

Matt dropped into the chair beside Kris and picked up his glass. He raised it in a salute. "Doctor."

Kris lowered her lashes, glanced up. "You're welcome." Her voice was soft, with just a trace of huskiness.

Matt forced himself to look at the table. It would be too dangerous to look at Kris, with so many people watching. A huge yellow cake held center stage, covered with candles. The tangy smell of lemon wafted to him.

"Marie, you didn't—" Matt's eyes widened in disbelief.

"Actually, I didn't," she agreed. "It is my recipe, but Kris made it for me—or for you."

"And the rest of the meal?" His sense of smell had returned with a vengeance and the aroma of Italian food was mouth-watering.

"Kris. Bill owes her an apology. She can cook, and very well, if I may say so." Marie beamed at Kris.

"I never doubted it for a moment," Matt said smoothly, turning to wink at Kris. Then, "When do we start. I'm starving."

"So are we," Kris said. "I thought you were never going to wake up."

"This calls for a blessing," Marie said. "We're all getting well again." She bowed her head and everyone else followed suit.

Kris felt her throat tighten as she heard herself included in Marie's list of things for which to be thankful. Tears stung her eyes and she blinked unashamedly when Marie said *"Amen"*.

"Where did you learn to cook Italian food?" Matt asked Kris as he passed around the lasagna.

"It was always Dad's favorite. His mother was Italian. Cooking was one of the few things I learned from her," Kris explained, her expression softening with the memory.

"I never knew that," Marie said. "Did you, Bill? Know that Hal was half Italian?"

"I never thought about it. I met his parents a few times while we were still in the service." Bill glanced at Kris. "My apologies, little one. You're a wonderful cook."

Kris bobbed her head in what would have been a curtsy had she been standing. "No apologies necessary, my lord."

Matt wanted to look at her, to see the smile on her lips that he heard in her voice. He was more touched than he cared to admit at her thoughtfulness.

The brief glimpse he'd allowed himself had snatched at his breath. She was dressed all in that soft green silk, a skirt and jacket over the turtleneck.

Matt thought the evening would never end. After the meal, everyone sang to him and Yanni lit the candles on the cake. Matt's eyes met Kris's for a moment before they closed, he made a wish, and blew out every candle. His lashes lifted to find her still looking at him, her lips parted.

After the cake, Yanni got out the packages he'd brought back from Fairbanks several days earlier. Tracy sent a sweater, Beth a scarf and woolen cap. Matt's nieces had made him a funny card. Tracy included a letter. There was even a card from Roy Ferguson.

"Where does Roy fit in?" Kris asked. She hesitated. "I know he's part of the family—the legacy. But why—or how?"

"Why?" Bill repeated. "He was our flight leader in Europe. Hal was his wingman. Ben was mine. The fact that we all managed to make it through the war, we owe to luck and to Roy."

Matt met Bill's eyes and nodded his agreement. He glanced at Kris to see her reaction.

She swallowed. "That's reason enough for me."

Matt turned back to his mail. He tore open Tracy's letter and scanned it. "Good news," he said, looking up. "About her car, that is." He began reading. "The insurance company decided to pay so Andrew is speaking to me again. There was a fault with the car. The steering mechanism failed and the manufacturer has admitted liability in this case, while refusing to admit to a defect in the design. I imagine their lawyers will fight out who ultimately has to pay. As much as I regret that you were hurt, Matt, you're probably the only one of us who could've survived a crash like that. Of course, neither of us would've ever gotten it up to a hundred and twenty miles an hour—" Matt folded the letter. "*Enough of that.* Little does she know that after the steering column broke, I was just along for the ride." He unconsciously rubbed his collar bone.

"Yanni." Kris looked up in remembrance. "I was wondering how much trouble it would be to clean and fill the hot tub. I think Bill and Matt could both use it for those aches and bruises."

Yanni shrugged. "No problem. It's ready now. I use it all the time."

Matt glanced at her, realized what he was doing and let his hand fall. "I'll give it a try tomorrow."

"You still have a couple of gifts," Yanni reminded Matt, pushing one across the table to him.

Matt tore off the tissue and Kris gasped in delight. Matt handed her the carving of an eagle in flight.

Kris touched it almost reverently. "Yanni, did you make this?" she breathed. "It's beautiful!"

"Of course he did," Matt replied. "Yanni has been turning pieces of wood into works of art for as long as I've known him. Some of his carvings are displayed in the museum in Fairbanks."

"It's wonderful," Kris said, handing it back to Matt.

His hand touched hers. *Would they ever be alone?*

"And here's something from us," Bill said. "Well, not exactly from us. Open it. *You'll understand.*" Bill cleared his throat.

Matt lifted the watch from the box and his eyes closed as his fingers tightened around it. Sitting beside him, Kris felt a tremor shake him.

"My grandfather's watch," Matt said. "The one he passed down to my dad. I hadn't thought about it—or wondered what happened to it. I guess I thought—" He broke off with painful abruptness.

"Ben left it here before his last flight. I assumed at the time that he'd forgotten it. Now, sometimes I wonder—" Bill's voice trailed off. He stood up. "You kids can stay here all night, if you want. But I think it's time to take these old bones to bed. That hot tub idea sounds like a winner, Kris. I'll try it out tomorrow."

Kris nodded and stood up. "Marie, do you need me to do anything—"

Bill helped his wife to her feet. "I can manage," he said before Marie could reply. He led her from the room.

Yanni stood up. "I need to get Salina home also. She is sleeping for two now, no?"

148

Kris smiled. "By all means. I'm glad you're feeling better, Salina." Kris held the other girl's hands for a moment in wordless communication.

Yanni slapped Matt on the shoulder. "Happy birthday again, my friend. I hope we see a lot more together."

Matt nodded and then Yanni and Salina were gone. Matt sank back in his chair with a sigh.

"Matt, did this wear you out?" Kris touched his face in concern. "I didn't think—"

He reached up and caught her hand. "No," he said. "What was wearing was having you so close and looking so beautiful and not even being able to look at you. I thought they'd never leave. I want to thank you for doing this. I know it was you."

Kris shrugged, trying to appear casual. "I didn't like the idea of your being sick on your birthday."

"You more than made up for it." He traced a finger down her cheek.

"Matt, this isn't a good idea," Kris said.

He pushed a curl behind her ear. "Then here's to bad ideas."

"I'm not sure—" Kris began.

"Don't think," Matt growled. He stood and drew her into his arms. His lips touched hers in the lightest of caresses.

"Matt—" Her breath caught. "Don't do this." She pulled away from him and turned away.

She took two steps before Matt caught her arm. "Why? Isn't it safe?"

"Safe?"

"Safe as in *am I still contagious?*" he asked with barely veiled patience.

"You should no longer be contagious," Kris said carefully. She looked up to meet his gaze. "But you know as well as I do that it isn't safe."

"For you or for me?"

"Definitely not for me. You've always been the one who pulled away. Whatever you think you feel for me has never been able to stand up to any tests." She drew a deep breath and let him see the turmoil that filled her eyes.

He held her jacket by the lapels. Now he tugged to draw her closer. *"Never again."* The words were a vow. He sighed. "You're pulling away this time. You have been ever since I got here." His gaze locked with hers.

"I have to," she whispered. "All the reasons you hesitated before now apply to me. I need time. I'm asking you to let me go."

"I don't know if I can." His voice was husky as he pulled her closer, still touching only her jacket. He bent his head and she could feel his breath warm against her lips. She trembled.

Kris closed her eyes. She had nothing left to fight with. She wanted Matt at least as much as he wanted her. *But not like this.*

"Matt, I can't resist you. I never have been able to and you know it. Please don't take advantage of that."

She felt his hands tighten on her jacket. "Do you want me to kiss you?" he asked.

Kris drew in her breath. "More than anything."

He froze and time stood still. Finally his grip relaxed and Kris pulled free. He turned away, running a hand through his hair. She saw his fingers tremble.

"I guess I have to be content with that knowledge," he said. Then he turned and pinned her with his gaze again. *"For the moment."*

Kris stood in the middle of her room, a hand massaging her stiffening neck. She had changed into pajamas and her hair tumbled around her shoulders. Pain racked her body from the roughhousing she'd taken from Buck. She needed something stronger than aspirin, but the only pain pills around were the ones she'd given Matt. She sighed. If she intended to get any sleep tonight, she'd have to ask for them. That meant admitting to Matt why she needed them. And worse still, if he was still in a mood to kiss her, she doubted she'd be able to refuse a second time.

Matt heard the knock on his door and stiffened. It must be Kris. Everyone else was long since in bed. He braced himself and crossed the room to pull open the door.

About to knock again, Kris let her hand fall and pushed her hands into her pockets. "I wondered if you still have those pills I gave you?" She couldn't bring herself to meet his eyes. She caught her bottom lip between her teeth.

A quick frown of concern crossed Matt's face. "You're in pain?" He drew her into the room and turned to look for the bottle.

Kris glanced at him. "You heard what happened—and saw some of the results. What do you think?"

"I think you're quite an actress after what I saw at dinner," he replied. "No one else knows, do they? And you aren't going to tell them?"

"Why should I? I don't want Bill and Marie to worry. And Yanni would feel terrible. It wasn't his fault."

"You seem to like him a lot," Matt commented. He found the pills and handed them to her.

"Who?"

"Yanni."

"Who wouldn't? For that matter, there seems to be a pretty deep friendship between you and Yanni." She turned away. "One that is a lot easier for me to understand than the one between you and Scott."

"We grew up together," Matt said.

Her eyes widened. "I beg your pardon?"

"I was about four and Yanni was two when he and his sister, Sozi, came to live with Bill and Marie. For the next seven years, until I moved to California, we were inseparable." His mouth twisted. "I think he wrote every week when I was in the Persian Gulf—" He broke off.

Matt could feel Kris looking at him and forced himself to raise his head. The compassion he saw on her face was almost his undoing.

"I heard Yanni mention Desert Storm when we arrived at the village," Kris said. "That was the first time I knew—well, how bad it was. He said something about the shrapnel in your shoulder. I saw the scars when you were sick. And you talked about it a lot." She glanced away from him as a shudder shook her.

"Don't feel sorry for me, Kris!" Matt said, his voice harsh. He didn't mean to sound so brutal, but he was afraid he was going to drag her into his arms. He knew she wouldn't resist.

He hadn't allowed himself more than a glance at her since she entered the room. It was an increasing strain not to reach for her, but at the moment he knew neither of them was up to facing the consequences of such action.

"That isn't what I feel." Kris shook several pills into her hand and returned the bottle. "I feel as if a part of me has been violated somehow." She walked out of the room.

Matt stood petrified, afraid that if he moved at all, it would be to go after her. Now he knew what upset her at the village. *Yanni and his big mouth!*

Matt walked over to stare out into the night. It was too easy to take his anger out on Yanni, but Yanni wasn't the problem. If he had been man enough to tell Kris about Desert Storm years ago, perhaps she would have understood. At any rate, she should have heard it from him.

The better he got to know Kris and the more he learned about her capacity for loving and caring, the more he believed she would have wanted him in spite of what he had seen as insurmountable obstacles. He had returned broken and scarred. But even worse than the physical damage had been the emotional. Bitter and disillusioned, he had seen her attempts to reassure him as pity. Loving her beyond reason, he could not bear the thought that all she might feel for him was compassion. It would be better for her to hate him.

Matt sighed. As badly as he had treated her, Kris continued to love him. He had convinced himself that with him out of the picture, she would go on and make a life with Scott. *Scott, who was perfect for her. Scott, with the perfect background, the perfect family. Scott, who had lied to him from the beginning about his relationship with Kris. Scott, who in his drunken madness, had beaten Kris into unconsciousness . . .*

Matt glanced down to find his hands clenched into fists. He forced himself to open them, reminding himself of the conversation with Bill and that it was not his place to deal with Scott. All he could do in that area now was in some way try and make it up to Kris. *No problem.* His mouth twisted into a grim smile. All he had to do was slay all her dragons and give her back the life she loved.

CHAPTER TWELVE

Marie turned from the stove to greet Matt as he entered the kitchen after a sleepless night. His eyes widened.

"Should you be doing that?" he asked in concern.

Marie shrugged. "Sure. Kris says I can do anything I feel up to. It's about time."

Matt poured a cup of coffee and dropped into a chair. "Where is she?" He sipped the hot liquid.

"Where is who?" Marie asked, busily stirring batter.

"Kris." Matt glanced at her, his eyes narrowed.

"She went to check on Salina. Yanni said she wasn't feeling well." Marie smiled as Bill came into the room.

"Morning, sunshine!" he greeted.

Marie poured his coffee as he sat down. She kissed the top of his head.

"Who isn't feeling well?" Bill put his arm around her.

"Salina. Morning sickness again." Marie returned to her cooking.

Bill looked at Matt. "What do you say we try that hot tub Kris recommends so highly after breakfast?"

Matt drank his coffee, stirred restlessly. "Why not? It can't hurt."

"We may even feel like working on your engine again," Bill said with deliberate slowness. "I've been thinking about those modifications we talked about yesterday."

Matt pulled open the door at one end of the hangar and glanced around. The approaching dawn hadn't made much headway against the darkness and he couldn't see into the depths of the building. He flipped on an overhead light and sighed as it illuminated the immediate area but threw everything else into even deeper shadow.

"Help me with these tools," Bill called from the Bronco. They brought the heavy box and put it down near Matt's plane.

"The first thing we need to do is pull the prop," Bill instructed. "Start removing those nuts."

They worked in companionable silence for several minutes, Bill finally beginning to relax. It would be only a matter of time before Matt noticed that Kris's plane was not in the hangar. He couldn't do anything about it now. It would take several hours to get his plane back together and in flying condition.

Bill knew the exact moment Matt registered the absence. He felt him stiffen, heard a muttered exclamation cut short, and felt Matt's gaze burning into his back.

"Where's the Cub?" Matt demanded in a voice that sent shivers down Bill's spine.

Bill glanced up in feigned surprise. "Oh." His voice was the epitome of innocence. "Kris went into Fairbanks. Didn't she tell you? She needed to pick up some medical supplies—things for Salina and Marie. You have to admit that between us we've sorely depleted her stock—"

"You let her go by herself?" Matt accused, raking a hand through his hair in agitation.

"Where would she put supplies if she had a passenger?" Bill asked.

"I can't believe you let her go alone!" Matt stared at Bill, his eyes smoldering.

"I can't believe you think I could've stopped her."

"I could have. Why didn't you tell me—?"

Bill looked at him. "You don't have that right." His voice was ominous in its quietness.

Matt stood frozen for a moment, then turned and slammed his fist into the door frame.

"Don't you think you have enough wounds and battle scars without inflicting any more upon yourself?" Bill asked as he saw Matt wince.

Matt flexed his hand inside the glove. "You made sure my plane would be down before I missed the Cub. Did Kris know I'd try to stop her—go after her?"

Bill nodded. "She thought you might."

"So she asked you to cover for her?"

"Something like that."

"When will she be back?" Matt persisted.

"She wasn't sure." Bill knew that answer wasn't going to be good enough for Matt.

"Say again."

"She had a lot of things to do," Bill said. "If she ran out of daylight, she said she'd spend the night with Sozi."

"She obviously left before the sun came up—while we were enjoying the hot tub, perhaps. The Jacuzzi would've drowned the sound of the Cub's engine." Matt sounded disgusted with himself, Bill thought.

"There's a full moon. She felt she'd be all right. She only needs light to land." Bill's voice softened as he looked at Matt's haggard face.

"Unless something goes wrong." Matt needlessly stated the obvious.

"I know how you feel about that." Bill's eyes filled with understanding. Sympathy. "Matt, don't you think it's time you put Ben's death behind you?"

Matt looked at him, eyes burning. "Have you?"

Bill shook his head and sighed. "No." There was nothing more he could say about Ben, but he felt he had to say more to reassure Matt about Kris. "You know, Kris isn't as fragile as she might look. In fact, she's one of the strongest people I know. It comes from a long history of independence and self-sufficiency."

"She told me a little about that," Matt said, allowing Bill to change the subject. "She never felt she could confide in either of her parents." His voice hardened. "Do you know they never told her about Joey? I mentioned him the other day, and she didn't know anything. I had to tell her—everything."

"Don't be too hard on them, Matt." Bill's voice grew sad. Heavy. "Losing Joey was devastating for them. I can understand a little now after what we've been through with Carl—even with him grown. I don't know how they survived. They each handled it in their own way, neither of which was good for Kris. Jean clung too tightly to her remaining child and Hal distanced himself—afraid of loving too deeply only to lose a part of himself again.

"Fortunately, Kris was stronger than either of them. She worked her way through what must have been a pretty barren childhood to emerge what she is today. In the end she and Hal became close—in spite of the fact that your relationship with him must have been hard for her to accept."

"I never knew until a few days ago that my friendship with Hal hurt her." A heavy sigh shook Matt. "I wonder if I've ever done anything that hasn't hurt her."

Matt spent the day working feverishly on his plane. At one time he would have found a quiet joy in this oneness with his machine. He knew everything there was to know about the sleek racer.

He and Hal had built the aircraft from a design of Ben's that sought to achieve the ultimate in speed and high performance. Hal had added a few improvements to the design during construction and over the years Matt had perfected it.

Matt's thoughts were melancholy as he thought of these two men who had meant so much in his life. The racer was their legacy to him.

But Kris kept invading his thoughts. Since he'd landed here a few weeks ago, and seen her again, he'd thought of little else. She had to be safe. He couldn't lose her now. He still had a ways to go, but she would be his. He had decided that when he made the decision to find her again. He had managed to rebuild his life. He could win the woman he loved. It was only a matter of time.

Matt dropped down on a stool, alone now in the hangar. Bill had grown tired and gone back to rest. Matt let his hands dangle between his knees and bowed his head.

Dear God, please take care of Kris and bring her safely back to me.

He knew it was time to confront Kris with his feelings. *Spell everything out.* Maybe she still didn't understand just how much she meant to him. He had to find the courage he had lacked in the past and go after what he wanted this time. Now that he finally had his priorities straight. He wouldn't let Kris walk out of his life again.

Tonight Beth said she loved me. I never imagined! I thought she and Hal had something going. When he introduced us, I fell for her like a ton of bricks. But I never thought she noticed.

Hal finally put two and two together. He realized I was interested in her, but wouldn't make a move as long as I thought she was his.

Tonight he and Beth staged an elaborate argument. She slammed out of the inn into the middle of a snowstorm! It must have been close to ten or fifteen below.

I couldn't believe Hal let her go! I told him he had to go get her before she froze to death. There was no where for her to find shelter. She didn't even have her coat. He glared at me and said if I was so concerned, I should go after her myself. I said I would do just that.

Beth was waiting outside the door, bundled into a fur coat, as warm as you please. She smiled and asked what had taken me so long--as if she expected me!

I stared at her, trying to think of a coherent answer, and she reached up and kissed me, asking how I could be so blind. She laughed very softly and touched my face.

"My dearest Ben!"

I finally found my voice. "Beth! What are you saying?"

She caught my lapels and looked up at me. "I know I'm not as fast or as sleek as those planes you fly, but I'm soft and warm, and I happen to love you. What does it take to get your attention, Captain?"

Matt looked up from Ben's journal. So—he had often wondered about the relationship between Beth and Hal. She had once told him they had been best friends—before and after her marriage to Ben. As soon as they met, Hal told her he had a friend he wanted to introduce her to—*Ben*. He said he had a feeling. He was right—only Ben's sense of honor and fair play kept him from going after the woman he wanted.

Matt stirred restlessly and got up to tend the fire. That all sounded a little too familiar. Had Ben almost made the same mistake he'd made?

Matt's thoughts returned to Kris. She had not returned that afternoon. Bill refused to worry, but Matt was ready to climb the walls. He reached for the journal again just as the radio came to life. He hurried to answer it.

"Bentley Base. Matt here."

"Matt, this is Sozi."

"Sozi!" His heart thudded. Why would she call unless something had happened to Kris? He swallowed, trying to stay calm. "Is everything all right?"

"Kris will not be coming back for a few days. She wanted to let you know."

"Where is she?" Matt asked, his voice strained. "What's wrong?"

"She is staying at my apartment. As far as what is wrong, she is black and blue all over, to begin with. I believe you know something about that. Franz came over to check her out and insisted on doing some x-rays. Nothing broken, but she has bad bruises to her ribs. He sedated her and she is going to rest for awhile. We will see what happens after that. She needs a couple of days, at least."

"Listen, Sozi, I'll be there tomorrow. I'm coming to get her—"

"That is not a good idea, Matt. She should not travel for several days. She could hardly get out of her plane when she got here. She was very stiff and sore and in much pain."

"Then I'll stay with her. It's the least I can do—"

"Kris is being well taken care of." Sozi's soft voice became firm. "On the other hand, Bill and Marie have not been doing so well. You should stay there for them."

"Yanni is here—"

"Salina needs him now."

Matt drew a hand over his eyes. *Sozi was right.* He fought the feeling of helplessness that washed over him. "Okay, Sozi. Just—take good care of her. Please. And let me know when she's ready to come back."

"Will do. Sozi—out."

Matt pulled up through five thousand feet. He felt the plane shudder on the edge of a stall, pushed it over and kicked it into a flat spin. His concentration was absolute. A man and his machine against all that the laws of gravity, physics and aerodynamics could throw at him. This was the third day he'd taken the plane up after completing the modifications. The performance was superb—even better than he'd hoped. He had no doubt he could win any race or aerobatic competition he cared to enter.

He recovered from the spin and leveled off at fifteen hundred feet. Next he executed a series of snap rolls above a frozen lake. He reversed course and did a set of eight and sixteen point turns. His plane was ready. What was missing was his enthusiasm for his sport.

Competition by nature was a lonely life—performing as he did mostly against his own standards. At one time he'd welcomed, *needed perhaps*, the solitude this sport forced upon him. Now, somehow, that was no longer enough. He turned his attention back to his practice. Only by such total concentration could he push aside those intruding thoughts of all that was missing in his life.

Sitting in the den, Bill and Marie glanced at each other as they heard Matt's plane fly over again. Day after day he returned, haggard, eyes bloodshot. They knew the limits to which he pushed himself and his plane.

They also knew the futility of saying anything. Countless times they'd seen the same pattern with both Ben and Hal as they encountered problems in their lives. They had to believe that Matt, too, would work things out in his own way and time.

Bill shook his head. They had to have faith in Kris, too, he reminded himself. It was uncanny how much of Hal he could see in her. *Just as Matt was so much like Ben.* The two men had been the best of friends, but the biggest threats to their relationship always came from their own volatile personalities.

Kris taxied to the hangar, throttled back to idle and switched off the mags and radio. She closed the fuel valve and removed her headset. Her body still racked with aches and pains, she climbed out of the plane and crossed to pull open the doors. Her breath caught as she stared at the spot where Matt's racer had been parked. *Gone!* She caught the side of the door frame and closed her eyes as a sense of loss swept over her.

Mechanically, she forced herself to put the Cub away. In the shelter of the hangar she unloaded the supplies and mail she'd brought from Fairbanks and waited for Bill.

The sound of an engine overhead drew her attention and Kris looked up to see a plane pull up into a stall, fall off into a spin and spiral down in a series of perfectly executed maneuvers. Only one pilot besides her father flew with such precision—*such beauty and grace*. She watched as Matt recovered from the spin and leveled off, entering the downwind leg of the landing approach. Her heart filled with unreasonable joy. *He hadn't left!*

Matt shut down his engine and pushed back the canopy. He pulled himself up, swung his legs over the side and leaped to the ground. Glancing up, he froze as he saw Kris standing in the hangar door.

Relief, hope, desire and passion swept over Matt in turn, but anger predominated as he stalked across the tarmac to tower over Kris. She stared up into the blue fire of his eyes and took a step back.

"Do you know what I've been through the last four days?" he grated. "Knowing you were sick and alone—"

Kris swallowed convulsively. "Sozi said she called you. I was with her. She and Franz took care of me." Her voice came out a hoarse whisper.

"So she said. If you'd stayed, I would have taken care of you." He grabbed her shoulders, unsure whether to shake her or pull her into his arms.

"I'm sorry. I needed some time and then I couldn't fly back until today." She wet her lips. "I—where's Bill? Didn't he hear me land?"

Matt nodded to a motorcycle. "I brought Yanni's bike so Bill wouldn't have to come down. We can ride back—"

Kris shook her head and pointed to the supplies. "I have to take those—"

"There's room." He removed a glove to touch her face. She closed her eyes, reveling in the feel of his hand against her cheek.

His thumb brushed her lips. "I missed you—"

Kris trembled. Her eyes opened. "Matt—could you—not talk—"

He froze. "What?"

"Just hold me." She held her breath as she waited for his response.

His arms closed around her and she melted against him. He buried his face in her hair. "Don't ever do that to me again," he groaned.

She raised her head and looked into his eyes for a moment. "I saw you flying," she whispered, barely able to think coherently, let alone speak. "It was beautiful. *Perfect.* I know Dad is pleased."

"Don't change the subject!" Matt felt his throat tighten as he looked down at her. "I've been so worried about you." His eyes roamed her face, drinking in every inch of it. "Don't you know how dangerous it is for you to fly alone? People crash—and may never be found. I—" His arms dropped and he stepped away from her, overcome with emotion.

"Matt, Marie told me about Ben—how he disappeared. I'm sorry. I had no idea." She reached out to touch his face.

"I have to get the racer in before it gets any colder," Matt said, turning away from her, shutting her out along with the pain. *Pain still too fresh to face.*

Kris picked up the bags of supplies and put them in the baggage compartment on the bike while Matt pulled his plane into the hangar. She started the engine to let it warm up.

"I'll drive," Matt said behind her.

Kris looked at him. "Gladly." She stepped off the bike and waited until Matt was seated, then climbed on behind him.

Matt threw her a glance. A corner of his mouth twitched. "You're *obviously* not feeling well."

"Obviously," Kris grumbled. "What made you notice?"

"That you'd agree with any order I gave, let alone *'gladly'* agree." He gunned the engine to find it still running rough.

"I probably shouldn't have come back today. I just felt that I'd been gone forever," Kris explained.

"Amen to that," Matt said.. He gunned the engine again, found it to his satisfaction, and the bike lurched forward. Kris grabbed for his jacket, and then wrapped her arms around him, nestling close to the shelter he provided against the cutting wind. Her eyes closed, her lips curved in a dreamy smile.

Matt didn't speak as they pulled into the garage. He unloaded the supplies and carried them inside. Marie came to greet them.

"Kris, darling!" Marie enfolded her in a hug. "Sozi called and said you were on the way!" She touched her face. *"Poor baby.* She didn't explain what was wrong with you, and suggested I not ask too many questions—"

Kris laughed. "Really, I'm fine. Just let me get out of these clothes. I picked up the supplies you needed and the mail is in one of the bags," she threw over her shoulder as she left the room.

Matt dropped the bags on the table. "Need any help?" he asked Marie as she began sorting through them.

"No, thanks, dear." Marie seemed preoccupied and after a moment Matt shrugged and went to look for Bill.

Marie found the small package she was looking for and drew a ragged breath. She sat down, turning it over and over in her hands, almost wishing it would go away.

"Is everything all right, Marie?"

Marie glanced up. Kris stood looking down at her in concern. Marie shook her head. "No, it isn't. I have to do something I'd really rather not do."

"It can't be that bad, can it?" Kris asked, sitting down across the table.

Marie held her gaze for a moment. "I have to tell Matt that they found—*Ben!*" Her voice broke, and Kris saw her eyes fill with tears.

"What do you mean—*they found Ben?*" Kris asked, not understanding the significance of what she had heard. "You mean the wreckage—?"

"*The wreckage. The body.* Ben went into a frozen lake. Twenty years under ice kept everything pretty well preserved. A few weeks ago Beth got a letter from the Department of Defense. Something about the latest in satellite technology. Anyway, they were able to make out the shape of the plane under the ice. We haven't got much rain the last few years, and all the lakes were at their lowest level—even this one. It was all a matter of everything finally coming together. It was time for Ben to be found—*for him to rest.*"

Kris felt her head spin. "What is this going to do to Matt? I know that at one time he needed this? *But now?*"

Marie shook her head, her eyes filled with pain.

"Oh, Marie! And you have to tell him?" Kris caught her hands.

Marie nodded. "Beth wanted us to. She felt we could do a better job than she could. I wish I believed that. I don't have a clue—"

"Don't have a clue about what?" Matt walked into the room and poured a cup of coffee. He glanced up to see both women staring at him with identical expressions.

"Matt—" Kris whispered.

Marie drew in her breath and Matt turned to look at her.

"What's wrong?" he asked.

"This package is from Beth," Marie said, as if that would explain everything.

"Mom? What—"

"Let me get Bill." Marie stood up. Her face had paled and she twined her fingers together in agitation. Matt reached down and caught her hands.

"Marie, what is it?" His voice was gentle, patient.

"Bill can help you." Marie touched his face. "He'll know what to say."

"Help me with what?" Dropping Marie's hands, he reached for the small parcel and saw that it was addressed to him. He tore it open.

"Matt," Marie's hands stilled his. She had run out of time. "They found Ben. They found your father a couple of weeks ago."

Kris saw the color drain from Matt's face. He reached inside the package and pulled out a metal tag on a beaded chain. The tarnished surface gleamed dully against his hand. Kris recognized it instantly. She kept Hal's tucked inside a pocket on her flight suit.

Matt drew in a pained breath as his fingers closed around his father's military identification tag.

CHAPTER THIRTEEN

"Beth called last week." Marie's strained voice broke a silence that was absolute. "They contacted her as Ben's widow and sent his things. She felt you should have this and wanted us to give it to you." She touched Matt's arm. "Matt, what can we do?"

Matt stood dazed. Kris put her hand over Marie's. "Let me." She gestured for Marie to leave her alone with Matt. Marie bobbed her head in relief and hurried from the room.

Kris led Matt to a chair and pushed him into it. She handed him the coffee he'd put aside. "Drink." She kept her voice firm, professional, hoping he would respond to it. "You're in a mild state of shock. This will help."

Kris sat across the table and watched as Matt obediently brought the cup to his lips. She took advantage of his preoccupation to study him, finding it almost painful, wanting him as she always had—*always would.*

Matt had the dark brooding good looks of which dreams were made, Kris thought, her mouth twisting. He fell just short of being too good looking, with just enough scars and rough edges to make him irresistible. She didn't think he knew that, however.

Matt wore his crisp black hair in a military cut as few men would dare. His lips were chiseled perfection, firm and sensuous. He stood a little taller than Hal, who had been an even six feet.

But one feature fascinated Kris above all others. His eyes were an intense dark blue—as deep as the ocean, as turbulent as the sky. She loved them when he was laughing or teasing; they held her captive when he was serious. Never, however, had she seen such raw pain reflected in them as she saw now. Her hand went out to cover his.

"Let's go in by the fire, Matt." The torn wrapper on the table drew her attention. "Beth sent a note. Do you want to be alone while you read it?"

His fingers tightened around hers and he looked up to meet her gaze. "No." He picked up the letter and his coffee and they walked into the den.

Kris sank down on the sofa. She'd forgotten her own aches and pains in her concern for Matt. So much had been explained once she learned about Ben; yet, she sensed there was more. His journal had hinted at some of the demons that plagued him. Somehow she had to get him to talk to her.

Matt stood before the fireplace, quickly reading the message from his mother. She saw his eyes close briefly and pain flicker across his face.

The silence stretched and finally Kris spoke. "When Marie told me about Ben, I understood why you don't like for me—for anyone to fly alone."

He looked at her then. Fully. "Particularly you," he said, his voice flat. "I've already lost one person I love that way." He closed his eyes. "At least I

169

finally know that Dad didn't suffer. He didn't die a cold and lonely death as he slowly froze, knowing no one would come." A tremor shook him and he opened his eyes to focus on Kris again. "I've had nightmares the last few nights. Just like I had then. Only you were the one dying a cold, lonely death— and I couldn't get to you."

Kris shivered. She had read about those nightmares in his journal. She opened her mouth to speak, could think of no words to comfort.

He knelt and put his hands on her arms. "Earlier, I tried to tell you what I've been through the last four days. I admitted to myself how I feel about you. If I got another chance, I knew I had to tell you and not run away."

Kris made a restless movement and looked away. She had wanted this for years, but now wasn't the time. "I don't think this is something we're ready to discuss, Matt. There are too many other things. Now that I know about your father, that explains a lot, but there's more. You have a lot of emotional and psychological scars."

"And you don't?" Matt asked, raising an eyebrow.

"Of course I do. I just never had anyone who cared enough for me to discuss them." She stood up.

"Kris?" Matt's voice stopped her. "Don't turn away. I know you're going to take some convincing, but I care."

He saw her bow her head, and put a hand to her face. He moved to stand in front of her. "If you won't come to me, then I'll have to go to you."

Kris thought she heard a hint of a smile in his voice and looked up at him through her tears. He reached for her and pulled her against him, wrapping his arms around her.

Kris relaxed as she nestled into his warmth. She felt as if she'd come home after a long absence. "This is nice—almost as good as I've imagined."

His breath stirred her hair as his head bent over hers. He kissed her forehead. "I missed you."

Kris smiled and traced his lips with her fingers. "You said that already." She moved away from him and stood before the fire. "But first, we have to talk about you."

He sighed. "Where do I start?"

"Your father. His death. We have to go full circle."

Matt sat down and clasped his hands behind his head. "You're right. I wish I'd talked to you before. But I've never been able to burden anyone—especially someone who mattered—with all the baggage that I've carried since I was a kid. I'm barely stable enough to handle my own company, let alone be around other people."

Matt drew in a deep breath, released it slowly. "But I've learned in the last few days that listening and caring and understanding is what you are—what you do. If I can talk to you—if you don't turn away—I may be able to heal." He looked at her. "*We* may be able to heal."

"Matt—" A sob tore from her throat as Kris knelt in front of him, catching his hands, bringing them to her lips. "I want to be here for you. I've always wanted that."

He drew her down beside him, cradling her close. His voice was cracked, dry. "I don't deserve this—deserve *you*."

She touched his face. "Talk to me."

Kris waited for Matt to begin his story. He started talking, hesitant at first, but as the story progressed, the words tumbled over one another.

"In her letter, Mom explains that she understood how hard it was for me, never having any closure on my father's death. Maybe that was part of it.

For awhile, since there was no proof otherwise, I pretended he was still alive. I even started my own journal, so I would be able to tell him everything that happened while he was gone." Matt paused for a moment and Kris stirred, guilt pricking at her.

"I know I was a challenge for Mom and Hal, but they never lost patience. They were always there for me. After military school I joined the Air Force. There was never a decision to make. That's what Dad and Hal and Bill had done. I'd follow in their footsteps. I functioned well in such a structured existence." His mouth twisted. "In Europe they flew P-47 Thunderbolts. I decided I wanted to fly the A-10—known as the Thunderbolt II.

"I had been flying A-10s for almost a year when we were called up for action in the Persian Gulf. I don't remember how many missions I flew. Mostly we looked for Scud missile launchers, tanks, or flew search and rescue. I was returning from Scud hunting when I saw a line of tanks and decided to go down for a bombing pass. I did some damage but apparently I overlooked a SAM site somewhere in the area.

"I didn't have time or altitude to take evasive action and a missile took out the left engine and exploded just behind the cockpit. Shrapnel came through the canopy and hit me in the shoulder. Fortunately, A-10s were built to withstand substantial damage and still fly. I wasn't worried about *it* staying in the air. I was worried about *my ability* to keep it there.

"My left arm hung useless and blood covered everything. Ejecting wasn't an option. I was still over Iraqi territory with a whole line of tank drivers down below and I'd just ruined their day. I would have been a proverbial sitting duck.

"I managed to stay in the air until I reached what I hoped was Saudi airspace and made a more or less decent landing. I'd lost a lot of blood by then, and even though I thought I was on friendly soil, there was no guarantee that the right side would find me—or that they would be in time. A couple of our pilots were already missing and presumed captured.

"I hadn't been able to raise my wingman and it wasn't until I was on the ground that I realized I'd lost all communications when shrapnel smashed into the instrument panel. I could only hope he wasn't far away and had seen what happened. Waiting became a nightmare. I drifted in and out of consciousness, either thinking or dreaming about Dad and how no one had come for him."

Kris felt Matt tense and touched his chest. *She had read all this in his journal, too.* His hand came up to cover hers and she felt it tremble.

"To distract myself from those thoughts, I would think about you. Somehow, that was even more painful—not knowing if I would ever see you again." His arm tightened briefly to draw her closer.

Matt swallowed. "I was in a bad way—both physically and emotionally—when Gregg and his team found me. I wasn't conscious of much for a couple of weeks. The first thing to register was being told my shoulder would never again be strong enough for me to continue flying for the Air Force.

"Six months later I showed up on Hal's doorstep—so to speak. I asked his advice on what to do with the rest of my life. I felt I was too young to have already used up all my options. He took me up in his trainer and we went through a few aerobatic maneuvers and I came down hooked." His mouth twisted. "You pretty much know the story from there."

Kris trembled and his arms tightened. He groaned and leaned his cheek against her hair. "Kris, I wanted you as I've never wanted anything, but I had nothing to offer you. I was still emotionally unstable, trying to adjust to civilian life for the first time since I was twelve years old. The scars from Desert Storm were too fresh. I couldn't expect anyone to put up with what I was, either physically or mentally. I tried to avoid you. Scott was still interested and, according to him, you returned his interest. The best course seemed for me to stay out of sight."

Kris lay still, her heart thudding painfully. She swallowed and tried to speak. Swallowed again. "I wanted to help you," she whispered, her voice thick with the tears she held back. "I tried—but you said it had all been a mistake—"

He crushed her fingers in his. "I know," he said against her hair. "I'm sorry. I was so torn between wanting you and not knowing who I was anymore. I focused on my training and completing the racer. Hal and I had started building it a couple of years earlier. It turned out to be my salvation—such as it was." His voice was tight with control.

Kris sat up and moved away from him. She couldn't bear thinking how it might have been—knowing Matt had cared all along. All the heartbreak and loneliness had been so unnecessary.

"Kris—" Matt hesitated. "About you and Scott—"

She drew in her breath, glancing at him, her eyes filled with pain.

"I'm sorry," Matt said, his voice brittle. "But I *need* to know. I thought you had everything in common. That Scott was what you wanted and needed. I left you alone, Kris, because I had none of what he had to offer you. I loved you so much that I wanted you to have the best—and that wasn't me. But, according to you, you never even noticed him. You weren't even friends, much less in love. Why not?" Matt's voice was hard, lest he betray how much he hurt. "If he wasn't good enough for you, how could I possibly be?"

Kris drew in her breath as anger shook her. "How materialistic do you think I am? I didn't notice Scott because he wasn't you and I wasn't in love with him. I didn't need him for anything he could give me. I didn't need you for that, either. *I still don't!*" She met his eyes, hers glistening with tears. "Do

174

you think it mattered that you had nothing? *That you think you had nothing?*"

"It mattered to me," Matt replied, his jaw set in a stubborn line. "You deserved more than I could give."

"Obviously." The bitterness in her voice brought his head up to look at her. "I only wanted you. I thought I deserved that much. But apparently you still don't have that to give!"

"Kris—"

She turned away. He caught her arm and turned her to face him.

"Kris—?" His face was white, strained.

"How can you and Scott be friends?" she demanded, asking a question that had puzzled her for years. Now that she knew Scott for what he was, it was unbelievable to Kris that he and Matt could have been so close.

Matt blinked. "Who said we were friends?"

"The fact that you were virtually inseparable speaks for itself—"

"Everyone always read too much into our relationship. We met at the academy when we were twelve. Scott was interested in me because I could fly—well, not legally, but Hal had given me lessons." He stopped speaking, lost in thought for a long painful moment.

"Scott was afraid of flying," Matt went on, "but he was more afraid of disappointing his father. He hung around me because I wasn't smart enough to be afraid of anything. I tried to protect him. Even felt a little sorry for him. I know I carry a lot of emotional baggage, but Scott has problems he doesn't even know exist. I didn't know who I was for awhile, but Scott may never know who he is because he lives in his father's shadow, afraid to be himself.

"Money was always able to get him anything he wanted, including instant fame when he started racing. I never had his name recognition because of his family, but I picked up several good endorsements along the way. I did all right." Again Matt paused for a moment.

"About a year ago Scott and I had a fight. He almost caused an accident with his careless flying. The other pilot was one of Hal's students. He's everything Scott isn't—a natural born pilot—if there is such a thing."

Kris smiled, a little sadly. "There isn't. Not according to Dad."

Matt grinned. "Hal came down from flying with Billy and apologized to me. He said Billy was already almost as good as I was and could be even better. He intended to see that he did. I feel I owe it to Hal to help Billy."

"And Scott?" Kris asked.

"I haven't spoken to Scott since. I lost my temper when I saw him almost kill Billy. I drove home a few truths that he didn't want to hear."

Matt looked at her. "I've been around Scott for twenty years. With his looks, his name and his money, he got every girl he went after. They never saw me. When you turned away from me that day in Hal's office—" Matt broke off. "Well, all I could see was Scott getting the girl again. It never mattered before. All I could do was pretend it didn't matter then, either."

"But it wasn't that way at all!" Kris said. "From the moment I ran into you that day in Dad's office, you were the only man I wanted." Her eyes filled with tears that she made no attempt to hide.

Matt jammed his hands in his pockets and turned away. "I know I've said this before, but Scott told me—"

"I remember. I guess what hurts so much is that you believed him—that I was sleeping with him—" She could not go on.

"Forgive me for being brutally frank," his voice was dry, "but that night in the hangar—you did nothing to discourage me."

Her breath caught and Kris swallowed convulsively. "I guess I didn't. I was too naive to realize how you would interpret my response. I only knew that you had finally noticed me—were kissing me—ravaging me—and it was the most wonderful thing I had ever experienced. When you pushed me away, I was devastated. But even then, I couldn't help but hope your actions—your kisses—had meant something."

Kris went to stand before the fire, holding her hands out to the flames. "For a year I waited for you to return. *Hoping. Dreaming. Praying.* Prepared for everything except the rejection I would get."

Matt made a restless movement. "When I saw you at Hal's funeral, and saw that Scott wasn't supporting you as he should, I knew that somehow I'd been wrong about your relationship. That he didn't deserve you."

"When you walked away from me then," Kris's voice was a strained whisper, "I'd never been so alone in my life."

"Neither had I," Matt said, looking up to meet her eyes. "I gave you a few weeks to adjust after Hal's death, and then I came back to see if you would give me another chance." He turned away, his back to her. "As usual my timing couldn't have been worse. Scott had—" He broke off and Kris saw him pass a hand over his face.

Then he turned to face her, his eyes burning with emotion. "Why wouldn't you tell me about Scott? Why wouldn't Roy tell me?"

"I—thought you were still friends," Kris said. "In spite of everything, I didn't want to come between you."

"That's not good enough," Matt said, his voice flat. "How could you think I would still want him for a friend after that?"

Kris brought her hands up, twining them together. "We were afraid—in spite of everything you said, I still couldn't convince myself that you didn't care for me. Especially after seeing you at Dad's funeral. We were afraid that if you found out, you might want to hurt Scott—maybe even—"

"Go on."

"Maybe even—kill him." Her voice was a whisper as she looked up to meet his eyes. "He wasn't worth it. We—I—couldn't take that chance."

"Of course I want to hurt him," Matt ground out. "I still do. What made you change your mind about telling me?"

"Bill. He said he would take responsibility. I trusted him to keep you from doing anything to Scott."

"*He's almost eighty years old.* What did you think he could do?"

"I don't think you should underestimate him," Kris said dryly. "He has a way of convincing people to do the right thing."

"And what is the right thing in this case?"

"Let it go. Scott isn't worth it."

"Why did you come up here, Kris?" Matt's voice was quiet.

She trembled. "Because if you had showed up back home, I couldn't have kept it from you. And you would have been able to get to Scott. Now, I've had a chance to put it behind me—and we have a chance to try and reason with you, before you go charging off on your white horse."

Matt looked at her for a long time. Finally he sighed. "You're right about Bill. He's already convinced me of the futility of beating Scott to within an inch of his life." He turned away. "You're wrong about the rest."

"What am I wrong about?"

"That you've put it behind you. You have Hal's death, the malpractice suit and Scott's attack all tangled up in your mind. You see going to court as the equivalent of Scott's attack, and losing in the same light as Hal's death—"

"Stop!" Kris put her hands over her ears. "Please! I can't listen—"

"Kris." He caught her arms. "I wouldn't let you help me four years ago. That was the biggest mistake of my life. I know you feel you have to work through this alone, but if I let you, that will be an even bigger mistake. I'm here, my darling! We'll get through this together."

"No!" Tears were streaming down her face as she tried to pull away from him. "You don't understand!"

"What don't I understand?" Matt's eyes narrowed as he watched her.

"If I go back, I have to do it alone. I can't offer you—*what's left of me!*" Kris stood with bowed head for a moment after she finished speaking.

"I do understand that feeling!" Matt's voice was dry. "Unfortunately, I know what will happen if I let you follow through."

"Please, Matt. I need—time."

"The clock is ticking. I won't promise anything." His dark brooding gaze locked with hers.

She stared at him for a moment longer, then hurried from the room.

CHAPTER FOURTEEN

Matt watched Kris walk away, emptiness sweeping over him. Regret stabbed through him at all the wrong decisions he'd made concerning her.

He reached for Ben's journal and it fell open in his hands. He stared at the date. *The day before Ben and the prototype plane disappeared.* Funny how today, of all days, he would reach that place in Ben's writings. He sat down and began reading.

Sometimes I wonder if I've been in the Air Force too long. If I hadn't been involved in the acceptance test phase of the new fighters, I would be in the middle of my third war now. And what a war. So different from the others. No clear enemy. No definition of victory. Not even an outright declaration of war. We just keep sending our kids over and they keep sending their bodies back.

Bill is happy with his air base and the inn. Even Hal is making a go of the flight school. It has filled a need for him since Joey's death. His success has been phenomenal as he turned Holland Aviation into the biggest aerobatics training school in northern California. I only hope he realizes before too long that he has a wife and daughter who need him.

Leave it to Roy to end up with one of the most prominent law firms in San Francisco! Thank God his steel trap mind is on the side of right rather than money. I have absolute confidence that his success is due to the fact that he cannot be corrupted.

Me—flying is the only thing I know. After thirty years I don't know if I can even fit into civilian life again. Beth has all the patience in the world with me. God knows why— or what I did to deserve her. I'm certainly not much of a catch. I'm too much of a loner . . .

Matt read far into the night. Wanting Kris was a physical pain and the ache enveloped him. He sought refuge in the pages of Ben's journal. He'd almost finished it and he knew that he would soon relive the events that led up to his father's final, fateful flight. Was he ready for that? He turned the pages reluctantly, his reading becoming slow and methodical as he neared the end.

Kris pushed open the door to her room, tears blinding her. Matt loved her. He always had, according to his journal. But he hadn't had enough faith in either of them to go with his feelings. That had cost them years of anguish and heartbreak.

She flung herself across the bed. How could she believe he would be any different now? That his love would stand up to any kind of test. At one time she had enough love and faith for them both, but that was before Hal's death. Before the malpractice suit. Before Scott—

She rolled over to distract herself from that train of thought and felt something hard and flat on the bed beneath her. Propping herself on one elbow, she reached for the parcel. A frown creased her brow. She remembered seeing the package in the mail and assumed it was for the Bentleys. Now she saw that it was addressed to her. She sat up and ripped it open.

A folded sheet lay on top of a bundle of letters. She picked it up and recognized Roy Ferguson's writing. She began reading, her frown deepening.

Kris, my dear, as you know I am continuing to sort through Hal's affairs. His records concerning his business are meticulous. Unfortunately, I can't say the same about most of his personal correspondence. In this case, however, I fear that I am more to blame than he. He gave me these letters for you just before his death. I have been waiting for the right time to give them to you. With all that has happened, I'm afraid they slipped my mind.

Needless to say, I have not read these letters. I don't have that right. I can only pray that I am doing the right thing by giving them to you now. I know that Hal loved you, although I'm not sure he was always able to show it, and that he would never do or say anything to hurt you. Whatever he wanted you to know at this time was written with the best of intentions. He was my friend and I loved him dearly. I love you as if you were my own. With my humble prayer that these last words to you will be of benefit, I remain faithfully yours, Roy Ferguson.

Kris trembled as she fingered the packet of letters. She and Hal had never had heartfelt father-daughter talks. He had never given her advice, seldom voiced his opinion even when she asked for it. Her hands shook as she untied the ribbon holding the letters together.

Each envelope was dated and in chronological order. Taking a deep breath, Kris opened the oldest one.

My darling daughter, today you soloed. You have no idea how proud I am of you, or how much I admire your strength and courage. That's my fault. I've never known how to tell you these things . . .

Kris continued to read, tears spilling down her cheeks as she read Hal's letters written to her at every milestone in her life. *Her mother's death. Graduation from college. Medical school. Residency. Her meeting with Matt in his office*—Kris stiffened, her tears drying as she scanned this page.

You ran into Matt again today. It has been years since you've seen each other, the most important years in your lives, the years that have turned him into a man and you into a woman. It was obvious from your meeting that you are both very much aware of that.

I'm not sure how I feel about this, at the same time realizing that how I feel isn't what's important. I love Matt like a son, but even at that, is he good enough for my daughter? And if he isn't, who is?

Matt's father, Ben, was my best friend, and without a doubt the finest man I've ever known. Matt has all Ben's strengths, but unfortunately, many of his weaknesses as well. I hope he has enough of Beth in him to keep him civilized and to smooth the rough edges.

For the most part, I would say Matt is the kind of man you need, someone with strength and courage to match your own. You have to be careful, my daughter, that you do not settle for someone lesser than yourself--someone without your honesty and clear-sightedness.

Kris put the letter down and saw that there were two more envelopes. She picked up the next to last one and read the date. Her heart thudded.

Matt finally returned from Desert Storm, beaten and broken. It is obvious that things did not go as you would have liked between the two of you. Give him time, my dear. He is defeated both in body and soul. Pride is Matt's greatest weakness. He wears it like a shield. He could never give you less than his best—as defined by him. He can't come to you except on his terms. Be patient with him. He loves you. I know him well enough to know how much he is hurting. But if he came to you now, it would destroy both of you, because he would have to sacrifice himself as a man. I doubt that, as a woman, you can understand this. But as hard as it is to stand by and see the two of you suffer, I have to believe Matt is right.

Eyes burning, Kris reached for the last envelope. The date was two weeks before Hal's death. *Had he known?*

My darling Kris—how can I possibly say to you now all the things I haven't been able to say during the last twenty nine years? No one could wish for a better daughter—nor a more beautiful one. When I look at you I am blinded briefly by your mother's beauty, and then my daughter shines through. Warm. Loving. Unique. My little Kristi all grown up. Beautiful Kristin—as befits the name. Kris, strong and dependable. There are so many facets to you that make you such a wonderful person. I am humbled that I played a part in that creation, and somewhat in awe of what you have become.

It saddens me that soon I will leave you alone—all alone, I'm afraid. I had hoped by now that Matt would have come to terms with his pride.

Today the doctors confirmed what I have suspected for sometime. I only have a short while left. I hope you will not feel betrayed that I have kept this from you, but one ailing parent is enough for any child to have to deal with. I cannot burden you with my illness and I have opted not to pursue the uncertain and painful treatment that could possibly prolong my life. I hope you do not see this as a lack of faith on my part, but as an act of love.

One more bit of advice concerning Matt. He loves you. My final prayer will be that he act upon that love soon. If in some future position I find it in my power to influence him, rest assured that I will set him on the right course! As for what you can do, I've been thinking that it might take some drastic action on your part to get his attention and keep it. I have faith that you will know what to do when the time comes. My final regret is that I will not be around to share the happiness you two will find together. But be certain I will be watching and cheering you on!

Kris let the letter flutter from her fingers and fall to the bed. She stood up and turned off the light and made her way to the window where she stood staring out at the healing darkness.

What was it about her that so intimidated the men she loved? Matt hadn't been able to tell her how he felt, until now, when it was too late. Neither had Hal. He even wrote that he had been in awe of her. If only she could have known how he felt while he was still alive.

Her childhood had been lonely and barren. She had never had any of the experiences a young girl should have. Beth Walker was the only person who seemed to understand her at all—the only one who had ever told her she was beautiful and encouraged her to let her blonde hair grow long.

Beth had taught her how to use makeup and helped her select clothes. None of that had done her much good, living in jeans as she did, but she had been grateful for the attention. Now she realized Beth had wanted to be closer, to help her as the contract dictated, but Kris shrank from such intimacy. Never having known it before, she had not understood Beth's motives.

Did Beth know she was in love with Matt? Kris wondered. And how did she feel about her in that respect? Did she think she was good enough for her son? Or would anyone be? A misty smile touched Kris's lips as she remembered Hal's musings about Matt.

What kind of drastic action did Hal have in mind? Kris reached out to trace a design on the window pane. *Something that would get Matt's attention and hold it.*

She turned at a light tap on the door. The knob turned and the door opened a few inches.

"Kris—are you awake?"

She swallowed. "Over here."

Matt stepped into the room, a silhouette backlit by the light from the hallway. He reached for a light switch.

"No," Kris said. "Please don't turn it on."

His hand fell and he pushed the door closed. "You've been crying?"

"Maybe." Kris brushed tears from her face.

Matt stood quietly, letting his eyes adjust to the darkness. He held up the book he carried. "I just finished Dad's journal. It has so much about Hal in it, I thought you might like to read it."

Kris nodded. "You offered before. Yes, I would. *Very much.*"

Matt shifted uncertainly. "At the end—" he hesitated. "I think Dad knew there was a problem with the plane. He had a feeling—" He stopped speaking as his voice broke.

Kris stared at him, suddenly realizing what he was telling her. "At the end," she repeated. "The last entry he made before the flight. Oh, Matt!"

She did not think. She could only feel. Matt needed her and this time he had acted on that need. She crossed the room and reached out to take the journal from him. Then she caught his hands in hers.

Matt drew her toward him, slowly at first, and then he pulled her into his arms. His hands trembled as they speared into her hair. His thumbs touched the corners of her mouth.

"Kris!" His voice sounded rough. "I love you. I want you—" The words were lost as he bent his head and his mouth closed over hers with savage hunger.

Only once before had Kris seen Matt lose control. That night in the hangar before Desert Storm intruded and ripped their lives apart. Then she had been too naive to understand anything except her response to him.

But this time she understood far more than she should. While fully understanding that it was Matt who held her, Matt who kissed her, the ferocity of that kiss startled her and she whimpered deep in her throat and struggled against his embrace.

Matt released her immediately and stood staring at her. He ran a hand through his hair as if awakening from a dream.

"Kris, I didn't mean—how could I have forgotten?" His voice was an anguished whisper.

186

"No! This has nothing to do with Scott." Kris reached out to touch his face.

They stood inches apart, tension throbbing between them. At last Matt raised his hand and traced a finger down her cheek. "What, then? You don't want me to kiss you?"

She shook her head. "I want you to kiss me—to love me. I've never pretended otherwise."

He quirked an eyebrow. "But?

"But I won't settle for being a distraction."

"Distraction?" He sounded rattled. "Distraction from what?"

"Forgive me if I'm out of line, but you just learned about your father. You finished reading his journal. You know about his fears and uncertainties before the flight."

"And what does that mean, Doctor?" Anger seethed in his voice.

"You may be a thirty-six year old man. You may be a wonderful pilot and a war hero. But you are still that eleven year old boy—"

Even in the darkness she could see the anger spark in his eyes. "You are out of line, Dr. Freud. Stick to your specialty in the future." He turned toward the door.

"Matt—" She held out her hand in a pleading gesture. "I thought— perhaps a friend could help." When he did not look at her, she felt her defenses collapse, completely and without warning. She turned away, a hand going to her face to stay the silent tears streaming down her cheeks.

"Why are you crying?" Matt's voice came out of the darkness.

"Because you won't!" She whirled to face him. "I'm crying for me. I'm crying for you. I'm crying for Ben and for my mother and father. And I'm

crying for the life together that you denied us!" She sank to the floor and rested her elbows on her knees, her face buried in her arms. "Go away! Just—go away! You're very good at that!"

"Not anymore, I'm not!" he grated. He dropped to his knees beside her, pulling her into his arms.

Kris struggled and pushed against his chest. Then she froze as a tear fell onto her hand. She stared at it for a moment then raised her face to Matt's to see his eyes glistening. A streak of moisture trailed down his cheek. She reached out to trace it with her fingertip.

"Are you happy—now?" Matt tried to tease, but the break in his voice betrayed the depth of his pain.

"Oh, Matt!" she whispered. She turned into his arms, her own going around his neck. "It's going to be all right. We're going to be all right!" She stroked his back and shoulders.

He dropped his head and she cradled it against her as she felt his tears sear her skin. Her arms went around him, holding him, giving him strength.

Matt opened his eyes and looked down at Kris lying against his chest. At some point he had picked her up and carried her to an arm chair. Their tears had stopped but occasionally a ragged breath still convulsed her. He reached up to cover her hand as she clutched his damp shirt.

He wouldn't be leaving. That had not been a consideration since the morning he stepped down from his plane and looked into her eyes again. A siren's eyes, he thought as a smile touched his lips. Eyes that lured and entrapped, but he wouldn't have it any other way.

No, he couldn't leave. Not now that he knew what it was like to hold her in his arms and be held by her in turn. Not now that he had felt her healing touch. What had be been thinking all these years when he had hurt them both so deeply? Kris was right. He had denied them a life together.

Well, no more. He had a lot of work to do, but it was time to make up for past failures.

He stood up, being careful not to awaken Kris, and carried her to the bed. He pulled the blanket into place and knelt to kiss her.

His lips clung to hers and he reluctantly raised his head and smoothed her hair back from her face. He had to talk to Roy and Bill. With any luck, he wouldn't have to wait long to make her his.

Matt crossed to his room, glancing at his watch as he stepped inside. A brief frown creased his brow. It was too late to talk to Bill tonight, but maybe he could still call Roy and get things underway. Now that he had a plan of action, he found it hard to sit still.

He turned to leave and swung back. Something white lying on the bed caught his eye. *An envelope.* He walked over to pick it up.

"Roy," he murmured as he recognized his scrawl. "I was just thinking about you."

He tore open the letter and unfolded the pages inside, his chest tightening painfully as Hal's neat script jumped out at him. He sank down on the bed as he began reading.

"Matt, my son, forgive me for reaching out from the grave like this, but I do hope to enjoy my eternal rest once I have earned it. The best way to assure that seems to be to try and tie up a few loose ends that have been dangling in front of me for years.

"Forty something years ago I watched your father fall in love with your mother and then fail to do anything about it. She had fallen just as much in love with him. I was as baffled as she because I had introduced them. It took awhile for me to figure out that I was the problem. Ben thought I was in love with Beth.

PROMISES KEPT

It took some elaborate manipulations on our part to finally get Ben to accept that Beth was in love with him and that I was just a friend—to both of them.

I don't think I am the problem this time, although that is a possibility. From watching Ben with Beth, I recognize the symptoms. You are in love with my daughter. At first I thought I understood your hesitation, but your reasons for holding back are no longer valid. If you really knew Kris, you would realize they never were. But I know your pride and stubbornness and even supported your reasons for not getting involved with Kris when you first returned from the Persian Gulf War.

Back to the reason I could be the problem. Do I consider you good enough for my daughter? If you doubt that for a moment, then maybe you aren't. Being a father figure to you these last twenty-five years has been both a blessing and a curse as I watched you grow into Ben—my best friend—the man who was closer than a brother could have been.

I know what you have to offer Kris, and what she has to offer you. I couldn't have arranged a better match had I tried. Now that I have removed myself as an obstacle, what are you waiting for? There has never been anyone else for Kris, and I fear there never will be. I know her too well. She may look like her mother, but she inherited my sensibilities. She will love once and forever. You are that love, Matt. Don't make her wait any longer.

I'm sure that by the time you read this, I will be flying formation with Ben again, breaking in my new wings and learning all the tricks he can teach me. We'll be watching you and Kris. If I taught you anything important about life, you won't let us down.

CHAPTER FIFTEEN

Kris stirred, a smile touching her mouth as she awakened by degrees. Eyes still closed, she flung an arm across the bed to touch—*nothing*. The smile vanished. At some level she knew she was alone, but in her dreams, Matt had been beside her, holding her, his lips brushing hers. Her eyes flew open to stop thoughts that brought only pain. How many times had she awakened from that dream, she wondered in frustration as she threw the covers aside and got up with stiff jerky movements.

She would not spend the rest of her life like a love struck teenager, Kris told herself as she began packing, her course of action decided. First, she had to return to California and clear her record of the malpractice charges. Roy had been hounding her for weeks, refusing to let her settle out of court. With that behind her, if Matt was still interested, she would be more than ready. If not, her life would go on. For now, she could only take one day at a time.

The packing finished, Kris went in search of Marie. She found her alone in her room, still wearing her robe.

"May I come in?" Kris asked from the doorway.

"Of course." Marie closed her book and motioned for Kris to sit beside her. "Bill got up hours ago. I think he's addicted to that hot tub."

"Is he doing all right?" Kris asked, too restless to sit down. She paced the room. "Any more problems since his fall?"

"None. You know, I think he may have been faking that." Marie's eyes were twinkling.

Kris smiled. "We suspected as much. He did it before, you know. To Dad and Ben. Matt read it in Ben's journal."

Marie studied her. "You aren't angry."

"No. What about you? How are you feeling? I've been away for several days, remember?"

"I'm fine—good as new. And Carl's doing great. He called yesterday. They plan to come here for Christmas."

"That's wonderful." Kris swallowed the lump in her throat. "Then it doesn't sound as if you need me anymore."

"What do you mean?" Marie's glance was filled with concern as her gaze swept over Kris.

"It's time for me to leave, Marie. There's a flight this morning out of Fairbanks to Anchorage and then on to San Francisco. I'll get home late tonight. Roy will meet me. The trial starts in a day or two. I've decided I want to be there. I'm grateful for all you've done and I apologize for running out like this—but I can't stay any longer."

Marie studied her. "Is this about Matt?"

Kris looked down. "If I'm honest, yes. I can't spend any more time wishing for what could be. I still have a life—according to Roy—and it's time I returned to it."

Marie sighed. "I hoped that if you could talk—you did talk last night, didn't you?"

Kris nodded. "We talked. We even cried—for what it's worth. I know he has a lot of problems to work out—*emotional baggage*, in his words. And I have just as many—more perhaps, right now. Maybe we've both been loners for too long." She paused for a moment then looked at Marie. "I don't want to see Matt before I go."

"Do you mean that?" Marie's eyes were warm with sympathy and understanding as they met and held Kris's.

"If I see him, I may not be able to leave. This is something I have to do. Whatever happens—well, I have to clear my name. Right now, I can't go to him like this, even if he should want me. I can't offer him what's left. I have to like myself again, believe in myself." She shrugged. "Meet him as an equal."

Marie nodded. "I can understand that. What do you need me to do?"

"Perhaps nothing. If I can get away before he wakes up, then you're free and clear. I'm going to leave the Cub and the ownership papers in Fairbanks for him. He wants it—and I think I'll like knowing he has it. He loves it as much as I do. It's something I can give him—" Her voice broke and she brushed impatiently at the tears that flooded her eyes.

"My dear—" Marie began, her own voice choked.

Kris made a dismissive gesture and drew a steadying breath. "I've packed everything. I can't take it all with me, but it's ready to ship. I left money to cover freight and if you could ask Yanni to take it to Fairbanks the next time he goes—"

"I'll take care of it," Marie promised.

"Then I'll say good-by. I'm glad I had this chance to get to know you and Bill. I love you both dearly. You're all I have."

Marie stood to put her arms around Kris. "Everything and everyone we have is yours, Kris. Including Matt. You two should have been friends, just like your fathers were. In fact, I think you are. I can see it, even if you can't. What you feel for him goes way beyond sexual attraction.

"To be married to your best friend is the most wonderful relationship in the world, my dear. It can withstand anything. Bill was my friend long before he became my lover. We've spent almost sixty years together—and still it seems such a short time. Think about that before you give up on Matt."

Kris smiled at Marie. "I've wondered about you and Bill. It's obvious that you're still so much in love. How did you meet him?"

Marie sat down again. "It's rather a long story. Do you have time?"

"I'll make time." Kris dropped into a chair beside Marie.

"I was a nurse and I still remember the commotion when they brought Bill into the field hospital. He was fighting to stay conscious, all the while insisting that he wasn't hurt. He had a bloody bandage around his head and his flight suit was soaked in blood. It seems his plane had been shot up and he caught some shrapnel."

Kris shivered. "I saw his scars. They're—much like Matt's."

Marie patted her hand, then continued.

"He was right that he looked worse than he was. We cleaned him up and the doctor put in a few stitches and gave him an injection for pain and a sedative. He had almost drifted off when there was another commotion." She glanced at Kris, a smile twitching her lips.

194

Kris's eyes widened. "What?"

"Guess."

Kris shook her head. "I don't know."

"His squadron buddies arrived. *Roy, Hal and Ben.* They had had a few drinks and needed to assure themselves that he was still alive.

"I had worked too hard to get him settled down to let them undo all my work. I turned them around and marched them out with strict orders not to come back before morning. I assured them he was fine and in good hands.

"When I returned to Bill he opened his eyes and smiled at me. 'You did that very well', he said.

"I stared at him and asked him why he wasn't asleep. He held out his hand and gave me the sleeping pill I was sure he had swallowed.

"I glared at him. 'What did I do well?' I asked, unable to overcome my curiosity.

"He laughed. 'You just pulled rank on a colonel and two captains. I've never seen them take orders from anyone before. I've always said if I met a woman like that who looked like you, I'd have to marry her'.

"I plumped up his pillow. 'Really? And how long have you been saying that, Captain?'

"He caught my hand. 'Since about two minutes ago. Will you marry me—' he glanced at my badge '—Marie?'

"I laughed and sat down beside him, enjoying his sense of humor. We talked and teased until he fell asleep. I went off duty and had a couple of days off. When I returned he had been released and was back with his squadron. But he left a note for me. *'I'll be back'*, it said, *'and the question still stands'*."

Kris smiled. "How long before you saw him again?"

"A couple of months."

"How long before you knew you were in love with him?"

"Almost as long as it took for him to ask me to marry him."

"That's such a beautiful story," Kris said, her eyes misty with emotion.

"No more so than Ben and Beth's or that of your parents. And you and Matt have one just as special," Marie said.

Kris rose from the chair, shaking her head. "There's nothing more I can do. Matt has to make some decisions. He'll be able to find me."

Marie smiled. "Then I presume I'm not to try and stop him should he decide to follow you?"

Kris returned her smile, her expression wistful. "I think I can trust your judgment."

Marie was busy in the kitchen when Matt walked in. She glanced up to see him stifle a yawn.

"Late night?" she asked, handing him a cup of coffee.

He dropped into a chair. "I finished Dad's journal early this morning. Then Kris and I talked again. I had a little trouble getting to sleep after that." He ran a hand through his hair.

"How about breakfast?" Marie asked after a moment, unable to think of a reply. "Pecan waffles and sausage?"

He groaned. "How can I resist? I was planning to do some flying this morning, but I guess that can wait."

Marie let out her breath. *She'd bought Kris a little time.* "Did you and Kris have a nice talk last night—this morning?" She asked to cover her nervousness.

Matt got up to refill his coffee. "Nice? Our talk was a lot of things, but I don't know if it qualifies as *nice*." He walked over to look out the window.

"Matt--?" Marie began, her voice hesitant.

He swung back to face her, his eyes dark and intense. "Marie, is there any hope for me with Kris? Have I blown any chance I might've had?"

She stared at him. "What are you asking me?"

"Marie, I love her. I always have—since she was two years old. But— well, I've let her down so many times." He shrugged. "I thought she wanted Scott. I'm still not sure I understand why she didn't. He had so much more to offer—on the surface, anyway."

"I think you're insulting Hal's daughter to insinuate she would only be interested in what's on the surface. Perhaps you would care to elaborate on what you think Scott had to offer her that you didn't." Marie raised her brows.

"Everything. I mean, she's so cultured, so educated, so classy, so— beautiful. He was all that. Me—all I know how to do well is fly. I'm scarred and battered. I don't even know how to conduct myself outside military situations. I like being alone too much. That doesn't add up to a whole lot to offer her. Will it be enough?"

"It's enough for Kris. What you have to decide is whether or not it's enough for you?"

"What do you mean?"

"Well, you could always use it as an excuse to keep running from what you feel. Make sure she spends the rest of her life miserable because you're the one thing she wants that she has no hope of getting." Marie's voice was flat, uncompromising.

"She could do so much better than me—" Matt began.

"She's the one you have to convince of that—not me," Marie said. "Personally, I'm beginning to agree with you. I wish there was some way she could forget you and get on with her life. But she won't. She'll spend the rest of her life alone. She has no reason to want marriage unless it's for real love— the kind that sweeps her off her feet and takes her breath away. She deserves a family, children, but you're the only one who can give her that."

Matt looked up, met Marie's eyes. He grinned. "I talked to Roy last night. I told him to do whatever it takes to get a marriage license and have it ready because I'll be bringing her back in a few days and I have no intention of waiting to marry her."

Marie caught her breath. "Matt—" she whispered.

He put his arms around her. "I'm tired of being noble. I can't go on without her. It isn't just that I want her. I like being with her. She makes me feel good. I like the way she teases me—and I like teasing her back."

"You're friends," Marie said. She touched his face. "Oh, Matt, I'm so glad—" She blinked and straightened. "Sit down. Your breakfast is ready."

"Have you seen Kris this morning?" Matt picked up his fork. "I'm afraid she was upset last night. I wanted to talk to her as soon as possible."

Marie froze. "Not for a couple of hours," she replied, suddenly torn by what she was doing. It'd been almost two hours since Kris left. She should be in Fairbanks by now, but her flight to Anchorage hadn't departed. Matt had to be delayed for awhile longer. After that, he could go after Kris if he wished. He'd be too late to stop her. She had to be given a chance to do things her way.

"She what?" Matt blazed as he stared down at Marie.

"I said she caught a flight out of Fairbanks," Marie repeated deliberately. "She's going back to California."

"Arriving when?"

"She said late tonight. I don't know what time or what airline."

Matt turned away and then swung back to face her. Marie read the accusation in his eyes. "How could you—?"

Marie held up her hand. "I'm sorry, Matt—"

"I could've stopped her in Fairbanks."

"I know. I had to give her a chance to leave. She didn't need any more pressure. She's hurting so much, Matt, not knowing what to expect from you. She has to know if you care enough to go after her—or not—"

"Of course I'm going after her. If I can leave in the next hour, I can get to San Francisco before she does, and meet her flight."

Marie gaped at him. "You can?" Her voice rose to a squeak. "But, Matt, she thinks she has to do this alone."

"She doesn't and she isn't going to." He was already on his way to his room, Marie trailing behind him. He grabbed his flight bag and began digging through it for sectionals. He grunted with satisfaction as he picked them up and took them back to the kitchen to spread on the table.

"I'll fly straight back," Matt said, thinking out loud for Marie's benefit, "stopping for fuel in Whitehorse, Prince Rupert and Seattle. The longest leg will be from Seattle to San Francisco. That'll be ten—eleven hours of flying, less if I have a tail wind. The airliner can fly faster, but will probably stop for a lay over in Anchorage and Seattle—maybe even change crews. With any luck, I can get there first."

Bill walked into the room, relaxed and refreshed from his stint in the hot tub. He glanced at the sectionals Matt was poring over

"What's going on?"

"Kris left. I'm going after her."

Bill looked at Marie and raised an eyebrow. She nodded.

"Have you thought about this?" Bill frowned at Matt in concern.

"I don't need to."

"Have you checked the weather?" Bill persisted.

Matt's hands stilled for a moment. "Not yet." He continued drawing lines on the aerial maps. "I'd appreciate it if you could do that for me. And maybe Yanni can help get the plane ready."

Marie sighed. "I'll find Yanni—and I'll pack for you."

Matt turned to give her a quick kiss on the cheek. "Thanks!"

"Just call me a hopeless romantic," Marie said as she turned away.

Bill hurried after Marie, catching her arm as she reached Matt's room.

"Can we stop him?" he asked.

Marie smiled. "Remember the first thing you ever said to me?"

"About Roy and Ben and Hal never taking orders from anybody?"

She nodded.

"And how is that relevant in this case?"

"Ben gave Matt life and Hal taught him to live. Through heredity and environment, he patterned his life after two of the most stubborn men ever created."

Bill grinned. "I guess I'd better check that weather for him."

Forty-five minutes later Matt and Yanni clasped hands and embraced as Matt prepared to leave.

"Don't lose her, Matt!" Yanni said. "Kris is special."

"I know," Matt said, his voice dry. "So what does she want with me?"

Yanni grinned. "Only God—and Kris—know. But she does. If you can't see it, you certainly have no business flying. You're as blind as a bat."

Matt laughed. "Bats fly, my friend," he reminded Yanni. "And very well, at that."

"So they do." Yanni regarded him for a moment. "Bring her back for Christmas, okay?"

Matt turned to the plane. "Marie already made me promise. I'm not to come back without her."

"You are going to use some common sense on this flight, aren't you?" Yanni asked. "I know why you think you have to go, but I really think Kris would like you in one piece."

Matt stepped up onto the wing and swung himself into the cockpit. "I always use common sense when I fly," he replied. "I'm not going off half-cocked, Yanni. This is virtually the same flight I made up here last month."

"And that took you how long?" Yanni climbed up on the wing also, and peered into the cockpit, scanning the instrument panel.

Matt sighed. "Three days."

"And you intend to make it in how long this time?"

Matt glared at him. "We've already been over that—"

Yanni held up his hand. "Give Kris a hug for me. She looked awfully alone when she left this morning."

Matt shot him a venomous look. "You knew she was leaving? And you let her go?"

"What did she have to stay for?" Yanni asked. "You're so bull-headed you'd lose her before you'd admit you need her, too."

Matt grimaced. "I've always known I could count on your faith in me. *Clear prop!*"

"*Clear!*" Yanni stepped backward off the wing with a wave and the engine roared to life. He watched as Matt put on his headset and closed the canopy. Returning Matt's thumbs up, he walked back to the Bronco. He reached for a note pad and scrawled down a number and the time, then watched as Matt taxied onto the runway and climbed toward the sky. His dark features creased into a grin of delight.

CHAPTER SIXTEEN

"I have to do this, Sozi!" Kris's eyes met the dark ones of the girl in the booth across from her in the airport cafe. "I know you don't understand, but I have to get my life back together. I told you about the malpractice suit a couple of days ago."

"But leaving Matt? He loves you, Kris. At least, Yanni thinks so. He says Matt is so crazy about you he doesn't think straight anymore."

Kris toyed with her food. "Then Matt will have to start thinking and decide if I have a place in his life. He's always had a place in mine."

"But this—" Sozi searched for words. "—is so crazy! To dash off madly with no warning. Back to California. It sounds as if Matt is ready to come around—and now you leave."

Kris smiled, a sad little smile. "I got a letter from my father yesterday—several letters, actually."

Sozi stared at her.

"In the last one, he told me that I might have to take some drastic action in order to get Matt's attention and keep it. I can't take a chance that Matt will talk himself out of a relationship again. Worst case, at least I will still have my pride. And I will get my life back on course."

Sozi shook her head. "I will pray that you are right—and that Matt will not be so stubborn, *or so stupid*, to let you go very far."

"Thanks for meeting me, Sozi. It would have been a long wait without you." Kris picked up her bag and slid out of the booth.

"I will see you again. *Many times.* That I know."

Kris smiled and embraced the native girl who had so quickly won her heart. She was every bit as warm, generous and loving as her brother.

Kris released Sozi and turned to walk back to her gate, hoping that this time her flight would indeed depart.

Kris watched the Alaskan countryside fall away beneath them and blinked at the tears stinging her eyes. Would she ever be back? Would she again experience the joy of flying the Cub along the Chena River and stopping at the Athabascan fishing village. No, she reminded herself belatedly. The Cub was now Matt's. She'd left the registration papers with Sozi, knowing she could trust her to see that Matt got them.

Sozi, Yanni's sister—and Bill and Marie's adopted daughter, was a pharmacist. Kris had liked her instantly, just as she'd been drawn to Yanni and Salina and all the native Alaskans she'd been privileged to meet.

Upon learning there would be a three hour delay in her flight, Kris called Sozi to see if she could meet her. They spent a leisurely couple of hours together with Sozi taking Kris to the museum to see Yanni's work. It was exquisite. Some small pieces were available in the museum gift shop and Kris bought a carving of a dog that looked very much like Buck—smiling wryly as she remembered her recent escapade with him.

Sozi confided to Kris that Bill planned to have Yanni take over Bentley Base when he retired. Carl had no interest in flying or living in Alaska. And although Bill loved Matt like a son, he'd never wanted him to feel obligated to keep the base going. Yanni had lived there all his life and loved it as Bill did. He was the perfect choice.

For herself, Sozi said she preferred to be a little closer to civilization. Fairbanks suited her nicely. She lived close enough to her native land and people to go back when she wanted. She was dating an Athabascan doctor. Franz planned to set up a practice in Fairbanks and volunteer part of his time to his people. From her voice, Kris could tell how proud Sozi was of him. She hoped everything worked out for them.

Kris realized the landscape had long since disappeared from sight and she'd been staring unseeingly at the overcast of clouds. She settled back against her seat, closing her eyes. It was going to be a long flight—well after midnight when she reached San Francisco. She'd call Roy from Seattle and tell him.

Matt tossed the empty potato chip bag into the trash as a voice on the other end of the phone finally answered.

"Yes, flight service," his voice deepened, became brisk and authoritative. "Matt Walker, seventy one bravo whisky, on a flight plan from Fairbanks to San Francisco, requesting current and forecasted weather and winds aloft between Prince Rupert and Seattle." He listened and made a couple of notes. "Thanks." He replaced the receiver and ran a hand through his hair.

"Excuse me?"

Matt looked up to see a tall young man with tousled blonde hair. He wore a battered leather jacket that Matt knew he had come by honestly.

"Matt Walker? I couldn't help but overhear. Are you flying the Walker Racer?"

Matt nodded. "She's out on the ramp."

The blue eyes glowed. "What would it take to see her up close? Begging? Shining your boots—"

Matt grinned. "Buy me a cup of coffee and you can help preflight."

The blonde thrust out his hand. "Joe Blankenship. That was too easy." His eyes narrowed.

Matt clasped his hand. Shrugged. "I need to kill fifteen minutes while a line of thunderstorms moves out of my path. It's just as easy to do it down here. Besides, I'm a little ahead of schedule."

Thirty minutes later Matt cursed flight plans, flight service and weather forecasters in general as he stared at the solid line of thunderstorms ahead of him. He wondered for the thousandth time why he even bothered to check the weather for all the good it usually did. The delay had been another exercise in futility. He was still going to have to divert around the storm system.

Roy Ferguson sat in the all night coffee shop at the airport and sipped his drink. From his vantage point he could see the gate where Kris would arrive. Fortunately she'd managed to get through to him from Seattle and tell him of the delay.

Only moments after Kris's call, Roy heard from Matt. He was about to depart Prince Rupert, British Columbia, and as he explained the situation, Roy

206

could hear the strain in his voice. Armed with the information he'd received from Kris, Roy was able to relieve Matt of some of the tension. Kris's flight had been delayed by three hours. That bought Matt the time he needed.

Roy smiled and took a sip of coffee. He felt a lot like Cupid. Matt had touched down about an hour ago and Roy had been on the ramp to greet him and take a quick look inside the cockpit. Inside the terminal Matt paced like a caged tiger as he waited for Kris. Roy felt confident that Matt had finally come to terms with his feelings and was ready to make the commitment Kris needed.

Of Kris he wasn't so sure. He knew she loved Matt. But he wouldn't be surprised to find that she didn't capitulate easily when Matt confronted her. She'd been through too much; she was still too uncertain of him. She'd probably take some convincing. Roy sat back to watch the show.

Matt strode back into Roy's line of vision and leaned casually against the railing separating those waiting from the arriving passengers. He wore his trademark black flight suit and battered leather jacket.

The lounge was crowded with families awaiting the flight so long delayed. Most of them were tired and in none too pleasant a mood, but Roy noticed that almost every female from twelve to seventy found time for a second glance at Matt. Arms folded across his chest, looking out at the lights of the airport, he was totally oblivious of the attention he received.

Roy saw Kris come through the door before Matt did. He marveled again at the perfect beauty of the girl. She wore jeans and a soft pink sweater, her wonderful blonde hair tumbling carelessly around her shoulders. Now Roy watched as all males present paused to give her another look—and perhaps again. As with Matt, she was unaware of the stir she caused.

Roy saw Kris glance up and see Matt, half turned away from her. She stopped dead. Matt raised his head and saw her.

To Roy it seemed an eternity before Matt straightened away from the rail and started toward Kris. She hadn't moved since catching sight of him. Good, Roy approved silently. *Make him come to you.*

Kris stood stunned. For a moment she thought she'd seen Matt. She shook her head to dispel the illusion. Of course he couldn't be here! She was about to move on when he looked up and she saw that it was Matt. *But how?* She couldn't take her eyes off him as he began walking toward her.

Matt stopped opposite Kris, the rail still separating them. Arriving passengers cast curious glances their way, but moved on quickly. The flight was late. All they wanted to do was go about their business.

"You're wearing that sweater again," Matt growled. "Do you have any idea how it affects my blood pressure—among other things?" God, she was beautiful! *Please don't let me screw this up*, he prayed.

Quick color stained her face and neck. Her gaze swept over him as if to assure herself that he was real. *Real enough.* And for whatever reason he was here, he seemed determined. Determined and slightly dangerous—and entirely too attractive. He didn't look as if he would brook any argument, she thought. *Please let him be here because he wants me*, she prayed.

"Matt, what are you doing here?" She sounded a little breathless, but she couldn't do anything about it. This was how she'd felt at that first meeting.

"You have to ask. *Because you're here.*" His voice was flat, matter-of-fact. She wasn't going to make this easy for him. Not that he had any reason to expect her to.

"But—" Kris could think of no reply, but continued to stare at him. She didn't have any reason to hope, as yet, except that he was here.

"Are you going to stay on that side of the rail all night?" Matt asked.

Kris stepped back. "It—might be safer." She tried to keep the words light, but her voice betrayed her.

In a heartbeat Matt cleared the rail and stood beside her. In an efficiency of motion, he took her bags and caught her arm to lead her out of the passage and into the waiting area. They were virtually alone now except for the single straggling passenger and the flight crew finishing its shift.

Matt dropped the bags. He stood close enough to touch, reached down and took her hands, leaned his forehead against hers. He closed his eyes.

"Kris," his voice was strained. "I love you. I want to be with you forever. Please say you want the same thing and don't ever leave me again!"

She drew back to stare at him, her hands still in his. She saw everything she could hope to see in his eyes, plus a vulnerability that humbled her. She felt her throat tighten.

"I must say, Captain, when you finally decide to make a move, you don't waste—any time!" In spite of the lightness of her words, tears sparkled in her eyes. Her voice caught.

His fingers tightened on hers. "I've wasted way too much time already. I called Roy a couple of days ago and told him to get a marriage license ready; that I'd be bringing you back within the week and I had no intention of waiting to marry you. All you've done is move the agenda forward a little."

She was still staring at him. "It's a nice thought," she murmured, "but there's a lot of red tape involved, to say nothing of blood tests."

"Trust me." Matt's hands moved to her arms. "Will you marry me, Kris?" Lines of tension etched deep grooves beside his mouth. His eyes were an intense blue that almost frightened her.

"Matt—" She made a restless movement and tried to pull away from him. "How can I be sure this is what you want?" Her eyes searched his face.

"Well," he drawled. "I have a few minutes to try and convince you before Roy comes looking for us. How's this for starters?" He drew her close. His head bent and his mouth closed over hers with exquisite tenderness.

Kris yielded immediately, her lips parting and her hands going up to clasp behind his neck. His arms tightened and she moaned deep in her throat. She'd wanted this since that first moment. This was heaven; this was home.

"Matt, please, say it again!" She drew back a little to look at him.

"Will you marry me?" His kissed her face, her throat. He couldn't get enough of her. What had be been thinking to have ever let her go?

"Yes—but not that—" He heard a hint of laughter in her voice.

Matt raised his head to look into her eyes. Hal's eyes. Eyes that he loved for so many reasons. Eyes that were smiling at him at last. "I love you."

"Yes!" She sighed against his mouth. "I love you so much, but I wasn't sure I'd never hear you say you loved me, and be certain you meant it."

"I love you, Kris, and I'll be saying it for a long time. I have a lot of catching up to do." He straightened. "Roy's in the coffee shop. I guess we've kept him waiting long enough." He bent to pick up her bags.

"Matt? Is that really you? *Matt Walker?*" Then as Matt and Kris both turned toward the voice. *"Kris?"*

"Kendra?" Kris recovered her voice first. "Kendra!" She stepped over her bags to catch the other woman in her arms. Then she stepped back to hold her at arms length. "Kendra, you aren't—"

The slender woman with the dark hair and compelling gray eyes nodded. "'Fraid so," she said casually. Too casually, Kris thought. "I've spend most of the day trying to get here from Seattle to catch a flight overseas."

Kris's eyes widened. "We must have been on the same flight."

210

"Could be. It was pretty crowded." Kendra looked over her shoulder at Matt. "Captain. Since you left us, I wasn't sure I'd ever see you again. I'm glad the rescue was successful."

"Same here." Matt held out his hand. "For both of us." His gaze swept over her. "Don't tell me you're still getting into the kind of trouble that it takes our Special Forces guys to bail you out?"

Kendra laughed, a low husky sound. "Just the one time."

"Well, from where I stand, once is enough. I know you can't tell me where you're going or what you will be doing, but good luck."

"Thanks. Luck is always good to have, but I'd hate to depend on it." She glanced at her watch. "I have to run. It was so good running into you." She was already moving away from them. "Maybe next time—"

Matt and Kris stood in stunned silence as they watched Kendra Allen disappear into the huge airport terminal.

Kris drew a deep breath. "I so hoped she wasn't doing that sort of thing anymore."

Matt shook his head. "Kendra Allen is one of the bravest people I've ever met. We need more people like her in our Country's service."

"True, except that's not the case," Kris said. "Kendra isn't brave. It's just that she isn't afraid of anything."

Matt looked at her, his mouth twitched. "There's a difference?"

"In her case, yes. She isn't afraid of anything because she doesn't care if she lives or dies. She thinks she has nothing to live for."

Roy stood as they entered. He drew Kris into a fond embrace and shook Matt's hand. Then he glanced meaningfully at his watch.

"Twelve forty-five. Do you have more luggage, my dear?"

Kris shook her head. "Just this."

"My car isn't far, but home's at least an hour away." He moved ahead of them. "You're both spending the night with me," he threw over his shoulder. "Since you live on opposite sides of town and hours away from where we have to be bright and early tomorrow, this is the only way. I took the liberty of picking up clothing for each of you."

Matt felt Kris tense as Roy talked. He slipped an arm around her and smiled reassuringly. After a moment she relaxed and her arm went around his waist. He felt a surge of protectiveness sweep over him.

They were in Roy's Cadillac headed out of San Francisco before either Matt or Kris could get in a word. Kris leaned forward and braced her arms against the front seat.

"What time does the trial start tomorrow?" she asked.

"Ten o'clock. We want to get there a little early." Roy hesitated a moment. "They selected the jury today."

Kris drew in her breath and Matt reached out to pull her back into his arms. He began massaging her neck and shoulders. "Will you relax?" he murmured against her ear, his breath stirring her hair.

"How can I? This is my life we're talking about." But she leaned against him, relaxing as he kneaded tense muscles. "I could get used to this."

"I'm counting on it," Matt said, his lips brushing the back of her neck.

"A couple of packages came for you today, Matt." Roy met his eyes in the rearview mirror. "I think they're the ones you've been waiting for."

Matt nodded. He and Roy had already talked. There was no need to say more. But he smiled to himself in the darkness.

Kris had grown drowsy by the time they pulled into Roy's garage. Matt helped her from the car and Roy held a door open for them.

"I arranged for a tray of sandwiches if you'd like a snack," Roy said. "Otherwise, I'd recommend you both get to bed as soon as possible. Like I said, tomorrow's going to be a long day."

"I'm starving," Kris said. "I haven't eaten anything since lunch."

Matt stared at her. "You're hungry?" His voice was incredulous.

"Yes." Kris threw him a glance. "You have—"

Before she could say more, a series of excited barks came from an adjoining room. She turned to Roy, her eyes shining with anticipation.

"Is that—"

He sighed. "*It is.* I suppose you must see them?"

"Please! It's been months."

"I doubt they'll quiet down without seeing you anyway. This way."

Kris and Roy left the room and Matt followed. Roy pushed open a door and an identical pair of Irish Setters immediately launched themselves at Kris. At her calming words they subsided and she knelt to put her arms around them, scratching behind their ears and under their collars.

"They look wonderful," she told Roy. "Obviously you've been taking good care of them."

"Did you expect less?" he asked.

"Well, no—" Kris met his eyes, saw the twinkle there. She smiled. "Thanks. I knew if anyone could love them as much as Dad, it'd be you. I appreciate all you've done—"

"We aren't finished yet," Roy reminded. "I suggest you get that snack. I'll take your bags to your rooms."

Roy left and Matt knelt to touch the silken heads of the dogs. "I'd forgotten them," he said, almost reverently. He met Kris's eyes and she saw an unnatural sheen of moisture in his. "They used to go everywhere with Hal."

Kris nodded, a lump in her throat. "I gave them to him a couple of years ago for his birthday." She stood up and Matt reached out to pull her close. *"I miss him so much!"*

"So do I," Matt whispered, wrapping his arms around her.

A half hour later Matt stopped outside Kris's room and drew her against him. "This is the last night I let you go into your bedroom alone," he said, his expression openly suggestive.

She raised drooping eyelids and startled green eyes met his. She toyed with the lapels of his jacket. "So why let me tonight?"

Matt laughed and tipped her face up to his. "Because it'd be a fatal blow to my ego to have you fall asleep during our lovemaking. Also, I have orders from Roy to let you get some rest."

She stared at him, wet her lips. "I—" She was at a total loss for words.

Matt's kiss was gentle. He turned her toward the door. "Inside— before I forget all my good intentions," he said, his eyes smiling down at her.

Kris slipped into an oversized T-shirt and ran a brush through her hair. She glanced at the clock and saw that it was two-thirty. Roy promised to wake her at eight. She groaned as she crawled beneath the covers. How could she possibly fall asleep with all that had happened today, *and all that was due to happen tomorrow?* She burrowed into the softness of her pillow and her eyes closed heavily.

Matt looked out at the night sky. He'd taken a shower to try and relax—to no avail. All the hours spent flying that day, nerves taut and faculties fine-tuned, guaranteed it would be a few more hours before he'd be able to unwind.

Matt turned at a knock on the door and Roy pushed it open. He came in holding a glass and a bottle of pills.

"I thought you might need these," Roy said.

"What are they?" Matt asked.

"A mild sedative and warm milk. Ben always had trouble getting to sleep after the kind of day you've had."

Matt grinned. "I'll take them under one condition."

"And that is?"

"That Kris never finds out." He popped a couple of the white tablets in his mouth and drained the glass. "It still tastes ghastly!"

Roy noted with concern the circles under Matt's eyes. "Well, better that than having you collapse on Kris on your wedding night."

Matt looked at him, belatedly remembering the trial. "Will I be able to go to court in the morning?"

"Were you planning to go?" Roy asked innocently.

"I have to be there for Kris."

"*I'll be there for her.* Right now, you have to take care of you. However it goes, we'll recess for lunch. You could meet us then."

"I want to be there. I have to be there." Matt yawned. "Roy, are you sure that was just a *'mild sedative'* you gave me?"

"Cross my heart," Roy said, and did.

Matt's head was swimming. "I guess I'd better lay down before—"

"Easy." Roy caught his arm and eased him down to the bed, pulling the covers back. "That's my boy," he said. He stood for a moment, looking down at Matt. *He was so much like his father.* For a moment the years rolled away and it was Ben there before him. Then Roy turned abruptly and left the room.

CHAPTER SEVENTEEN

Kris took a nervous sip of coffee and turned to Roy. "Could you—" she hesitated. "Could you tell Matt that it would be better if he didn't go to court with us this morning? I—this is something I have to do alone. Do you think he'll understand?"

Roy nodded. "I gave him something to help him sleep last night. He'll be sleeping in."

Her eyes widened. "He willingly took medication? He must have been even more tired than I realized."

Roy's eyes twinkled. "He was thinking of the future."

"He looked so exhausted," Kris said. Her expression softened. "I can't believe he flew all that way to meet my flight—"

"What did you think he'd do?" Roy asked.

"I had no idea. I just couldn't stay there any longer, and not know—" she broke off.

"He's talked to me several times a week since he's been in Alaska, always about you. He loves you very much, Kris."

"Everyone seems to know that better than he does," Kris said, her voice even, matter-of-fact.

"He knows it now," Roy said. His hand covered hers.

Kris glanced at her watch. "If we aren't waiting for Matt, then I'm ready to go. You said we have to stop by your office?"

"Yes. A couple of forms you need to sign. Then I'll drop them off and we'll go to court. I must say that you look quite lovely this morning, my dear." Roy slipped into his jacket.

Kris kissed his cheek. "You always have been an outrageous flirt," she teased. "But thanks. I need all the help I can get."

"Flirt?" Roy looked wounded. "I deal in facts. And although I know you're carrying the weight of the world on your shoulders right now, I've never seen you more beautiful. It has to be love."

Kris caught her breath. "I do feel different. I feel beautiful just knowing Matt wants me. Does it really show?"

"It shows." Roy pinched her cheek. "I wish—" His voice trailed off.

"Wish what?"

"Looking at Matt last night, and seeing how much like Ben he is, I got a bit nostalgic. I wish Ben and Hal were here to see the two of you together."

Kris swallowed. "So do I," she whispered.

Kris sat stiffly, her hands clasped in her lap. She found the silence and formality of the courtroom oppressive. She wanted to clutch Roy's arm, to hide her face against his shoulder. But pride kept her from betraying her concern, her vulnerability.

Everything seemed unreal as she listened to murmurings and paper shuffling of the court coming into session. The judge hearing the case was introduced as the Honorable George Evans and everyone rose as he entered. The bailiff read the charges against her. Although she thought she was prepared for this, Kris felt the blood drain from her face at the stark reality of what she was hearing. *These people actually believed she'd committed murder!*

Roy had tried to prepare her for what she faced as they drove to court. He told her of the witnesses appearing on her behalf, and about a security tape he wanted admitted as evidence. None of it meant anything to her, numbed as she was by the whole scenario.

For six months she'd been torn between betrayal and guilt. Betrayal that she'd done the best she could and was still being sued; guilt that perhaps somehow she hadn't done enough to save the little girl. Every night she dreamed about the surgery—relived it. It always came out the same. She'd done everything she could. Neither she nor Melinda had had a chance. But last night she hadn't dreamed. Was that somehow significant?

Roy made his opening statement to the jury, his voice mesmerizing them as he explained what had to be proven in order for them to find Kris guilty. He meticulously defined criminal negligence and willful neglect.

Kris suffered through a short recess and then court resumed. Roy called his first witness. The complainants had no witnesses. They didn't need any. This was a civil case and Kris had to prove her innocence. Most doctors didn't bother to fight malpractice lawsuits. The expense was too great and they were insured against such charges. For Kris, however, this had become personal. Much more than her career was at stake here. Her whole future hung in the balance.

The first witness was Russell Court, the hospital administrator who had accepted Kris as a raw intern. Under Roy's questioning, he expounded on her credentials and her skill. Never once did he or Roy refer to Kris as young or as a woman, merely as an experienced surgeon.

Not so during the cross-examination by the plaintiff's lawyer, Jeffrey Hill. In condescending and mocking tones, he tried to hound the administrator into admitting that Kris was young and inexperienced. He repeatedly referred to the fact that she was a woman. Mr. Court was obviously becoming irritated, and finally, in reply to a last persistent question, he looked past the lawyer, straight at the jury.

"No, I repeat, an additional twenty years experience or a gender change wouldn't have made a difference in the outcome of the case in question." His voice was dry. "Dr. Holland's performance, under very trying circumstances, was exemplary. A Medical Review Board could find no evidence of negligence or over-sight." He swung his gaze back to the lawyer with a penetrating stare until Jeffrey Hill looked away and cleared his throat.

"No further questions, Your Honor."

Kris sat up with interest during this exchange as it became evident to her what the lawyer's tactics were.

The next witness was Laura Grey, the nurse who worked admissions the night of the crash. She told Roy and the jury what a madhouse the emergency room had been. She remembered the complainants. They'd signed a parental consent form. The original wasn't available, but she'd scanned it into her computer before going off duty at midnight. She then left on a two month pregnancy leave and was unaware of the missing form until her return. Upon hearing of the malpractice suit against Dr. Holland, she'd re-imaged the form and forwarded it to Roy Ferguson with a note of explanation. Roy asked her to identify the form and had it entered as evidence.

Jeffrey Hill, furiously angry at this turn of events, asked the nurse how she could have possibly not known about the lawsuit for two months. Was she an imbecile? his tone implied.

Taking her cue from the hospital administrator, Laura looked past the lawyer to the jury. "My husband travels a lot. I went to Nebraska to stay with my mother until my child was born. Two weeks later I returned here. When my leave was up, I went back to work. Dr. Holland is someone I enjoy working with. When a few days passed and I hadn't seen her, I asked someone where she was. Only then did I hear about the lawsuit." She looked back at Jeffrey Hill, her gaze narrowed.

"No further questions, Your Honor."

"I now call Dr. Kristin Holland." Roy's voice resounded through the courtroom.

Kris stared at him. She'd expected him to call her, but so soon! She got to her feet and somehow managed to walk the distance to the witness stand. In a trance, she was sworn in and responded automatically.

"Dr. Holland," Roy's voice was calm and reassuring. "Will you tell us your recollection of the events relating to the crash on the night in question? The crash in which Melinda Morales was fatally injured?"

Kris looked up, expecting to hear an objection from Jeffrey Hill. She saw him scribbling furiously, apparently not paying attention to the proceedings. When no objection came, she drew a deep breath and began speaking, her voice firm and clear. She remembered those events well. She'd relived them every night since. When she came to the part where Melinda was brought in, her voice faltered. She described how the little girl was already in shock, her blood pressure so low that she could not immediately detect a pulse. She remembered Melinda's parents clutching at her, begging her to save their child.

"Dr. Holland," Roy interrupted. "Are you bilingual? Do you understand Spanish?"

"I understand the language. I do not speak it fluently."

"Please continue."

Kris described the decision to rush Melinda to surgery. Her condition warranted moving her ahead of several of the less seriously injured. One of those victims, a woman who'd been on the bus, threatened Kris with a malpractice suit if she didn't attend to her facial injuries at once. Kris's mouth twisted with irony as she related this.

"And did this woman sue you?" Roy asked.

"No. Within minutes doctors from surrounding hospitals responded to our call for help. Time was not as critical for any of the other patients as it was for Melinda."

"But even so, Melinda didn't have enough time, is that correct, Doctor?"

"That is correct." Kris's voice was wooden.

"Objection!"

"Overruled. Proceed, Counselor."

"Had she been brought in earlier—even immediately, would it have made a difference for Melinda, Doctor? Your professional opinion, please."

Kris stared at him. She'd never allowed herself to believe that there had never been any hope for the little girl. But now, under oath, she realized with startling clarity that it had been too late for Melinda from the beginning.

222

"I—" Kris tried to speak and tears began streaming down her face. She drew a harsh sobbing breath. "No." Her voice was brittle with control. *"It wouldn't have made a difference."*

"Objection!"

"Overruled! There will be a brief recess. All parties, return in twenty minutes."

Roy helped Kris from the witness stand and led her out of the courtroom. When they reached the corridor Matt saw them and hurried over.

Matt threw Roy a dark look. "Nice work, Colonel. They wouldn't let me inside once court was in session. Kris, darling, what—" He enfolded her in his arms, his eyes searching Roy's.

"It's all going quiet well, actually," Roy said.

"Then why is she crying?" Matt asked, his arms tightening around Kris.

"Because she just had to admit that she isn't God, and shouldn't go around assuming his responsibilities," Roy explained, his voice bland. "I'm going for a cup of coffee if you'd care to join me." He threw this over his shoulder as he walked away.

Matt turned to follow him, keeping his arm around Kris.

After a moment Kris stopped and turned to Matt. "Could you hold me for a moment?" Her eyes shimmered with tears.

He drew her close. "I've never been able to refuse a beautiful siren anything." His lips brushed her forehead.

"Melinda never had a chance," Kris murmured.

"Of course she didn't. If she had, you would have saved her."

She nestled against his chest. "You make it sound so simple. I never wanted to admit that I couldn't save her."

"Even if it cleared you of any wrong doing?"

"I never saw that as an option," she whispered.

"Dr. Holland, why were you the surgeon assigned to Melinda Morales that night?" Jeffrey Hill began his cross-examination.

She frowned. "I had emergency duty that weekend. I wasn't assigned to anyone. *I was there.*"

"Have you performed many surgeries on children, Ms. Holland?"

Kris stiffened. So, he intended to ignore her professional credentials. "I have."

"Why is that, do you suppose?"

Kris looked at him, glanced at the judge. "Your Honor, I don't understand the question as posed."

"Clarify the question, Mr. Hill." Judge Evans's voice was curt.

"Do you suppose you've performed so many surgeries on children because they're considered of less value than adults?"

Kris stared at him. "I'd never suppose that. Besides, I've performed at least as many surgeries on adults."

"But, surely, Ms. Holland—people pay for experience."

"I beg your pardon?"

"You're all of what—thirty, at most?" He peered down his nose at her, a slight sneer on his lips.

"I daresay that makes me a couple of years older than you," Kris said with a voice that dripped sweetness and eyes that flashed green fire.

"Ms. Holland—"

"*Dr. Holland,* if you please."

His face turned a dull red. "Dr. Holland, why do you perform so many surgeries on children?"

"Because of requests, referrals—"

"And why is that?"

"Because children are comfortable with me. They trust me." Kris held his gaze.

"Did Melinda Morales trust you?"

Kris drew a sharp breath. "No. She couldn't have."

The lawyer's smile was triumphant. Predatory. "And why is that?"

"Because Melinda didn't have a chance to know me. She was never conscious in my presence."

Kris saw a flash of annoyance cross his face. "No further questions, Your Honor."

Kris stepped down from the witness stand and made her way back to the table where Roy sat. Roy gave her a reassuring smile and stood.

"Your Honor, at this point I would like to present a hospital security video of the night in question. This tape was kept in the archival files instead of being reused because of the crash and the overwhelming number of emergencies. It was felt that useful information for handling such future incidents could be gotten from studying this video. During one such review, a hospital board member realized that it contained information that might be helpful in Dr. Holland's defense and I was contacted. A security guard is here today with the original tape. Most of what you'll see should be familiar after the testimonies of Ms. Grey and Dr. Holland. But we'll also ask the security guard to take the stand to clarify any points that may come up."

"Objection!"

"Overruled. Proceed, Counselor."

The courtroom was silent as the nightmare described earlier began to play out on the large screen television set up for the jury. Kris hadn't been paying attention. She knew the scene too well. And then a collective gasp from the jury brought her gaze to the screen.

"Stop the tape and replay the scene in slow motion," Judge Evans ordered. His voice was cold and hard.

Kris held her breath as the scene was replayed. Then she saw Jeffrey Hill's face emblazoned across the screen.

"Continue."

The tape resumed and Jeffrey Hill could be seen going from one accident victim to another, "ambulance chasing", as it were—a practice of drumming up business that went against all codes of legal ethics and professional conduct in most states. Even where it was not illegal, as in California, it was frowned upon.

The tape ended and Judge Evans swept the courtroom with his glance. "I want to see the lawyers for both parties in my chambers at once. Court will recess until one o'clock."

"But, Roy, I didn't want a mistrial!" Kris said, her eyes sparkling with tears. "I wanted to be found innocent!"

"But you are, my dear," Roy explained, his voice calm and soothing now, so different from his count room growl. "It wasn't a mistrial. Judge Evans threw out the case. There is no evidence against you. Melinda's parents were coerced into suing you by an unscrupulous shyster. It's over."

She sighed. "You're right. It just seems anticlimactic to have it end this way." She turned to Matt. "Are you sure you still want me? I feel—"

"Want you?" He touched her face. "When I saw the video of the emergency room—well, I never encountered that kind of carnage in Desert Storm. You were so calm, so competent. And you face that every day, I feel ashamed that I haven't been able to put my personal Hell behind me and get on with my life. I not only want you, I need you. I'll never be complete without you. Are you sure you're willing to take on a project like me?"

Kris's smile was radiant. "Not only willing, but ready and able!" She looked at Roy. "Can we get out of here, do you think?"

"Soon. Someone has been asking to speak with you. I promised her she could." Roy moved aside and gestured to a young woman to come forward.

"Laura." Kris stepped to meet her and caught her hands. "How can I ever thank you? I—"

"It was the least I could do. Just come back to work soon. I've missed you." Laura Grey smiled through her tears.

Kris nodded. "Very soon. I've missed all of you more than I can say."

"I'm afraid it may be a while yet," Matt drawled behind them. He stepped forward and clasped Laura's hand. "I want to thank you for your help on Kris's behalf. But for the next *several* days, she's taking time off for a honeymoon."

"Honeymoon?" Laura's eyes widened. "Who is she marrying?"

Matt grinned. "The name is Matt Walker. Better get used to it."

Laura looked at him for a moment, liked what she saw. She returned his smile. "You know, I could use some help taking care of her."

CHAPTER EIGHTEEN

Matt tore the wrapper off a small box and sighed in satisfaction. He turned to Kris and coughed discreetly to get her attention.

She looked up, a faraway expression in her eyes. "I'm sorry. Did you say something?" She put her cup on the desk.

"Not yet, but I'm about to." Matt turned in the swivel chair in Roy's office until he faced her.

"Matt, what—" Kris met his gaze, an uncertain half smile on her lips. The expression in his eyes erased every coherent thought from her mind.

"I had Mom send these. They originally belonged to my grandmother." He held out the box so that Kris could see the contents. He removed a ring and reached for her hand. "This one you get now." He slipped it onto her finger. "The other you'll get in a couple of hours. This may qualify as the shortest engagement in history."

Kris stared at him, lips parted. She looked at the ring, caught her breath. "Matt, what is this? I don't—"

"You're going to marry me, my darling," he said. *This afternoon, to be precise.*"

"Oh, I am, am I? Did I agree to this?"

"You must have. Roy said you signed the application for a marriage license this morning. That's all we needed to go forward."

"So that's what he had me sign! He was pretty vague about it all—"

"We figured we'd better catch you when your defenses were down, when you were distracted by the trial." Matt's eyes were warm and teasing.

"What about blood tests?" Kris said, always practical. "Don't you need blood tests to get a marriage license? And what about a waiting period?"

"California doesn't require either. I had Roy check several days ago."

"So—you've been planning this? With Roy's help?"

Matt nodded. "So how about it? Are we going to let all his efforts on our behalf go for naught, or will you marry me—today?"

"I suppose Roy has it all arranged?"

"Of course." Matt glanced at his watch. "We're on a schedule."

Kris laughed, a soft musical peal. "How can I refuse? This is actually very romantic."

"It is?" Matt searched her face, unsure whether or not she was teasing.

She kissed him. "Yes, it is. I can hardly wait."

"Hardly wait for what?"

"To be Mrs. Matthew Jordan Walker—and everything that implies." Her voice was husky, no longer light and teasing.

Matt reached for the other package and ripped it open. "I have a wedding present for you before we go," he said, his manner suddenly all business. He removed several sheets of paper and scanned them. Satisfied, he handed them to Kris.

Kris took the papers, glanced at them, then sat up in amazement. "Matt—it says here that you bought Holland Aviation." She looked at him, her hand going to her mouth. He saw her fingers tremble.

"I'm trying to give you back your life," Matt said. His gaze held hers.

"But it'll be yours anyway—if you want it. You don't have to buy it—"

"*But I did.* I talked to Bill about it for a long time. We both agree it's time I do something with my life besides compete. I want to teach others what Hal taught me. I know I'm good enough. Hal helped me get my instructor's license just before—about a year ago. I want to help kids like Billy. Pick up where Hal left off."

He caught her hands, his eyes searching hers. "The flight school will be mine, to succeed or fail. About a third of the money came from my investments, Andrew threw in some, and we borrowed the rest. With it," he picked up the check attached to the papers, "I want you to have what you want. *Your own practice.*"

Kris stared at him. "How can one day make so much difference? Yesterday, I had nothing. I even left the Cub in Fairbanks for you. I guess that's your wedding present."

"Kris, you can't—"

"But you wanted it. I thought it was all you wanted." She blinked away tears. "I was jealous of an airplane!"

Matt smiled and reached out to cup her face between his hands. "I never wanted it as much as I wanted you. I was hoping I could have both."
230

"It looks like you will," Kris whispered, raising her face to his. Her eyes closed as his lips touched hers.

"We'll go back in the spring and fly it home—a belated honeymoon," Matt said, raising his mouth from hers a fraction of an inch.

"Oh, Matt, could we?" Her eyes were shining.

"Why not? It there something else you'd rather do?"

She shook her head. "That sounds just about perfect!"

Roy came into the room. "Are you ready to leave? We mustn't keep the good justice of the peace waiting."

"Justice of the peace?" Kris echoed, rising to her feet.

"Only for now," Matt said. "We'll do this right later."

"What do you mean?" Kris turned to him as he stood up.

"I thought we'd have Bill marry us properly when we're there for Christmas, with all the family present. You know he's an ordained minister? For now, forgive me, but I have no intention of waiting that long."

Kris looked at him for a moment, smiled. "Captain, your ideas keep getting better and better!" She reached out to straighten his tie, the same shade of blue as his eyes, with tiny red and gray stripes. She let her hand rest against his chest. "Have I told you how handsome you look?" Her eyes swept over the heather gray suit and white shirt. Her eyes danced. "I didn't think you could look better in anything than you do in your flight suit, then I saw you in jeans." She sighed dramatically. "And now this!"

Matt's smoldering gaze traveled over her. "You aren't half bad yourself." He ran his hands down the arms of her ivory silk blazer. The matching skirt ended just above her knees, the split in the back allowing him a tantalizing glimpse of thigh. Her silk blouse was a pale jade. His eyes came back to hers, a wicked gleam in them. "But don't throw away that pink sweater!" he whispered.

Behind them Roy cleared his throat.

Matt winked at Kris. "I told you we were on a schedule!"

Roy's silver Cadillac whispered to a stop before a large Tudor style house with trees lining the driveway. The street was quiet and peaceful, the sidewalks recently drenched with rain. He turned to look at the couple in the back seat.

Kris sat with her eyes closed, her head on Matt's shoulder, one hand clasped in his. His other arm cradled her against his side. He looked out the window, a slight frown creasing his brow. As Roy watched, Kris raised her head, aware that the car had stopped.

Roy smiled fondly at them. "This is as far as I go. The cleaners were here yesterday and I told them to stock the refrigerator as well." He seemed thoughtful for a moment before he cleared his throat. "We've been a long time getting here, and I'm pleased that I could play a small part in bringing you together. I know your fathers would be happy—as I am." He blinked a couple of times.

Kris leaned forward to kiss his cheek. "What would I have done without you and how can I ever repay you?"

"We've already talked about that," Roy replied, his voice gruff to cover his emotion. "Be happy, and take care of this guy." He looked at Matt. "And you already know you'll answer to me if you don't treat her right." His voice held a subtle warning.

Matt saluted smartly. "As you say, Colonel." He opened the door and reached inside to help Kris from the car.

Roy still looked over his shoulder as of reluctant to leave. "I'll give you a call in a few days. See if you're ready for me to bring the dogs over." He turned the key and the engine caught.

Matt closed the door and they stood on the sidewalk and watched the car disappear. He reached out to draw her close.

"Do you think we can do it?" he asked.

"Do what?" Kris murmured.

"Meet his expectations? Be as happy as he wants us to be?" Matt's voice sounded strained, tight with control.

Kris looked at him, unsure what he was asking. She decided there would be no more pretending on her part. "I know I want to try. I think—I know there's a better chance now—than I had before." Her gaze held his. "Tell me you aren't having second thoughts already!"

"Never." Matt looked into her upturned face, kissed her softly. "Let's go inside," he whispered, his arm tightening.

Kris handed him the key and they turned to walk up the curving drive to the house where she'd been born. Matt pushed open the door and turned to sweep her into his arms. He stepped over the threshold.

Matt's gaze swept the entry as he set Kris on her feet. "It's not as big as I remember. But then, I haven't been here since—" he broke off abruptly.

Kris turned to look up at him. A puzzled frown marred her brow and then she remembered. *Matt hadn't been in this house since Joey died!* She drew a sharp breath. "Matt, I'm sorry! We can go to a hotel. My car—"

He shook his head, reached out to pull her close. "No, my darling. This is our home." He glanced up at the massive beams in the cathedral ceiling. "It's just that it was a bit more impressive from an eight-year-old perspective."

Kris reached up to trace her index finger across his lips. "I'm finding that I like it much better from a thirty-year-old viewpoint." She loosened his tie. "I've decided I don't like this suit much, after all. It's a good thing it has served its purpose."

"What do you mean?"

She slanted him a glance from beneath her lashes. "I liked you better when you were wearing Carl's pajama bottoms. You looked like a pirate."

"A pirate?"

She nodded. "I kept having fantasies about being kidnapped and carried away to some deserted island—just you and me. There were palm trees, the sun and surf—"

His arms tightened. "I could get into a fantasy like that—with you."

She shook her head. *"That's my fantasy.* You have to come up with one of your own."

He held her away from him, looked into her face. "This isn't exactly a fantasy. *More like a wish."*

"Tell me, anyway."

"It's the same one I made on my birthday. Most of it has come true. You're mine at last." He kissed her, the softest brush of his lips against hers.

"What part—hasn't come true?" Kris found it hard to speak. She could feel his breath warm against her lips.

He drew her against him, pressed her face against his shoulder. "When I kissed you that night in the hangar, before I left for the Persian Gulf—"

Kris trembled and Matt's hand tangled in her hair. "I've relived that kiss a million times, feeling your lips warm and quivering beneath mine, seeing your eyes cloud with desire. That part will happen again," he promised.

This time Kris pulled back and looked up at him. "No doubt." She wet those same lips. "What else?"

Matt shifted, suddenly restless. He reached up and pulled his tie free. "The part that I fear is gone forever is the trust you had in me that night. You would have let me do anything I desired with absolute confidence that I would never hurt you."

Kris stared at him, not daring to breathe. Finally, she nodded. "Yes. And as much as I didn't want you to, I understood why you stopped—the way you did. You thought you were protecting me."

He swallowed. "I couldn't start something, knowing I might never be able to finish it."

"So what's stopping you now." Her husky voice dared him. "You have all the time in the world to finish—anything you might wish to start!"

He leaned his forehead against hers, reached down to catch her hands. "But I've hurt you so much. I don't have your trust."

"I do trust you. I—only feel complete when I'm with you. Before— that kiss, I had never wanted anybody else. After it, there couldn't be anyone but you." She moved away from him to stare out a window. She stood with her back to him and wrapped her arms across her chest.

"I don't know if you want to hear this, but I'll be thirty in a couple of months." She closed her eyes. "There's never been anyone else, Matt.. I didn't know if you would ever want me, but I've never wanted anyone else, so it wasn't really all that hard to wait—*for you*." This last in a whisper.

She heard a strangled sound behind her and turned back to face Matt. The blood had drained from his face.

"Kris." His voice sounded strained. "You—can't mean that."

Tears stung her eyes. "Why can't I?

"Because—dear God, Kris!" He reached her in a couple of strides and crushed her against him. He kissed her lips, her eyelids. She could feel him trembling. *"Because, my darling, that is a fantasy beyond my ability to even imagine!"*

Her eyes shimmered with tears as she looked up at him. As he watched one spilled over and slid down her cheek. "I love you." Kris whispered. "Do you at least believe that?"

"I believe that." He caught a tear on his fingertip. "It has taught me to believe in miracles!" He bent his head to capture her mouth again, completely this time, feeling her lips tremble and part beneath his.

After a moment he raised his head to see that her eyes were smoky and sensuous. "Yes," he whispered, running his thumb across her mouth. "We can make this work." He lifted her into his arms, took a couple of steps and came to a stop. He gave a dramatic sigh.

Kris opened her eyes to find him smiling down into her face. "As much as I'd like to follow through," he said, amusement dancing in his eyes, "I don't have a clue where I'm taking you!"

Kris put a hand behind his neck and pulled his face down to hers. She kissed him slowly.

"Up the stairs," she said. "And through the door. The master suite occupies the entire second floor."

"How convenient." His voice was a lazy drawl. "I'm beginning to like this house!"

CHAPTER NINETEEN

Kris wrapped her arms around Matt's neck and buried her face against his shoulder as she felt him mount the stairs. She counted the steps and knew when they were standing outside the bedroom door—*their* bedroom door. He shifted his hold on her, turned the knob and stepped into the room. She felt him stiffen.

"I don't believe it!" He put her on her feet.

Kris raised her head and saw him looking at the room behind her. She turned and felt shock rock through her. The entire room seemed to be filled with flowers. Baskets and pots and vases occupied every available surface.

"But where did they all come from?" Kris asked in wonder. "Who knows besides Roy?" She picked up a card from the nearest basket of flowers. *"Wishing you happiness and love. Bill and Marie."* She looked at Matt.

He turned over a card. *"Much happiness. Yanni and Salina."*

"Roy's better than a telegraph service." Kris bent over another arrangement. *"Carl, Celia and Mitch."*

"Mom and Alex." This on a dozen red roses.

"Tracy, Andrew and the girls." Kris smiled at the two bears embracing in this assortment of flowers, candy, and balloons. She touched the velvet ribbon.

"And the champagne and fruit—*from Roy.*"

"They're all here for us." Shaking her head in wonder, Kris looked up to meet Matt's gaze. She saw love, tenderness and banked passion. "So the contract is for real?" She gestured around the room, still awestruck at this outpouring of love from people she scarcely knew.

"As real as it gets." His eyes caressed her, promising more to come. "Where were we?"

Matt stood by the window looking out at a steady drizzle. He and Kris had been married for an entire day and so far they had not gone downstairs. They'd eaten fruit and cheese and drank champagne. Most of the time they had spent in bed.

He sighed. Sooner or later they had to face the rest of the world. As far as he was concerned, it should be sooner. He was starving. *For food.* It wasn't very romantic, but he was beginning to realize that it was harder than it sounded to live on love alone.

Kris came up behind him and slipped her arms around his waist. She rested her forehead between his shoulders.

"Why would you choose a time like this to decide to be modest?" she asked, her voice slurred with sleep.

Matt grinned and turned to pull her against him.

"This is better." Her fingers began roving across the expanse of chest exposed by the open pajama top. He reached up to catch her hand.

"And what are you wearing?" Matt held her away from him. "Hmm. I can see that I'll never view that shirt in quite the same light again."

Kris looked up at him, started to speak.

"What?" His eyes smiled down at her.

"Promise you won't laugh." She lowered her lashes.

"Cross my heart."

"I'm hungry."

"That's impossible." Matt tried to hide a grin. "You ate half the fruit basket—"

"I know it isn't very romantic, but I want real food," she said. "Pizza. Steak. Oriental—"

"Roy said the frig was stocked. Shall we check it out?"

"Please!"

"Should we get dressed?"

"Why?"

Matt shrugged. "Just a thought. *Obviously not a very practical one.*" He followed her down the stairs, almost missing a step as his eyes followed the gentle sway of her hips, the slender length of her legs.

Kris stopped on the bottom step and looked back at him. Matt deliberately bumped into her, his arms circling her. "I'm not interested in eating anymore." He nuzzled her neck.

"I am." Her voice was firm.

"Where's your sense of romance?"

"It needs food to recharge it."

Matt released her with a reluctant sigh. "All right. The frig—"

The doorbell, only a couple of feet away, chose that moment to buzz insistently. They both jumped and stood staring at one another.

"We're not dressed," Kris said, her eyes wide.

"That was your idea." Matt moved to peek out a side window.

"Who is it?" Kris whispered.

"A pizza delivery boy."

"No, who is it really?"

"A pizza delivery boy."

"Did we order a pizza?"

"Let's find out." He started to open the door.

"Matt!" Kris caught his arm. "You aren't dressed!"

"I'm better dressed than you," he pointed out. "Do we have any money?"

"For what?"

"Pizza."

"We didn't order pizza."

"So why is someone trying to deliver one?" Matt pulled open the door.

"Good afternoon, sir! A complimentary pizza from Mr. Roy Ferguson, and a rose for the lady." The delivery boy tipped his cap as he handed the box to Matt. He ran down the steps, then turned and waved as he got into his car.

Matt stood stunned. He turned back inside and closed the door. Picking up the single pink rosebud, he handed it to Kris.

"From Roy," he said as if he'd expected nothing less.

"How perfectly romantic!" Kris breathed. Then, "Do you think he moonlights as Cupid, or something?"

Matt grinned. "Who could do a better job, now that you mention it?" He carried the pizza into the kitchen. "Still hungry?"

"Starving."

"Roy!" Kris threw open the door and Roy caught her in a bear hug. Two streaks of dark red bounded past him.

"Sami! Shah! Sit!" Kris turned her head to speak sternly to the Irish Sitters who obeyed instantly and looked up at her with adoring liquid eyes.

"I'm impressed!" Matt drawled from the doorway to the kitchen, looking at the dogs who appeared to be auditioning for *Pet of the Year*.

Roy and Kris turned to look at him and Roy whispered something to Kris. She giggled.

Matt's eyes narrowed. "Colonel," he nodded in greeting. "Still flirting with my wife, I see."

"Matthew, my boy," Roy returned. "You know, as they say, rank has its privileges. But, for the record, this *is* the first time I've flirted with *your* wife."

Matt grinned and came forward to shake Roy's hand. "I guess it is, at that. Would you like some coffee?"

Roy glanced at Kris, still standing in the curve of his arm. "You haven't managed to break him of that habit, yet?" he asked with mock disapproval.

"Not yet," Kris confessed, "but he is drinking decaf."

"Does he know that?"

Matt looked at his cup. "He does now," he said dryly.

"In that case, I'll join you." Roy winked at Kris and followed Matt to the kitchen.

Kris called to the dogs, dropped to her knees to hug each one, then opened the sliding doors to let them out into the yard. They bounded out with yelps of enthusiasm.

She entered the kitchen as Matt handed Roy his coffee. He sniffed it appreciatively and took a sip.

"Sit down," Matt invited. "You can stay awhile?"

"As long as I'm not intruding." Roy sat back and studied the young couple before him. His gaze shifted to the single pink rose in a vase in the center of the table, now opened to its full glory. His mouth twitched. "Did you enjoy the pizza?"

"Very much." Matt grinned. "What made you think of that?"

"My mother."

"Your mother?" Kris asked, her eyes widening.

Roy smiled. "When Mary Beth and I got married, my mother brought over a Shepherd's Pie and cornbread. She had packed it all in a covered basket and left it on the steps. She rang the doorbell and left. When we opened the door and smelled the aroma—well, suffice it to say, that was one of the most welcome gifts we ever received.

"After I dropped you off, I began to wax nostalgic—I believe that is the correct term, and wondered what I could do for you along those lines. The owner of the Pizza Restaurant is an old friend. I told him what I wanted and he handled it from there."

"It was most welcome," Kris said. "And thanks for the rose, too!"

"I wish I could say I thought of it, but that was Gorgio's idea." Roy reached out to touch a delicate petal. "I have been giving some thought to something else, however."

"What?" Kris and Matt asked in unison.

Roy looked at Kris. "Your setting up your own practice."

"And?" Kris held her breath.

"It seems to me the ideal way is to take over an established practice."

She stared at him. *"Yeah, right."* She stood up to pace a few steps. "And I might like to live on the moon—"

"Sit down, my dear. Hear me out."

Kris dropped into a chair beside Matt and he caught her hand in his.

"I have a friend who is a pediatric surgeon and he is thinking of retiring soon." He watched Kris's face. "He's looking for someone suitable to come in as a partner and eventually take over his patients."

Matt felt Kris squeezing his hand and gently pried her fingers loose and smoothed them between his. He felt her shaking and saw her wet her lips.

"What does *'suitable'* mean?" she asked Roy.

"Why don't you meet him and ask? He's free for lunch tomorrow."

Her hand started to clench and Matt pressed it more tightly. She glanced at him and he gave her an encouraging smile. She pulled free and stood up to begin pacing again.

"You can give me an answer before I leave," Roy said casually. He watched as she slid open the door and stepped outside, then turned to Matt. "Have you been going over Hal's records? Any questions for me?"

Matt leaned back in his chair with a lazy smile. "Actually, I have glanced at a few of them. Not that I've had much time, you understand. No questions, so far."

Roy studied him. This was a Matthew Walker he had not seen. *Laid back. Casual. Happy. Relaxed.* Always before, Matt had possessed a nervous intensity and drive that made it almost tiring to be in his presence. Roy felt his lips twitch in a smile.

"What?" Matt asked, his eyes narrowing in suspicion.

"I'm just thinking that marriage—or Kris—perhaps both, certainly seem to agree with you. I've never seen you look so—content is the word that comes to mind."

Matt drummed his fingers on the table in a brief return of the restless energy before mentioned. Then he raised his head and grinned at Roy.

"I can't deny anything you've said. It's just too bad it took me so long to realize what I wanted—what I needed."

"Hal and I discussed you at length and reluctantly agreed that you have all the best traits your father possessed—along with a few of the worst."

Matt's fingers drummed again. "Yeah? I've heard that before."

"He was one of the best men either of us knew."

"I've heard that as well. I realize it's a tall order."

"What is?"

"Filling his shoes—living up to his reputation."

"A worthy ambition, but hardly necessary. You're doing okay in your own right. And just as Beth was the best thing that ever happened to Ben, Kris is the best thing that could happen to you. I'm glad you finally realized it."

"So am I." Matt looked up. "Thanks for sticking by me."

"Glad to help. Now, call Kris back inside. I have something for her."

Matt stood, stretching lazily, and again Roy marveled at the change in him. He went to the door and a moment later Kris rejoined them.

"Walk me to my car," Roy said to her.

She nodded and followed Roy outside. He unlocked the trunk of the silver Cadillac and reached inside for a large flat box.

"You will want to see about getting this cleaned and restored, perhaps altered, although I doubt that will be necessary." He put the box in her arms.

"What is it?" Kris looked at him in bewilderment.

"Your mother's wedding dress. I thought you would want to wear it next month when Bill performs the ceremony for the family."

"What a beautiful thought!" Kris said as tears filled her eyes. She blinked, unable to wipe them away.

"No more beautiful than you deserve," Roy said gently as he brushed away a tear and dropped a kiss on her forehead.

"Will you do one more thing for me?" Kris asked, her voice hesitant. "You've already done so much."

"Ask." Roy's voice was gruff with emotion.

"Will you give me away? You know I don't have anyone else—"

"You don't have to ask. I had every intention of insisting. It will be the easiest thing I've ever done, knowing you will be in good hands from now on." His eyes twinkled. "And I meant what I said earlier. Whatever you're doing, keep it up. Matt looks wonderful!"

Kris laughed and blushed adorably. "Thanks, I will! You haven't given me bad advice yet."

Roy winked and got into his car. Then he rolled down the window and stuck his head out. "About lunch tomorrow?"

"Set it up. As I just said, you haven't given me bad advice yet."

"I almost forgot—here's your mail." He laid a bundle on top of the box in her arms. "I took care of everything that didn't look personal."

"Thanks, Roy." Kris stood on the sidewalk and watched him drive away, then turned back toward the house.

The door opened as Kris reached it and Matt took the box from her. "What do we have here?"

"My mother's wedding dress."

Matt whistled. "Roy does think of everything, doesn't he? I wonder how he knows to do just the right thing at the right time." He placed the box on the coffee table.

"It isn't so much knowing as caring," Kris said. "And after he lost Mary Beth, it's the only thing that makes him happy."

"I've never heard him talk about her. What's their story?"

"It's beautiful, but tragic. They were only together for twelve years before she was killed. They didn't have any children, but Roy adopted her daughter from her first marriage. Susan became his whole life after he lost Mary Beth. She's a lawyer, too, and about to make partner in his law firm."

"A father-daughter lawyer team. Sounds impressive."

"I don't think so. Roy is talking retirement."

"You're kidding! Aren't you?"

Kris laughed. "Susan is about to make him a grandfather. I think he has plans to do a lot of baby sitting for his high powered lawyer daughter. But don't worry. I've been assured he will always be there for us."

"Good. I've learned to rely on his advice."

"So have I," Kris said. She glanced through the packet of mail, and a frown creased her brow.

"Something wrong?" Matt asked.

"Just a postcard from Kendra. *Sent before we saw her the other day.* She says she got the brochure I sent on *Extreme Expeditions*—you know, Jared Hall's survival training program. Thinks she might check it out when she gets back from this mission."

"So why the frown?"

Kris shrugged. "Kendra is—fragile."

"Kendra?" Matt laughed. "She might be a lot of things, but fragile is not one of them. She's as tough as they come."

"Physically, maybe. But not emotionally. And Jared—well, jaded is the best word I can think of to describe him."

"Do you realize they know each other?" Matt asked.

Kris stared at him. "No. *Jared and Kendra.*"

"I'm not saying there's anything there—just that they know each other. His unit rescued her group when they were captured in Kuwait."

Kris frowned again. "I wonder if he's *her Major.*"

"Her what?"

"She's had a secret crush on some Major ever since she came back from the Persian Gulf." Kris shook her head. "I hope not."

"Why not?"

"You've heard of the Irresistible Force meeting the Immovable Object? I believe that accurately describes those two."

Matt laughed. "Well, nothing is impossible. Just look at us. And my money is on Kendra."

"I just don't want her hurt. She's been through a lot." Kris looked at Matt. "And like someone else I know, she's never learned to deal with it. She handles it by living too close to the edge."

"If that's the case, then there's no one better than Jared to catch her should she fall."

As if on queue, a mailing tube rolled off the coffee table and landed with a soft thud. They both laughed.

"Speaking of which." Matt bent to pick it up. As he saw the return address, a frown passed briefly over his face.

"Now you're frowning," Kris said.

Matt handed it to her. "From your partner in crime."

She looked at it. "From Gregg! Maybe it's my map—or their wedding pictures." She sat down and began removing tape from the end of the tube.

"Wedding pictures?" Matt dropped down beside her. "Gregg? What kind of girl would marry him?" He teased.

Kris glared at him. "Well, I might have if he'd ever showed any interest. But he's always known about you. Besides, Karen is perfect for him. She's the kind of challenge he needs." She withdrew a photo and held it so Matt could see.

"*Karen—McGraw? And Gregg Watson?* That's harder to believe than Jared and Kendra."

"That's right. She did mention that she interviewed you once. She was quite suitably impressed." Kris teased him. She shook her head. "She and Gregg had a rough go of it, but things finally worked out for them. She agreed

248

to marry him while I was there last summer. In fact, they were thinking there might be a triple wedding in the works."

"Triple wedding?" Matt watched as Kris pulled out another photo and smiled in satisfaction.

"That's right. *His mother and his former partner.*" She handed that photo to Matt and pulled another from the tube. "*Her step-father and her aunt.*" She picked up a smaller photo. "And it looks like they decided to adopt Michael and Amanda." She drew a satisfied breath. "It looks like Karen got everything she wanted." She reached into the tube again. "Ah, my map!"

Kris went into the kitchen and spread the map on the table. Matt followed to look over her shoulder.

"This is fantastic!" She said, tracing the route she had flown from California to Alaska with the tip of her finger.

"This is a nightmare!" Matt said at the same moment. He bent to turn the map for a better look, squinting at the little graphics that Gregg had added along the route. "You never told me about thunderstorms. And what's this? You didn't tell me—"

Deciding it was time to distract him, Kris turned and stepped into his arms. "I guess I didn't. Tell you what. We can plot the course you flew back from Alaska on the same map and frame it."

He nuzzled her neck. "And why would we do that?"

"Someone might want to know about it one day." She began unfastening buttons on his shirt.

"What are you doing?"

"Following Roy's advice."

"Which is?" His voice was husky as he reached out to pull her close.

"To keep doing whatever I've been doing. He thinks it's good for you." She slipped a hand inside his shirt.

"Uh-huh. Seems I've heard that before." His lips brushed hers. "Good old Roy!"

CHAPTER TWENTY

Matt leaned against the doorframe and surveyed the cozy scene in the den. He wondered again how, in the space of six short weeks, his life could have changed so drastically—and so wonderfully.

He sighed and massaged his neck. The last week here in Alaska had been filled with emotional highs and lows. Chief among these was a memorial service for Colonel Benjamin Walker with full military honors.

Bill, Roy, Yanni and Matt flew their own missing man formation in honor of a fallen comrade. The funeral behind him, Matt could lay to rest the shadowy fears about his father's death that had plagued him since childhood.

Also notable was the wedding ceremony he'd promised Kris. Performed by Bill, it united Matt and Kris in the eyes of God. Kris wore the wedding dress her mother had worn when she married Hal Holland and everyone was there to bless the union and welcome her into the family.

Kris had asked Sozi to be her maid of honor and Yanni was Matt's best man. Roy gave away the bride and Beth was delighted with her new daughter.

Appropriate for the occasion, Bill had slightly reworded the contract signed so long ago, and it became the marriage vows that united Matt and Kris. It would continue to be honored for at least another generation.

Matt's eyes rested on Kris now as she read to his nieces. The twins, Sara and Kara, sat on either side of her, Mitzi at her feet. Kris looked like a princess in a green jumper and white blouse, her golden hair curling softly around her face.

Matt let his gaze sweep over the other occupants of the room. Beth and Marie chatted with a pregnant Salina over tea, overwhelming her with advice concerning her impending motherhood.

Tracy and Celia plied the convalescent Carl with all the attention any man could desire. He caught Matt's eye and winked, basking in all the attention.

Across the room Andrew talked with Sozi and her fiance, Franz. Matt knew that he was giving Franz advice on financing his medical practice.

Matt frowned. A sizable portion of the family was missing. Where was Yanni? Bill and Roy were no where to be seen. Neither was Alex, Matt's stepfather. Come to think of it, he hadn't seen them since early afternoon.

Matt suppressed a surge of resentment. Those missing were all pilots. Mitch was gone, too—no doubt hanging onto their every word. Why hadn't they included him in whatever they were up to? Matt wondered. Didn't they know he was going stir crazy?

He looked around the room again. All this domesticity was fine, but a man could only play so much Scrabble and stay sane. He almost wished Christmas was over. He was ready to have Kris all to himself again and get back home to his new flight school.

Matt felt Kris's eyes on him and looked up with a guilty start, as if she could read his thoughts. The past six weeks had taught him that she could hit pretty close to home when it came to knowing what he was thinking. She gave him a sympathetic smile and handed the book to Mitzi. A moment later she extracted herself from between the twins and walked over to him.

Kris pulled him around the corner into the kitchen and out of sight of everyone in the den. She stood in the circle of his arms, her hands flat against his chest, seducing him with her eyes. Matt groaned.

"I've been thinking of you as a princess," he said, touching her nose with his. "But my original analysis was more accurate."

"And what was that?" Kris asked, her eyes shining with happiness.

"You're a siren. I read somewhere that they had green eyes."

"I like that," Kris said. "The sirens in mythology were part woman and part bird. Rather fitting, don't you think?"

"I was thinking more in terms of their seductive charms," Matt said.

"And what could that possibly have to do with me?" Kris tilted her head to one side, her eyes wide and innocent.

"I rest my case!" He kissed her. "Is there any chance—?"

A commotion in the den drew their attention and they looked around the door to investigate.

"We were right," Bill said. "It won't be official, but Roy and Alex believe they can get it published."

A cheer went around the room. Matt looked at Kris and saw her smiling at him, her eyes filled with pride.

"What's going on?" he asked, puzzled. He noticed that Yanni, Roy, and Alex had returned. Mitch, too.

Kris pushed Matt into the room. "Bill, you've kept him in the dark long enough."

Bill drew Matt over to the fireplace and stood beside him. He cleared his throat. "Six weeks ago, when you made a made dash for San Francisco in order to intercept a certain young lady, you and your newly modified plane set a speed, efficiency and endurance record that won't be broken for years in the annals of racing. Unfortunately, as I said, it won't be official, but Alex and Roy, as long time members of the racing association, believe they can have it listed as a milestone. Congratulations, Matt! Ben and Hal would be proud, as we all are." He clasped Matt's hand and then embraced him unashamedly.

Matt looked dazed. He ran a hand through his hair. "Well, I guess that's as good a way as any to retire."

In the silence that followed, a log crackling on the fire might have been a grenade. Matt looked up to see all eyes riveted on him.

He shrugged. "I'm a flight instructor now. I already hold a speed, efficiency and endurance record."

"Yes, but—" Bill broke off.

"And I intend to train the pilot who will break that record." Matt looked up and met Yanni's eyes. In them he saw the understanding he sought. "What you don't realize is that I'd never again have the same motivation." His glance swung around to rest on Kris, to see the love and approval in her eyes.

"We understand," Alex said, watching the play of emotions across his stepson's face. "And we support your decision. But the record is still yours. We wish you the best, son." He reached out to clasp Matt's shoulder.

Congratulations from the rest of the family followed as they surged around Matt. He heard from Yanni, Bill, and Roy how they'd called ahead and asked friends at each of Matt's stops during his flight to record his arrival and departure times and the hours on his engine. All this information was then sent to Bill. Yanni had recorded the first readings, Roy the last. From this, Roy and Alex did the calculations that established the record.

When he was finally able to break away and go in search of Kris, Matt found her setting the table in the dining room. It would soon be filled to capacity with the crowd gathered for Christmas. She looked up and smiled.

"Hey, Champ!" Her eyes were gently teasing.

"The credit is all yours," Matt replied, his hands going to her waist. "Only you could have inspired me to put myself through that." Then, before they became too serious, "When's dinner?"

"About thirty minutes, according to Marie and Beth." Kris made a face. "I can't wait. I'm starving!"

Matt looked at her. "Aren't you hungry a lot lately?"

She threw him a glance. "Well, maybe I'm getting more exercise than I used to."

"Hmm. I was thinking of another reason." He watched as she picked up a stack of plates. "And you seem to be sleeping a lot, too."

"Well, that could be jet lag," she replied absently.

"Wrong direction! Besides, you were doing it back home."

"Doing what?"

"Eating nonstop and falling asleep without warning—"

She stopped to look at him again, put the stack of plates on the table. "What are you trying to say?"

He put his hands on her arms and turned her to face him. "Kris, listen to me. I think you're pregnant."

Her breath caught. "That's impossible—I think!"

"Impossible!" Matt laughed. "I hardly think so. Not only is it *not* impossible, I would say it's highly probable—"

"Wait! Stop." Kris put her hands against his chest. "I'm trying to think. You—you could be right!"

"Don't you want kids?" Matt asked. "We haven't talked about it—but after seeing you with Phillipe—and then when you suggested we might want to keep that map of the routes we flew—"

"Of course," Kris said, playing with the front of his shirt, unwilling to meet his eyes. "Boys would be nice—especially if they looked like their father, or even one of their grandfathers."

"I've been thinking more in terms of a little girl—with blonde hair and green eyes." He touched the tip of her nose.

She glared at him. "I don't think I could stand the competition. I'm already jealous enough of the dogs." A smile curved her lips as she remembered how Hal's dogs had been smitten with Matt on sight. He'd fallen for them just as hard.

Matt tipped her face up. "Kristi, you're not serious—"

She laughed. "Of course not." She studied him for a moment. "How is it that you notice all these things that are going on with me—and I'm totally unaware that they're happening?"

"Well, I have a theory about that," Matt said. "You're so busy taking care of the rest of the world, their comfort and well being, that you totally ignore any messages your body is trying to get through to you. Me, on the other hand—all I have to do is watch you. I pick up on these subtle little changes."

"Well," she turned back to her task. "I'm still not convinced that you're right this time. It could be any number of things. I—"

She broke off in horror as the plates she'd picked up slipped from her hands and crashed to the floor, pottery shards flying in all directions. She looked up to see Matt collapsed in laughter, holding onto the back of a chair.

"What's so funny?" Her eyes sparked with resentment.

"You doubt that you're pregnant? I think you just made it official. Don't all the women in this family publicly announce impending motherhood by breaking dishes? Remember Salina?"

As Kris stared at him, Marie poked her head around the door. "What's going on?" Then she saw the broken dishes and her eyes lit up. She looked at Kris. "My dear, I'm so happy for you—"

As Matt drew his blushing bride into his arms and pressed her face against his shoulder, the room filled with the rest of the family. He looked at them over her head, a smile lighting his face.

"Our legacy has come full circle," he said, his eyes going from Roy to Bill and Marie, then traveling to meet and hold his mother's gaze. "We're having a baby!"

END

About the Author

Growing up in a dysfunctional home long before such terminology existed, the author found escape in books. She attributes the wholesome characters created by such authors as Emilie Loring and Grace Livingston Hill with giving direction to her life. After a successful career as a chemist in Houston, today she lives in a private airpark in San Angelo, Texas, with her airline pilot husband of 35 years, two dogs, nine cats, lots of deer and wild turkey—and oh, yes—airplanes!

In the **HEARTland Series**, Eva O'Connor creates the characters for the books *she* wants to read. She strives to keep them wholesome enough for the daughters and granddaughters of all her friends to enjoy as well. If you enjoyed ***PROMISES KEPT***, please look for ***ON THE EDGE*** coming soon to lulu.com.

www.ingramcontent.com/pod-product-compliance
Lightning Source LLC
Chambersburg PA
CBHW031218020726
47499CB00002B/636